CAPTAIN BUTTERFLY

a novel by
Bob Leuci

A SIGNET BOOK

SIGNET
Published by the Penguin Group
Penguin Books USA Inc., 375 Hudson Street,
New York, New York 10014, U.S.A.
Penguin Books Ltd, 27 Wrights Lane,
London W8 5TZ, England
Penguin Books Australia Ltd, Ringwood,
Victoria, Australia
Penguin Books Canada Ltd, 2801 John Street,
Markham, Ontario, Canada L3R 1B4
Penguin Books (N.Z.) Ltd, 182-190 Wairau Road,
Auckland 10, New Zealand

Penguin Books Ltd, Registered Offices:
Harmondsworth, Middlesex, England

Published by Signet, an imprint of New American Library,
a division of Penguin Books USA Inc. Previously published in an
NAL Books edition.

First Signet Printing, May, 1991
10 9 8 7 6 5 4 3 2 1

PUBLISHER'S NOTE
This is a work of fiction. Names, characters, places, and incidents either are the product
of the author's imagination or are used fictitiously, and any resemblance to actual
persons, living or dead, events, or locales is entirely coincidental.

BOOKS ARE AVAILABLE AT QUANTITY DISCOUNTS WHEN USED TO PROMOTE PRODUCTS OR SERVICES.
FOR INFORMATION PLEASE WRITE TO PREMIUM MARKETING DIVISION, PENGUIN BOOKS USA INC., 375
HUDSON STREET, NEW YORK, NEW YORK 10014.

There is Brooklyn, and within Brooklyn there is a neighborhood called Red Hook. It is a very small place and could not accommodate all the action described in my novel. Like the setting, the characters, too, are fictitious. This is in preface to remarking that all the situations are products of my imagination. Any resemblance to actual events, or to persons living or dead, is entirely coincidental.

There is not now, and as far as I know there never has been, a New York City Police command bearing the name of Brooklyn South Command Office, or BSCO.

One of the principal occupations of men
is to divine women.
—LACRETELLE

Many smile who bite.
—COTGRAVE

Prologue

The Alberta Clipper flew all the way from Canada and scored a direct hit on Red Hook. Folks didn't know how to act. Snow came, then more snow came on an unholy northern wind that dropped temperatures forty degrees, exploded water pipes, sealed doorways, and frosted winos who thought they'd found prime spots in cardboard boxes under the Gowanus Expressway.

What a celebration went on at Sanitation Department garages!

Jehovah's Witnesses, in the Watch Tower up in Brooklyn Heights, saw the storm as the beginning of the end.

Garbagemen went looking for investment counselors.

New York City Police Officer Ramon Rivera loved the eighteen-inch snowfall because it brought silence to the Brooklyn South Command.

"Pleasing," he said as he hummed and grinned and tapped the dashboard of the Sector Charles car as if it were a bongo on wheels.

Monty Adams, Ray Rivera's partner, couldn't stand him when he talked like that. So Adams didn't answer.

Ramon took another swing at it.

"The snow is pleasing," he said.

Adams gave him his left profile, which was sharp and hard-edged. When he was upset, the muscle in Adams's cheek danced a warning.

"Sucks," he said. "I already told you the fucking snow sucks, and any piss-ant fun-seeker that likes it is a snapping asshole in my book."

"C'mon, c'mon, c'mon, lighten up. You've gotta admit this here sure is different."

Adams felt his face go red, knew Ramon was watching his face redden, and hated that dumb, blank, Latin grin.

Officer Rivera had a dark and evil look when he was serious. Adams liked that, loved the sinister quality of his partner's face.

But now Ray was grinning, his lips moving, grinning—grinning, pissing Adams off, knowing all the while he was pissing him off, playing greaser, spick games with him.

"Lighten up," Ramon repeated, and Monty Adams nodded.

Ramon Rivera's complexion was the color of walnut, and he wore a heavy Pancho Villa mustache. Born and raised in the barrio of East Harlem, Rivera's friends thought he would blossom into a hit man—a shooter. It told you something when you saw him going for the eyes and throat in a street fight; it told you a lot.

Rivera maneuvered the Sector Charles car through narrow South Brooklyn streets that were clogged with cars veiled in snow. It was late, the neighborhood deserted. The few remaining trees on the Hook were bent, ready to snap. Overhead, electrical wires, sleeved in ice, sagged low; some touched street signs, then exploded, red-yellow and blue.

As the car churned along Union Street it threw chunks of ice and snow into the air. A few residents, who in normal weather had trouble finding their hands and feet, watched as the sector car did a neat figure eight onto Gene Street.

Under the harsh light of a half-moon Gene Street resembled a dead planet.

Sliding up, Adams pointed to the Bombay Bar at the corner of Columbia Street. A few junkies wandered in and out of the bar. One had a bandanna tied around his head.

"Look at them turdbirds out on a night like this," Adams said.

Rivera smiled. "The great habit knows no season," he said.

Adams pursed his lips and wagged his head.

"Christ Almighty," Adams said. "I hate it when you talk like that."

The wind-driven snow was piled high in the intersection.

"I've never seen so much fucking snow," Monty Adams declared.

"Ohhh, man, it's beautiful, so white, so pretty." Even though Ramon Rivera had been raised on the hard streets of upper Manhattan, there were times he'd affect a distinct Latin accent.

Adams wanted to say something but decided against it. Ramon was his steady partner, and they were here to do a simple job, a favor.

Adams did favors for people. You could say he was famous for doing favors. Monty Adams was a law unto himself. An Old Testament man, he did not believe in a merciful God.

Ramon nosed the car to the edge of a monster snowbank just south of Columbia Street.

"It's about that time," said Adams. "No more smiling, no more laughter. Now I find out what you really got swinging between those PR legs of yours."

Ramon sat up, looked at the tenement just on the other side of the snowbank, and saw that there were lights in the first- and fifth-floor front apartments; the third and fourth floors were dark.

"Okay, c'mon, it's gettin' late," Ray said. "Do it."

Adams took hold of the portable transmitter, pushed the send button, and spoke briskly. "Charles of BSCO to Central-K."

Silence, some static, more silence. Adams would bet he'd have trouble getting through. Whenever he really needed the radio, he'd have trouble.

"Fuck," said Adams.

His thumb hit the send button again. He clicked it a couple of times just to get the feel, hearing Ramon say, "Hell, they must be busy, all this snow and all."

"Sector Charles of BSCO to Central. *Charles to Central-K*," Adams shouted.

Ramon didn't say anything, just wagged his head. He seemed to know something.

A woman's voice responded. "Central." Adams put on his gloves and rubbed his hands together.

"Central," he said, "we got a job here at 1402 Gene Street. A report of a woman screaming for help. We're on the scene and going in."

"That's a 4-Charles. You want a backup at this time?"

"Negative, Central."

Out of the car, knee-deep in snow and followed by puffs, then streams, of vapor, they rushed toward the five-story walk-up. To their right was New York Slim's rib joint. Adams noticed that the place was well lit, and in the entranceway he could make out the shape of a huge man.

"Check out the alligator in the doorway," he told Ramon.

"I seen 'em. There's four more in a Gypsy cab just up the street."

The alligators in the car and the one in the doorway were something to worry about, Adams thought. He'd better be quick, he'd better be quick and careful—fuckin' alligators.

Alligators were what Monty Adams called street people; alligators and turdbirds.

Ten years younger than Officer Rivera, and a two-time New York City Golden Gloves Heavyweight Champion, Monty Adams, at six-feet-four and two hundred and twenty pounds, was the precinct's equalizer. The Prince of Pain himself.

As he neared the building he passed soft white statues created from bulging garbage pails standing motionless in the yellow light from the street lamp. The light threw a harsh glare into the tenement alleyway, and his shadow swept across the front of the building like a ghost. He couldn't explain it, but there was something about the shadow that made him feel good; a thrill seeped through his nervous system, and a voice whispered in the back of his head: "Go get 'em, lawman."

Officer Rivera followed Adams to the steps of the building. He was a bit unsteady.

Now it occurred to Adams, as Rivera moved past him, that ol' Ray was probably enjoying this as much as he was. After all, it was his nephew the creep had grabbed. Then again, every pigskin-eating Puerto Rican in the precinct was somehow related to ol' Ray.

For a moment Monty Adams became aware of the dark stillness of the building, and he was embarrassed by the giddy excitement that rose like a surging tide in his chest. The moment refused to pass, and he felt a tightening in his shoulders and arms. Beautiful was this feeling, a fine, manly thing to do God's work with a good solid partner. Just to find a good, solid stand-up partner took some doing these days. He wanted to say, to tell Ray, "Hey, buddy, I'm glad I found you. I'm happy you're my partner."

The February blizzard wind was strong, but Monty Adams's brain and blood were bubbling, so he didn't mind.

Across the street, B-Eye, a big purple man, stood in the doorway of Slim's rib joint going through his pockets for his little screwdriver.

B-Eye spent his days ripping gold chains from white people in Park Slope; his nights were spent on the Hook, waiting. B-Eye would have liked to know just where the cops were going. He'd like to know because once the cops snatched whatever freak they were going to snatch, he could then lean on the door and, with his little screwdriver, maybe claim the room. B-Eye decided to wait. He'd lay in the cut, and see.

Ramon opened the vestibule door with a key. Adams

lit a cigarette, put it out; took a blackjack, a good twelve-
ounce slapper, from his tunic, checked the spring, and
slipped it back into his pocket.

He said, "We shudda jacked this turdbird up weeks
ago, got it over with."

"The bum moved," Ramon said. "I hadda find him."

Gray water, melting snow from their boots, followed
them up the stairs. They held the banister and touched
the cracked, moist green walls for silent balance. It was
just past midnight.

Ramon took a deep breath, Adams smiled, then they
moved to the fifth floor and stopped at 5F.

Outside, stuck in a drift just ahead of the police car,
Girl-Girl, Mr. T, Ronnie, and V-Ting sat in the Gypsy
cab with some fine dope they'd copped east of Avenue A
on 1st Street. They knew the dope was fine because there
was Chinese writing on the seal of the half-spoon bag.
They'd held their breaths as the cops scooted past, and
watched when they turned into the building. Girl-Girl
took a handful of cornstarch from the pocket of her coat
and began to chew. She'd been eating a whole lot of
cornstarch lately, which meant she was probably pregnant. Girl-Girl always ate cornstarch when she was
knocked up, or when she was frightened. Right now she
was scared silly. The cops had come close. And V-Ting
had a new pistol and was dead sick. Nobody was going to
bust him, not as sick as he was. That's what V-Ting said,
and Girl-Girl believed him.

Ramon tapped the apartment door with the back of his
hand. No answer. Adams punched it with the flat of his
fist. He punched it in the sweet spot above the two-by-
four crossbar and said sharply, "Police, open up."

"What police? There ain't no police out tonight! Who
you kidding! Get away from my door! I'm crazy and I got
a gun. I'll kill your fucking asses, you don't get away
from my door!"

Adams shouted, "There's a police car parked in front

of your building. Go take a look at it. We understand there's a woman in this apartment who called the police."

"Bullshit, there ain't nobody in here but me."

Adams kicked the door. A cockroach disappeared into a crack in the wall like a ghost.

"Hold it, man. Jesus, you'd better hold it. Don't kick the door."

Monty Adams grunted. He took his blackjack, raised his right hand, and slammed the door. "I'm getting real tense standing out here," he said. "I'm telling you I'm a police officer, and I have reason to believe there's a woman in there who called for help. You got maybe two seconds to open this door, or I'm gonna kick this fucker to Queens. You hear me?"

A small voice said, "But there ain't no woman in here."

"If that's the case, then we'll leave. But we can't do that till we have a look for ourselves. Ya understand what I'm telling you?"

"Actually," Ramon Rivera said to the door, "why don't you take a glimpse out of your window. You'll see an official New York City Police ve-hi-cle parked directly in front of your building. Once you're satisfied and feel safe and secure, you could respond to our request and open your apartment door like a good fellow."

"Ray," Adams whispered, "I want you to understand something." He paused, rubbed his hands, and went on. "I fuckin' hate it when you talk like that."

Ramon Rivera smiled a wide, closemouthed smile, and shrugged. A few seconds later the door to apartment 5F opened.

Adams slammed the door behind him. A smell of sweet, musky cologne hit him in the face, and he tried not to breathe.

A stride back from the door stood Felix Falco, and the sight of him made Adams twitch. He could feel the hot bitters roll from his stomach, creep up into his chest, flow into his mouth, and drop in his throat. He found it hard even to speak, though he did, telling Ramon to get in and check the other room.

Felix Falco was a large man, fat, and the blue dress he wore made him seem all the rounder. He wore a green beret with a red feather that curled out from the side. The dress was really a nightshirt, a long one that covered his feet, but to Monty Adams, Felix Falco wore a dress, pure and simple.

Adams kicked Falco in the side, kicked him good, sending him spinning across the room, and Falco swirled, doing a cute little pirouette—a dancer in a blue gown. He came to rest on a couch and screamed. He screamed some more, then again, each scream joining together and becoming one wail. He looked at Ramon, then back to Adams, too numb to move.

"Why you wanna—" Felix Falco cried, then his hand went up to his face, but he was way too slow. Monty Adams threw a left. It caught Falco at the bridge of the nose and sent him flying over the couch, rolled him to the wall. Falco crawled along the floor, and Adams let him go just a little, then caught him again in the corner. Helpless and pinned, Falco tried to cover up. Adams delivered three sharp slaps. One to the back of the head, one to the shoulder, the third to the neck.

"Don't kill him," said Ramon.

"Man fucks children, needs to be killed," Adams said. "But I ain't gonna kill ya." He kicked Felix Falco again.

"Stand up," Adams said. "Get up."

Falco rose, first to his hands and knees, then rolled back on his haunches. He was on one foot, holding the wall, when Adams's right hand caught him flush on the mouth.

Blood gurgled, then streamed from his mouth. It ran over his lips and splashed on his blue nightshirt. He slammed against the wall, then slid to the floor, his green beret in his lap, the feather gone. In terror he called on God.

Adams and Falco looked at each other for a long second.

"You're a murderer," Falco said, "a crazy murderer. Look what you did to me. Why you wanna kill me?"

"Because you're a short-eyed, baby-fucking piece of shit, and I'm here to give you the only justice you'll ever get in this piss-pot city. Get up," he said, and he pulled Felix Falco to his feet.

"To the kitchen table," he said, and he dragged Falco across the room.

His rage increased, and he could picture it all quite clearly. A little dark-haired boy, bent at the waist, his pants down around his knees, gleaming oil on a tiny mocha ass. Monty Adams lost it.

He grinned down at Felix Falco.

"You're a discredit to the human race," he shouted.

Falco muttered some words.

Officer Rivera went into the bedroom.

Felix Falco was in shock; his eyes were glazed and he was trembling. At first he wept imperceptibly, then the sobs came in convulsive blasts. He tried to speak, but before he could say a word, Adams reached into the collar of his nightshirt and ripped it down.

Falco dropped to his knees, his head bowed. He couldn't get enough air and he gasped.

"You fuck little boys in the ass, don't you?" Adams screamed.

Falco shook his head.

"You perverted scum, you'd better think carefully and answer correctly," Adams whispered. "You fuck little boys, don't you?"

Falco nodded.

"Well, you fucked the wrong one."

Now Falco really began to bawl.

"Do you know what the Ayatollah would do to you?"

"W-who?" Falco said, stammering.

"All right," said Adams, "stand up and put your dick on the edge of the table."

Felix Falco did what he was told. He trembled, he fumbled, he moaned, but when Monty Adams said, "I'm gonna put my gun up your ass, you fat fag, if you don't move quicker," Falco did what he was told.

"On the corner, near the edge," Adams said in a very calm voice. Then he slipped the good twelve-ounce slapper from his pocket. He could use the blackjack fast, like a whip.

Chapter One

Marjorie Butera told Charlie to sit on the living-room sofa while she brought him a cup of tea just the way he liked it, laced with a hefty shot of light rum and two teaspoons of sugar. Then she sat yogalike in a chair opposite him, folded her arms, and cocked her head, all ready to open up.

Outside, the city was cold and snowy, icy and bleak. Silver shadows grew on the windowpanes. In the kitchen down the hall, a light burned.

Charlie knew it would be wise to be silent and listen, but he didn't. "Marjorie, we both know just how good an investigator you are." He said this while sipping the tea, inhaling the fragrance of the rum, feeling that good, warm glow begin to spread. "Sure, you're good, sweetheart, but this is one case you'll never clear."

"I'll do the best I can. I'll do my job, I won't do less. I couldn't," Marjorie said without enthusiasm.

A prizewinning journalist, Charlie Rose was anything but a timid man. Still, he'd learned from past experience that when that line began to form around Marjorie's mouth, thoughtless chatter could bring trouble. So he sat, sipped his tea, and felt the hair bristle on the back of his neck. Marjorie could do that to him, raise the hair on his neck at the same moment she could put weight in his dick; she could do that to him with a look.

A beauty, like her paternal grandmother, Marjorie was tall, with dark auburn hair and brown eyes. Sometimes when the anger came, her eyes flashed black. Years of biking and tennis had made her body lithe and strong. And she was stubborn, quick to anger. Nineteen years of police work can do that to you. To some she seemed remote, quiet, judgmental. To Charlie she was warm, tough, sexy. His feelings for her were close to mystical.

"Charlie," she said slowly, "I've told you before, and it's vital you understand, that if there's good enough reason, I'll go after anyone. Do you remember my saying that?"

"Oh, sure I remember," Charlie said, now slouching a bit, looking amused. "But you never screwed around with someone like Janesky. Right now, Marjorie, no one in the Department is in a stronger position than Inspector Janesky, except maybe the people who are ready to protect him. I can't convince you of that, can I?"

"Screw Janesky, screw the son of a bitch. I'm gonna get him, Charlie. Don't underestimate me—don't *you* make that mistake too."

They sat for a long second in the center of her living room just staring at each other. Charlie in his rumpled suit, his tie still straight and neat; Marjorie in her sweats, her hair pulled back and tied. Then she stood up and turned toward the kitchen. Charlie got up from the couch. He caught her, took hold of her shoulders, and held her firm. His face was full of intensity, and she knew there was no resisting Charlie when he was like that.

"You've been with the force for nineteen years—nineteen years, Marjorie—and apparently you haven't learned a whole lot."

"You think so?" Her voice was tense.

"If you think you're going to get Janesky on your own, you haven't learned a thing."

His left hand absently went through the soft, blond tangle of his hair.

Marjorie went back to the chair. She had never liked journalists much, and with good enough reason. Marjorie was a New York City Police captain, and it was real tough for her to remember a police story a journalist wrote that was half accurate. Forget fair.

But Charlie Rose was different. From the moment they'd met, he had talked to her about justice, real justice. And it wasn't bad. For a journalist it was pretty damned inspiring.

Charlie had been assigned to do a piece about her for *Metropolitan* magazine. On that occasion they spent hours together, at lunch, walking, Marjorie answering questions, Charlie leading her around the Upper West Side, holding her elbow, taking her to places with a lot of oak and green glass and brass and copper doodads hanging from ceilings and walls.

Metropolitan magazine did a lot of police stories. Way too many as far as Marjorie was concerned. "Pick on somebody else, why don't you?" she'd told Charlie. "Go pick on the dancing mayor, or the City Council, or any of the other sulking, complaining, empty suits in the City, and give us a break."

Charlie had taken her to a prizefight at the Garden. When the match was over, they'd stopped at Manny's to raise a drink for the winner. Marjorie had asked him what he thought about the fight. Charlie answered her, saying, "It makes my blood freeze to see two black kids whale the shit out of each other while an audience of white folk cheers and laughs." He saw her look of surprise. "You asked, so I told you. And what did you think?"

"I think the one in red had nice teeth and a great ass," she rejoined.

That night was the first time they'd gone to bed. Marjorie knew that getting into bed with a journalist could end up presenting her with no small set of problems. But she did like what Charlie Rose had to say, the way he said it. Softly, with no illusions. Charlie was intelligent and intuitive, and his ass, well—it was world-class.

To Marjorie's astonishment, when the story about her appeared, it was better than good, it was accurate.

He'd described her as the Department's rising star,

doing a job everyone hated, hating everything the job represented, doing it better than anyone ever had.

"Investigating policemen is what this special lady does. And the policemen? Some call her the Dragon Lady, others Madame Butterfly, playing on her name. But Captain Butera takes none of it too seriously," Charlie had written. "Still, when the cops speak of her, they speak none too kindly. As a captain in the Internal Affairs Division, Marjorie Butera has learned a great deal about loneliness."

Marjorie fell in love.

For her, new lovers were major events in her life. Something funny went on as she approached her fortieth birthday. Still, Marjorie thought she knew what she was doing. Captain Marjorie Butera always *thought* she knew what she was doing.

Years earlier she had made the choice between a career, which she was good at, and relationships, which she was not. Marjorie had been lonely a long time. Then came Charlie.

Charlie loved to love; he made love teenage-style, with loud moans and great enthusiasm. Still, more often than not, the sounds of Charlie pleased her. And when his time came, there was a little hollering—short, sharp calls for God. Charlie would narrow his eyes and take a long, solemn look off into the distance, as if life's questions had answers and those answers were written in script on the wall above her headboard.

They both knew that it would have been wiser to pass on the lover relationship and simply remain friends. A cop and a journalist, an explosive mix. A year ago Friday, dancing to a jukebox after a few beers, Charlie had said, "Yeah, explosive, sure, but that's the beauty of it."

There was a goodness in Charlie that was convincing, an awareness that was enlightening. He made it easy to see things with his eyes. And although Marjorie sometimes disagreed violently with his view of things, she had come to love him, and the loving frightened her in ways she couldn't explain. *Maybe,* she thought, *I'm meant to be alone, just a loner, that's me.* It was a hard thought.

Now Marjorie got to her feet, went to her briefcase, and took the file folder she'd meant to read. Charlie had left the room. In a moment he was back, walking up to her, taking her hand, putting the folder down on the sofa, telling her, "You're going to read another report about Chief Janesky. You're going to read it, get pissed, swear and stammer, and carry on. Janesky's going to take you to school, m'lady. Take my word for it, you're in way over your head and alone on this one."

"Who said that I'd do it alone? I have colleagues, Charlie, people who'll come around and help. I won't give them a choice, they'll have to."

He smiled.

"I suppose you're talking about Carow."

"For one, yes."

"He's a ball-less wonder, Marjorie, for God's sake. The man's a lush."

"He drinks less than you do, Mr. Hero Journalist. I wouldn't be so goddamn quick to find fault in that area if I were you."

Charlie looked at her as though he were very tired.

Marjorie bit the inside of her mouth and thought about the confidential report she held. She decided she wasn't handling this right.

"C'mon, Charlie, it's getting late. Let's get into bed." She smiled at him tenderly.

"You mean to tell me"—he sounded angry— "that this is it, no more discussion? It's over, right? Why the hell don't you let me work with you on this?"

"We've talked this to death. My God, we've talked about it for months. I'll not be your Deep Throat in the Department, Charlie. Now what do I have to do, write it in blood on my chest for chrissake? This is my case, Charlie, mine. And you of all people know how I feel about the press. I'd hang a cop that went to them regarding an ongoing case."

Charlie looked down at Marjorie, blinked, and smiled. He was blessed with a beautiful face, deep gray eyes, and light brown hair. *He's tired,* Marjorie thought, *really exhausted. I'll take him to bed, make him sleep. Then I'll read the report later.*

It was as if he'd read her mind; he shook his head. Marjorie's anxiety quickened, and her mind raced, trying to find a way to end the discussion. The planning made her sad. Charlie, she knew, loved her, only wanted to help and protect her. The thought made her want to please him. But she didn't want his help, and she certainly didn't need his protection. She'd gone too far on her own; put up with, and put down, enough bullshit to sink Manhattan. No, she didn't need Charlie's help, not his or anyone else's.

Later, in the bedroom, both undressed, lying on the bed, Marjorie played her fingers along Charlie's cheeks. Charlie, getting into it, kissed her. She felt a rush of warmness for him; it was a good feeling. She took hold of Charlie's neck and tucked her head into his shoulder.

Marjorie didn't really feel like making love that night, and she never simply fucked. She wanted Charlie to be still, so she could hold him, comfort him, get him to sleep.

"Baby," he said, "you don't want to make love. And, sweetness, neither do I. I'm exhausted and I'm worried."

"Don't worry about me, Charlie. It makes me nervous."

Charlie Rose was thirty years old, a bit of a diet and workout freak. He'd won a Pulitzer for a series he'd done on the homeless. Said it didn't mean a thing. The people he most cared about had no idea what the prize was. He knew the City, knew its dark places better than anyone Marjorie had ever known, cop or civilian. Someday, Charlie had said, he wanted to write a play, tell the story of the City in a play. Another reason for Marjorie to love him. He knew many things, Charlie Rose did. He was wise. But he didn't know the Department like she did; he wasn't part of it.

Marjorie couldn't tell how long it took, but it was a matter of seconds before Charlie's body relaxed and his breathing came on in quick, steady whispers. Marjorie was amazed to see his total collapse, and how he hugged her as if she were life itself. There was such relief in his sleep, such satisfaction, it poured out of him easily and smoothly. It was one A.M., and all New York City Police Captain Marjorie Butera could think of was that she had a hell of a lot of work to do, and she wanted to get to it. Charlie was asleep, and the truth was that whatever thrill the night held for Marjorie lay in her briefcase on a sofa in the next room.

As silently as she could, she slid from beside him; she did not want to wake him. She turned her head, a half turn, and flicked her eyes over her shoulder. She was surprised to feel anxious, truly anxious. It was her apartment, after all, her bed, and her kitchen she wanted to get to. The light in the kitchen was on, and for that she was grateful.

Marjorie sat along the edge of the bed listening to Charlie's steady breathing. The rhythm was unbroken. As her feet touched the floor she thought that in such a vicious world it was odd that Charlie could sleep so snuggily.

Smoothly, without a sound, she slipped from the bed.

She made it to the bedroom door.

"You need my help on this one, Marjorie. I can't believe that you have no notion of what you're letting yourself in for."

"You're awake! You've been awake all the time! Charlie," Marjorie said, taking a step toward him, "only children and rummies pretend to sleep when they're awake."

"And only fools take on a battle they can't hope to win. C'mon," Charlie said, "please! You're playing with the big guys here. Not some nobody cop on the take." Charlie was up on his elbow, pointing at her with his index finger, a gesture she was less than fond of.

"Janesky and these people all have a lifelong, vested interest in the status quo. They're the music makers, Marjorie, and they'll force you to dance to their tune, because if you don't, they'll pick you up and spin you around till you don't know which way is up. Normally I couldn't care less what it is that you are working on. For me to insist you back off is in some ways an affront to my standing as a journalist. But I'm not going to sit still and watch you get battered. I love you too much. And I know what getting whipped will do to you. It'll put out your fire, change you, till you're one of them. Just another one of the boys in the band. And I'm not about to let that happen."

Marjorie could see, even from where she stood, that Charlie was angry. She smiled at him; it was a kind smile, meant to diffuse that anger.

"I have to put on some clothes. I'm freezing," she said.

If he heard what she said, he gave no indication of it. Charlie sort of grunted and said, "You can't do this through the Department. When you put a light on Janesky, it'll bring more heat on you than it will him."

She did not want to quarrel with him, so she chose her words carefully and spoke softly. "Things are different nowadays, Charlie. You're talking about the old Department, pre–Serpico, pre–Knapp Commission."

She looked at him, his wide shoulders above the quilt. "Don't be angry, Charlie, don't be. But I've always believed that the Department should clean its own dirty linen. Going to the press is a betrayal of everything I believe in. So please, please, Charlie, let's drop it, huh?"

"Nothing changes in this city, Marjorie. To believe that it does is wishful thinking. Fighting the good fight is bullshit—winning, survival, is all that counts."

She was too tired to think that one over, and so she just sighed and walked out of the bedroom.

Marjorie went through the bedroom door with the idea of putting on a pot for tea. In the hallway near the bookcase, she stopped to take a heavy cotton sweater from the chair; her nipples were as hard as diamonds, and sensitive to the touch. Carefully she put on the sweater and then padded through the hallway, toward the light in the kitchen.

Gooseflesh covered her legs, and she realized that she was naked from the waist down. Her feet were cold, but her slippers were in the bedroom closet, and she wasn't about to go back there and chance another speech from Charlie. She heard him approach; she could feel him watching her. She lifted her leg and rubbed her knee with the bottom of her foot. Her foot was cold and she shuddered. When Charlie walked into the kitchen, she thought it best not to look his way.

"Would you like more tea?" she asked calmly.

Charlie looked over at the kettle of water and the two cups that she had set out, then he looked down at her legs. His eyes stayed on her legs. He caught himself and sheepishly looked up at her.

"I only want to help," he said.

"If that's true, then you'll stay out of my business. I don't tell you how to write a story, don't tell me how to conduct an investigation. Okay?"

He stared at her with a warm grin, and for an instant Marjorie's eyes locked on his. She turned away quickly, moving down the hallway toward the bedroom. Charlie followed, calling after her, "I won't mention Janesky again. You want my help, you'll let me know, all right?"

Marjorie knew that Charlie wasn't about to let go of the subject, but she nodded, anyway.

At the foot of the bed she found her bathrobe and wrapped it around herself. In the closet was a pair of old, worn running shoes that served as slippers. Tea in hand, she returned to the living room and made herself comfortable on the sofa.

Charlie was lying on the floor. A South Side Johnny tape was playing—"Without Love."

When the piece ended, she asked Charlie to turn off the stereo. She glanced at her watch. It was 1:30 A.M.

Charlie Rose was tall, his hair longer than the current

style. He lay on the floor with his legs crossed at the ankles, hands twined behind his head. He was breathing softly and staring at her. It struck Marjorie that his face, in this light, was perfect, too perfect for a man. She gave him a look, a slow shake of the head, saying, "I've been with the Department for nineteen years. Till you, there wasn't a reporter that I'd talk to. Till you. To me they were all whores, all of them. The best of them's gonads would shrivel and drop off if they had to face for one minute what a street cop faces in a career. And still you all make judgments, twenty-twenty hindsight from a table at the Lion's Head."

Charlie drew in his breath wearily.

"To me, Charlie, you've always been the enemy. A bunch of half-assed elitists who don't have a clue about the real world."

Charlie polished off his tea, saying, "What horseshit." He smiled at his own remark.

"Is that right?"

"Do you know what this city is really about, Marjorie? D'ya know the answer to that heavy question?" asked Charlie.

Marjorie looked at him as if to say, "What are you talking about?"

"Well, I know the answer," Charlie told her. "First off, you have to know that this city is a circus, and that the mayor is a clown. He's a clown, and the ringmaster of the biggest, flashiest, bust-out circus in the world. Knowing that, from the get-go, solves everything."

Marjorie smiled and shook her head.

"People in this city," he said, "rich beyond description, step over their fellow citizens who sleep and shit in the street. Am I right?" he asked in his racy Sam Donaldson voice, which he normally affected for people he didn't know.

"My God," Marjorie said, "it's going to happen. You're going to talk all night. Did you take a drug?"

"Listen, this is not funny," Charlie said. "Just give me

a minute. In one ring of this five-ring circus we see fourteen-year-old drug dealers doing a little crack-a-doo on the front steps of a tenement. They take time out from their endeavors to shoot the mother of four in the face because she had the audacity to complain to the police about the creeps who infest her hallway and stoop."

"I read your story, Charlie. I told you what I thought at the time. It was a tragic, horrible story. What's the connection between the Gomez woman and my investigation?"

"I passed by Mrs. Gomez's building today, and ya know what I saw? I'll tell ya what I saw—they were there, the crack-a-doos, doing their slipping-and-sliding routine on the front steps of poor Mrs. Gomez's building, just like nothing happened."

"Is this going to be a justice-system-doesn't-work speech?" Marjorie asked.

"The point here, Marjorie, is simply that nothing changes in this city. Anyone that's awake knows it, and it all seems perfectly natural," Charlie declared. "It's a circus. You think of the City as a circus, then it's all just one big laugh, with a few oooohs and ahhhhhs thrown in for a head rush, a little coolness."

"So?" said Marjorie, thinking, *I don't believe I let myself in for this, a night of speech-making by the world-class cynic, Charlie Rose. Shit.*

"When the idea finds a home in your head that this city on the Hudson, this city of jewels, is a circus, you can sit back, laugh, and applaud while the talent walks off with all that's not nailed down. Then you wait awhile, the circus moves on, soon a new one comes to town. New acts, younger, more frisky elephants and tigers. But the same ol' fucking clowns."

"Charlie—"

"No—no, wait, listen. If you think you can pull their plug, if you think you can throw shit in their game, by your lonesome, dear heart, then you rank pretty high in the loose-head department."

Charlie was staring at her, his hands still laced behind his head, biting the inside of his cheek. A signal.

Marjorie knew that for the remainder of this conversation she'd have to move carefully. She looked down at him, and he looked up at her. Gently she fingered the border of her robe to open it. She'd always marveled at the way Charlie's mouth dropped open at the sight of her legs.

"I hear you, Charlie, I do," she said. "I know you want to be helpful. But now *you* hear *me*, huh? I've long since forgiven this city for being what it is. I have tons of stories of brutality and treachery. Every cop does. And what I can't change, I live with. Still, I reserve the right to be an honorable person. I believe in what I do, and I don't give a damn about politics. I'm a cop, Charlie, and there it is. I'll do my job, and I'll do it the best I can, my way. And the deal is"—and this she said with as much strength as she could muster—"I do my job alone. Okay, my love?"

She watched his face change, and she didn't like the change she saw. It occurred to her, against all good sense and reason, that she did in fact need Charlie. If nothing else, he was truly an enemy to dullness. And God knows, life had been pretty dull before him.

"We've been together, what, a year now?" he said. "I figure that entitles me to make an assumption as to when you do or don't need my help."

"You'd be wise not to assume anything, Charlie."

It would be possible, she thought, to describe Charlie as a regular man-about-town. Lunch at the Russian Tearoom, dinner at Elaine's, a nightcap with the boys and girls at The Lion's Head. Snappy stuff, real glitz, bright lights and bullshit. When he made that particular round, Charlie had long since given up asking her to come along. Still, it remained a part of his world, and she had told him, great, okay, go ahead, enjoy, call me when you get home.

Except that Charlie wasn't really like that. There was

always the suggestion of a street tough about him. Like he always knew just what was happening.

Yeah, ya can't bullshit ol' Charlie, been around too long, seen too much pirouetting by the silky snakes of the ol' Big Apple.

Except that Charlie wasn't like that, either.

Not a wiseass.

"C'mon, Charlie," she said softly. "Let's be kind to ourselves and end this conversation."

Charlie fell silent, wagged his head, thought for a moment, then said, "I'm going back to bed."

"Good," Marjorie said with a neat turn of her head. "That's good."

Later, Marjorie didn't feel happy. She wasn't unhappy, she just didn't know for sure how she felt.

She put her feet up on the sofa, rubbed her eyes, reached for her tea, then reread the report from her field associate.

The report described Janesky as a lunatic.

That was exactly what the field associate had written: "I believe that the inspector is a lunatic."

The field associate was a rookie cop, three months out of the Academy, assigned to Janesky's command, no street experience at all. He was describing the man in charge of the most active precinct in the City. The man who, many plugged-in people believed, yearned to be police commissioner; some said FBI director. Marjorie had always figured Janesky wanted to be mayor. In her mind he was a dangerous man, and not because he was ambitious. His ambitions had nothing to do with Inspector Janesky's dark side. He probably *was* a madman, Marjorie thought.

Ronald Janesky had been named Cop of the Year. His picture had been on the cover of *Metropolitan* magazine. He was dazzling, the toughest, best-looking cop to come down the pike in years. She had seen him interviewed once on TV. He had come on like a cop's cop, hot after drug dealers, whores, muggers, and any other perv you'd want to name. Janesky had a fire in him, he exuded an almost sexual kind of heat. But Marjorie believed that Janesky traveled around in a mask. That he was in fact a power-and-violence junkie, a man who used people to attain high rank, and she suspected he was a stone-cold racist. She studied Janesky's career, interviewed men and women who had worked for him. Janesky had no business being a cop, much less an inspector of police. The thought of him becoming police commissioner wobbled her knees. Marjorie had been assigned to the Internal Affairs Division for over a year, and in that time she'd taken on a mission, and that mission was to nail Inspector Ronald Janesky.

The field associate reported that the precinct cops loved Janesky.

She kept reading, and later, when she thought about it, it made sense that Janesky would stack his command with cops that were reflections of himself.

Marjorie rubbed her forehead with the heel of her hand, feeling the tiredness spread. She sensed a shift in the tone of the report, just enough to realize that the young cop was losing it. It was amazing; the officer was a college graduate. He wrote as if he were on drugs. Maybe, she thought, he was simply frightened out of his wits. Maybe he was right to be.

"A war is going on in this precinct," the memo read, "and we take prisoners. Some of the prisoners are beaten in the basement of the station house in a place called the gym set. The main headbuster is a psycho they call the Prince of Pain. His name is Monty Adams, pronounced *Mon-tee*. He's Janesky's personal favorite."

Marjorie sipped her tea and read on.

"Inspector Janesky is a tight-lipped crazy; he condones what goes on here—supports it, even. I'm afraid of them all. I want out of here. I didn't volunteer to do this kind of shit. I'm not a good spy; I don't fit in. They all look at me sideways.

"By the way," the memo continued, "in case you're interested, and you certainly should be, the TS man and the Broom are having an affair. Need I tell you that they are both male officers. *This place is a loony bin! Get me out of here. Transfer me or I'll quit this shitty job.*"

The memo was signed, "F/A 119 a.k.a. Ken."

Field Associates did tend to be a bit dramatic. This one in particular, Officer Ken, she thought, had a special flair.

She'd been his contact for three months, and during that time he had come up with more than one bizarre story. Like the one about the gorilla masks. Ken once reported that the cops in Janesky's precinct, on the late tour, wore full-head gorilla masks. They'd stop motorists and go on family disputes wearing their masks. They were selective as to whom they stopped. It was always persons unlikely to complain. She had checked that allegation herself, couldn't substantiate a thing. Nevertheless Ken swore it was true.

She had to remember just who she was dealing with. Ken had a habit of following up an accusing memo with the news of a sudden change. Which meant, of course, he was probably exaggerating in the first place. Well, F/As were hard to come by, very difficult to recruit, and impossible to keep working for an extended period of time.

God, she remembered the story he'd told about the gay motorcyclist, the one who had led three sector cars on a merry chase all over Brooklyn. Ken reported that when the cops caught up with him, they stuck a curtain rod in his ass and tied a flag to it. Another one of Ken's allegations she was unable to prove. Apparently the motorcycle daredevil didn't mind, because he never made a complaint.

The most recent case was the arrest of Felix Falco by Officers Adams and Rivera. The defendant in the case had a broken nose, a broken jaw, and a ruptured penis. But this time she had a complainant. This time, with

Ken's help, she just might be able to make a case. Maybe Felix Falco's splattered dick was a godsend.

In any event, come morning, she would meet with her commanding officer, Chief Carow, and the chief of operations. The meeting would be secret, and the entire agenda would be concerned with Chief Janesky. Everything at her command was secret. Internal Affairs was famous for its secrets. Despite that, she was sure that enough people knew about the meeting to start a bowling league. Janesky was too important. He was the mayor's favorite cop.

Marjorie returned to the bedroom and quietly crawled back into bed. Charlie opened his eyes, smiled faintly, and began to hum a song. Marjorie thought it was "New York, New York."

"Still not sleeping, eh?" she whispered. "And just what are you smiling about?"

"It's close to three o'clock," he said.

She looked at the clock on the nightstand and saw that it was true. And that bad news presented her with a knotty problem. Because when Marjorie had pulled back the bed covers, so as to get back into bed, she'd looked at Charlie's body and made a decision.

"You are virtue, Charlie. That's what you are to me—living, breathing virtue. Now, if you'll promise to be good, I will give you such a blow job, you'll scream till they hear you in Chinatown."

Marjorie bent over him and moved her hand along his body.

"Sometimes I think you're a little sick—ya know, mentally," Charlie said with an enormous smile.

Without hesitation she took hold of Charlie's dick and balls, held them in her hand, and bounced them, as if the weight alone would tell her something.

"Hmm," she said in an ominous tone, making it clear she was more awake than he. "Crazy, am I? Well, then, I can't be responsible for what it is that I do."

She bounced Charlie's balls in the palm of her hand.

Charlie crossed his feet at the ankles, and his hips began to move up and down. He had that faraway expression on his face.

"I know why they call you Madame Butterfly," Charlie said in a hoarse whisper.

She looked at his beautiful, open face, and wide gray eyes looked back at her.

"You're a bit of a poet. You should understand such things."

She was kneeling alongside him now, gently stroking him. Waiting and watching.

"I love you," he said. "I do, I truly do."

"Shh," she said, and Charlie dropped his arm across his forehead, closed his eyes, and opened his mouth. He looked to Marjorie as though he were wounded.

Marjorie permitted herself a small smile and whispered, "You're a sweet, gentle soul, Charlie."

She lowered her head, her mouth covering Charlie, and moved herself as though she were in a hurry. The sounds of Charlie filled the room.

And afterward she took hold of Charlie's shoulder and prepared herself to sleep. Charlie wrapped his arms around her, held her close. Marjorie was eight years older, and that thought made her heart drop.

He had options; she knew that Charlie had choices. Still, he was here in her arms.

She lay still beside him and stared at the dark, square bedroom window; somewhere beyond it there was a siren, and in her head she heard the screams of victims. She felt lonely again, and a little frightened. She wanted the good dream, not the nightmare.

Marjorie slid smoothly through the surface of sleep, and the good dream came.

When childhood friends had played with dolls and teacups, dreaming of a domestic future, Marjorie had dreamed of adventure, of cruising the islands of the Caribbean, riding the trades along the coasts of Haiti and Puerto Rico, sailing the boil of Bocas del Drago.

The images were quite clear: the wake lying whitely against the blue water, the hot sun, the cooling trade winds, and over the bow she could make out green palms rising to shadowed mountains.

Her dream made her smile.

Chapter Two

"Listen, way back when, in the ol' days, ya know what I mean, back when Christ was a cowboy, in the ol' jaaaab we had standards, and they were high. Nowadays, man, you can be a midget. A midget with three collars, or an eighty-five-pound broad what smokes dope on her swing and lets the boys go by, and ya can still get on the fuckin' jaaaab. The jaaab's gone ta shit. And there it is, there ain't no more, that's the fuckin' story."

Police Officer Ken Malloy loved it when he had a chance to ride on the late tour. To be off the street and in a warm car when there was a mean sea wind howling through blocks where even at midday the sun never hit the sidewalk was a boon.

But to spend eight hours locked in a box on wheels with Officer Ben Paris, a guy who talked nonstop and said *jaaaab* instead of *job*, well, that can tickle the dark side of your nature. Especially when the conversation never went past a great hero sandwich, a great Bruce Lee flick, a great place to retire—the greatest hockey fight of all time, no less—and you had to pretend interest. Well, you can learn from older, more experienced people, any fool knows that. But this—this never-ending, mind-numbing roll of bullshit from Paris made Malloy's long back muscles tense and his forehead go numb from resting it against the window. Paris, his slow speech, highlighted now and then with a sickening cigarette cough, his breathing labored a bit, was not his idea of a great partner.

The whole thing was ridiculous, really, when you thought about it; roaming in the sector through the night, hoping that you're not too successful. Rolling through a forest of tenements and alleys, shining light into rear yards near the docks.

Sometimes the radio would fall into a long, blessed silence. The longest silence of all came between three and six A.M. That's when the pendulum stopped swinging, and peace came to Sector David.

It was exactly five A.M. when there was a rush of static from the radio, then the CB operator took over and the call began.

"David, Sector David in BSCO K—"

"David," Ken Malloy said to the radio.

"126 Water Street, that's 1-2-6 Water, we have a Signal 31, burglary in progress."

Officer Paris hit the roof-light switch, and Ken Malloy ran the back of his hand across his nose. Then he adjusted his gun belt.

The dispatcher came back, a touch more excited this time: "David, we got a second call. Man with a gun. Heads up, guys. All other available BSCO units respond. K—"

Blessed silence gone, the blue-and-white did a neat U-turn and roared off.

Paris nodded his head.

"We got one," he said.

Malloy was thinking, *My first gun run—is it for real?*

Red Hook dogs, two of them, howled when Malloy hit the siren switch.

The patrol car slowed. Paris gave a glance at Ken and asked, "Ya want maybe a bugle and flag, make sure the shithead knows we're on our way?"

Malloy wasn't offended. He shut the siren off, sat still, and narrowed his eyes.

"Sorry," he said.

Except for an occasional car, the streets were deserted. They ran through one red light, then another, and picked up the pace down a one-way street. With one hand braced against the dash and the other on his pistol grip, Ken Malloy looked out the window. The buildings had lost their shape—the quiet, empty street suddenly looked mean.

"David of BSCO," the CB operator called.

"David," Ken shouted into the radio.

"We have multiple calls from Pier 3 on that man with a gun."

Multiple calls means it's for real. Multiple calls means there's a guy out there for sure, and for sure he's got a gun. Probably a bigger and better gun than yours, Ken thought.

But who called? It's five o'clock in the morning; there's no warehouse open at five o'clock in the morning. There's no one around, just the burglar. Maybe *he* called, maybe he wants some action, a little duel. *Well, fuck him,* Ken thought. *I got a bulletproof vest. But what if he's an expert, an Olympic shooter, and shoots me in the face? Oh, shit, not in the face, anywhere but the face. Man, fuck this job.*

What you hoped for when you were heading on a gun run, when you were flying along the street racing to the piers, searching for a warehouse on Pier 3, where someone had broken in and was seen to have a gun, what you hoped for were other cops' voices.

You came to love those voices, each one. You knew you were part of something special. No wonder the old-timers loved the feeling. It was marvelous; everyone cared. At no other time in your life did so much seem to focus just on you. At no time did so many people tell you they wanted you to stay alive.

The sector car moved through the South Brooklyn streets like a thunderbolt.

"David, slow up. This is Charles, we're on our way."

"Adam read direct."

"Frank read direct."

"This is the sergeant's car BSCO to all responding

BSCO vehicles. Watch those side streets and intersections, cowboys. Everyone's moving. Wait for us, David."

"Give 'em a four, hah, partner," Ben Paris said. "Let 'em know we heard 'em."

"Ten-four," Ken said into the radio.

"Don't worry," Paris said. "Take my word for it, there won't be anyone around when we get there."

Suddenly Ken felt the worst chill he'd ever felt, as if ice were rising in the marrow of his bones. One hand frozen to the dash, the other to his gun butt. He was glad they weren't there yet, because he couldn't move. If it happened now, this instant, he would freeze and that would be it. Just like the policewoman he'd heard about in the Bronx, the one who rolled on a man with a gun in a gas station. Right off, the perp shot her partner. She screamed, "Oh, no," dropped her gun, and ran. The perp used her gun on her and two other cops.

Ken knew this was for real. It didn't make a whole lot of sense, he thought, to rush like crazy to a place where someone might kill you. He wanted to shout at Paris, "Hey, slow up, you're being reckless."

Ken stared straight out the windshield. They were on Water Street. Pier 3 lay maybe two blocks ahead. The Hook's streets seemed to be full of demons and ghosts.

They should slow down and wait for the other cars, Ken thought. Because God knew eight cops were better than two. He should tell Paris now, "Okay, slow up, let's wait for the others."

He had the right to say it. Paris was a cop like himself, not a sergeant, not a boss of any kind, just another cop. He should express his own thoughts. He had things to say. Fuck, this was his life too. And he was a college graduate. Ben Paris had never gotten out of high school. Right, he'd tell Ben just what was on his mind, except that when Ben shouted for him to get on the horn and tell 'em there's a van parked in the alley—an olive van with New Jersey plates—none of it seemed to matter. And there it was, right in front of him now, just sitting there, with its back doors open . . . no people . . . not a perp in sight.

Shit, the side door to the warehouse was wide open. The huge parking lot they'd crossed had a car parked here and there, but it was pretty empty. Anyone could see you coming for miles. And no people, not a soul around, not even a security guard at the gate they'd passed. Should have been a security guard there. Maybe he was the one who had called. Maybe he's hiding, afraid of the man with a gun who would use it on the security guard in a flash. It occurred to Ken that maybe the security guard was already dead.

Ben Paris slammed on the brakes. They ran toward the open side door to the warehouse, toward the building with the olive van parked in the alley. Ken couldn't remember if he'd mentioned that over the air. He must have, but he couldn't remember.

At the van—it was new—Ken looked inside. It was empty, and he looked back to see Ben Paris motioning for him to move to the open warehouse door.

He was just going to take a peek inside; that's what he'd do, take a little peek inside, then get back behind the van and wait. He could do that. A little peek was no big deal. *Careful, take off your cap, just a little peek.*

Then he saw them rush through the door. Ken Malloy knew one thing for sure, he was dead meat if that damn vest didn't work, because they came out shooting. *Dumb,* Ken thought. *This is the stupidest thing I've ever seen. They're shooting at me, a cop, and there's about a billion other cops coming right behind me. Even if they kill me, there's no way out. Dumbest damn thing I ever seen.*

It seemed to take so long to bring his gun up. Why was he so slow? Finally he squeezed, then jerked, and jerked again. An explosion hit him. It spun him around. Something pressed against his throat. He stiffened with the shock. *I'm not afraid. When you think of all the cops coming—six cars, maybe—why should I be afraid?* Figures appeared and disappeared in front of him, beside him. His mind was still working enough that he could ask himself, *Who are these people that they want to kill me? What the fuck are they doing here?*

He heard the sounds of a little boy crying. When the wailing became more intense, he coughed, gagged, and felt a hot stream run through his nose. The crying stopped. *It's me,* he thought. *It's me acting like a stupid kid. But I'm not afraid, I was never afraid.*

Chapter Three

She hadn't slept well, anyway, so it was no great shakes for Marjorie to be out at seven A.M., in her car, and on her way downtown for the Headquarters meeting.

The Upper West Side southbound avenues were filling with traffic. In a half hour, Broadway would be thick with cars; West Street and the West Side Highway Extension were already wall to wall. A typical Big Apple morning.

She had dressed quietly, letting Charlie sleep, not bothering with breakfast. At nine or so she would phone to make sure Charlie was up and out. He would sleep till noon if she let him. She smiled, thinking how well Charlie slept. As if the universe was at long last in order.

Heading east on Seventy-ninth, she crossed the park at Seventy-second and hesitated about which route to take south. She finally opted for Second Avenue. At Sixty-fourth Street, she hung a quick left and scooted onto the FDR Drive.

Maybe she would make Headquarters in fifteen minutes; an hour was more likely.

Marjorie despised New York traffic, hated to drive in it. At rush hour in this city, only the strong need show up. At least Marjorie had a Department car. And when you had a new Chevy, with citywide frequencies and a special frequency at your command, you had a certain amount of freedom. And it made sense to stay off the mystery- and surprise-filled subways.

She snapped on the radio, tuned just past NPR, and

found one of the all-news stations. Before she rolled beneath the U.N. overpass, just before the radio signal faded into the morning air, she heard it.

The radio commentator said that two policemen had been shot in Brooklyn, one DOA at Downtown Medical Center, the other in critical condition at Beekman General. The Police Department, as of yet, had not released the officers' names.

Marjorie eased the Chevy out of the traffic lane into the next turnoff and rolled to a stop. She sat staring through the windshield, searching for something, concentrating, not looking around.

She made an effort to breathe slowly. Her throat was dry as dust. *We're getting pretty shaky,* she told herself. Cops get shot in this city all the time; six already this year, and it was only March. Why should she think that this shooting was anything special?

Because it was in Brooklyn! At BSCO, that's why.

She knew all right; it was eerie how she knew.

Marjorie shut off the AM radio, picked up her transmitter, and called the IAD base.

Sergeant Flynn, the morning man working base, told her that Chief Carow was waiting. Told her he'd left a message at Headquarters for her to report forthwith to IAD.

Flynn said Chief Carow did not look good, did not look good at all.

Marjorie said, "I'm on my way."

At Forty-second Street she hit the lights, and at Twenty-third the siren.

The Internal Affairs Division of the NYPD occupies an entire building on Poplar Street in Brooklyn Heights. Few officers could guess at the size of the place, but those who have been there would tell you that you can get lost in the building. Most divisions have only an office, or a series of offices, like the Homicide Division or the Rape Squad or the Crimes Against Senior Citizens

Unit. She considered the IAD building a monument to bureaucracy.

The structure itself, a somber, four-story, gray-granite box, was an ancient police station. The windows of the street-level floor are crossed with heavy black bars. On the vestibule wall someone, a long time ago, had written, "Justice has nothing to do with the law."

IAD has the power to put snakes into the stomach of the toughest cop. Line officers see the IAD as a home for anticop cops. They think of it as a perverted unit, stocked with ball-less wonders, afraid of the noise and pain of the street, a real gang of hoopels.

The very day Marjorie was made captain, she was assigned to the IAD. She knew its reputation. It was hardly a secret. But she also knew it could be her break-out command. From there she could get her Eagle, then her Star, then two Stars. She could soar from the IAD; become the highest-ranking woman ever in the NYPD. Marjorie could make history. And if it took an assignment to the IAD to make it work, then so be it.

"Look at it this way," Inspector Carow had said. "Promotion, promotion, promotion. All you have to do is drop the hammer on a few deserving cops. Think of yourself as a holy launderer. Dirty linen. You know."

Marjorie got off the elevator on the second floor and walked around to the front of the building. The place reminded her of a Bulgarian State Institution—pea-green and gray walls, municipal construction, substantial, heavy, old, depressing. Small wonder cops' hearts tried to eat their way out of their chests when they entered this building, she thought.

From an open office door, the sound of country music. Farther along the hallway, the office of Inspector Andrew Tony Carow, her boss. She walked up to the doorway; the room was dark but for a few lines of bright sun that slid into the room behind a pulled and tied drape.

With a sense of sadness she observed the rounded

shoulders of her commanding officer slumped over a case folder. Carow, the man in charge of the unit that policed the police of the nation's largest police department, sat at a glass-topped metal desk surrounded by a dozen case folders, a dab of butter from a half-eaten bagel crowning his nose like a tiny golden horn.

It was early morning, not quite nine A.M., and already he seemed pretty far gone to Marjorie.

She looked at Carow, half expecting him to get up.

"I suppose our meeting at Headquarters has been canceled."

"Your F/A was shot this morning. Did you know that?"

"Malloy?"

Carow looked at her for a moment, let his shoulders sag, then exhaled slowly.

"Yeah. Right. Malloy. How many field associates are assigned to you, Captain?"

"Two," she said.

"Maybe I'd feel better, Margie, if you'd express a little concern."

"Andrew! Jesus! I heard the radio report. I got the message from Flynn and came into the office." Her voice had gotten louder. "How in the hell was I supposed to know it was Malloy?"

Chief Inspector Carow could pull rank; he was a chief inspector, after all, and Marjorie merely a captain. But it would be no contest. They had known each other too long, had worked together for years. Marjorie always spoke her mind to Carow. And he knew that she knew; she was quicker. She would rout him in any shouting match.

Carow shook his head. He squinted at her as if she were something tiny, hard to make out. And he looked at her a long time.

"Come in and sit down," he said finally. His voice had become pleasant, almost casual.

Marjorie looked straight at him and said, "Would you like me to get you some coffee?"

After an outburst Marjorie always managed to return Carow's ego to the head of the table.

"Just had some, thanks," he said, and pointed to his cup.

He looked less healthy than usual, Marjorie noticed. She worried over friends, and Chief Inspector Andrew Tony Carow had been her friend since the days of the old Policewoman's Bureau. The old days, when women were not permitted to take promotion examinations, when to be a policewoman meant that you body-searched dead females or live hookers. Maybe, if you were lucky, you could be a clerk typist somewhere, or be a detective in the Missing Persons Bureau. Little else.

The Policewoman's Bureau was where it all began for Marjorie. She always knew it wouldn't end there: she knew there'd be changes.

Still, during all those years—Carow as sergeant, Carow as lieutenant, Carow as captain, Carow as deputy inspector, then assistant chief inspector, then chief inspector—he'd treated her with respect. No small thing in the Department of the sixties and seventies. She had not forgotten it.

Chief Inspector Carow had a scar on his face, the kind men get in knife fights. He'd gotten his in a car wreck. And he'd sit in his office for hours talking about it with Captain Gleason, or his driver, Officer Martin, or anyone else who would sit and listen.

"The gook forced me off the damn road," he'd say. "It's the way they drive. You ever see a gook drive, or worse yet, a Pakistani? It might have been a Pakistani that got me," he would explain, squinting, sitting hunched over his desk, nodding his head and rubbing his cheek.

He had taken to drink years ago when he was in command of the Public Morals Unit—around the time his son was killed. It was not true that someone had forced him off the road. Long Island cops said they found him in the arms of a scrub oak at Exit 40 of the Expressway. He was stewed to the mickey, half his face in his hands. "It was a damn gook," he'd yelled. Trouble was, the Long Island police had been on him for ten minutes. They had clocked him at seventy, saw his Department car pirouette off the center divider and loop-de-loop into a tree. Fortunately it had happened at four A.M., and the only people out and about were cops. Three of them; two in a patrol car and the Chief Inspector in a tree.

Once Marjorie had seen him standing in front of a mirror, staring with fascination at the red, jagged line that ran from the center of his forehead, across his right eye and cheek to a spot behind his ear where it disappeared into what was left of his brown hair. He'd muttered quick curses and traced the red line with his pinky finger.

"Ya know," Carow said, now sagging back in his chair, "I'm a loser. I identify with all the world's losers. You know the kind of people I mean, don't you, Margie? The ones that jump into holes too deep and slimy to get out."

Marjorie smiled a tight smile and nodded.

Not her mother, not her best friend, Emi, nor her ex-lover Jeff, not even Charlie, had ever called her Margie. Her name was Marjorie. For fifteen years she had been telling Carow that her name was Marjorie. And she had said it often through clenched teeth. Finally she had stopped protesting. Instead she had taken to calling him Andrew—a name he never used. Even that didn't help. Marjorie would always be Margie to Andrew Tony Carow.

"Oh, hell, don't tell me you suspect that Malloy was shot because he worked for me," Marjorie said.

Carow set his coffee cup by the stack of file folders on his desk, and handed her the Unusual Occurrence Report. "Of course not," he said.

At the surprise in Carow's tone Marjorie already felt relieved.

"Amazing Grace," sung by Willie Nelson, drifted into the office from down the hallway. Marjorie listened for a moment, then said, "They play that damn radio too loud."

"Malloy wasn't killed. He's shot up bad, but he wasn't killed. His partner, Paris, took three in the chest and died at the scene," said Carow.

"Office Malloy will be okay," she said after glancing at the report.

"Okay? He took one in the throat. That's not too okay. Then again, you've always had a curious way of looking at things, haven't you?"

"He'll live," Marjorie said softly. "He was damn lucky."

"Yeah, well, his partner wasn't."

"Shot three times. Died within minutes. And he was wearing a vest, huh?"

"Keep reading," Carow said. "Teflon-coated bullets, they went right through."

Marjorie nodded. "One arrest and they're looking for three more people?"

"Homicide's holding one of Castro's swimmers."

Carow looked at Marjorie now. "Guess what?" he said.

Raising her eyes slowly from the report, Marjorie regarded him. "What?" she said.

"Chief Janesky has given Homicide forty-eight hours to break this guy. If the Cuban doesn't ID the other perps by five o'clock Wednesday, he wants him brought to BSCO where he can interrogate 'im himself."

"You're kidding. He can't do that. Can he do that?"

"Who's going to tell him he can't?"

"Chief Hess, that's who. I know Chief Hess. He's a tough old bird. He won't go for that."

"Chief Hess wants to break this cop killing as soon as he can. If Janesky can help, then why not?"

"If Homicide detectives can't bend this character, what makes Janesky think he can?"

"Janesky told Chief Hess that Homicide is full of shit. He said he'd have the names of the other three perps fifteen minutes after they deliver the Cuban to him."

"Really?"

"Sez Hess. That's what Janesky told him."

"The man's a loony," Marjorie said, cutting in. "What's he going to do, torture the guy?"

"Probably. The main thing is, he'll get his way, they'll give him a shot."

"Janesky is dangerous, Andrew. He's a loony. You should read some of the interviews I've done."

"I've seen them," Carow said vaguely.

Goddammit, Marjorie thought to herself, *he thinks I'm a fool.*

"And the chief of operations," she said, "he doesn't want to talk to me now, I suppose?"

"Now! You want to talk to the chief of ops *now,* about a precinct where they just shot two cops? You wanna tell him *now* that his favorite precinct commander, who has to bury one of his officers, needs to be driven from the job? You want to tell him that *now,* Captain?"

Carow spoke with regret, and enough amusement to tighten Marjorie's jaw.

"Right now? Of course not right *now.* But it's not going to go away, Andrew. I'm not going to let it go away."

Carow sighed.

Marjorie could hear people walking down the hall outside. She looked at the warning coming together in Carow's eyes and said, "We agree on this, don't we, Andrew? I mean, you do believe that Janesky needs to be stopped?"

Carow sat still, glanced at her, then looked down at the report on his desk.

"With Malloy gone, you have no line into BSCO," he said.

"Oh, yes, I do." Marjorie winked. "Trust me."

Carow looked bewildered and a little sad. "You do?" he said.

Marjorie nodded; watched Carow and just nodded.

"Just remember, what goes around comes around. It's

an old line, but in Janesky's case you can bet it's for real."

"Meaning?"

"If Chief Janesky finds out you're out to nuke him, if he hears that you're trying to cross into a place he figures you were never meant to be, he'll come after you. And let me tell ya, sweetheart, he'll know. The man has friends, plenty of friends."

"Screw him," Marjorie said, and she said it with a fine smile, a neat turn of her head.

That cute little move was lost on Carow; his features suddenly went blank.

Marjorie stood at her office window looking down at Ace, an informant from her days in PMD. Ace stood in a vacant lot across the street. She watched him drop wood into a fire barrel, watched as smoke rose and thousands of sparks exploded, then fell.

There was all sorts of garbage in the lot, and it was covered with sparkling ice and snow turned gray from sand and salt.

Two other men stood beside Ace; a family circle of winos. All three men were black, and they stretched their hands over the barrel as if it were the local deity.

Marjorie wondered where Ace spent the frozen nights.

Stepping back from the window, she glanced at her reflection in the office's glass partition. For a moment she was paralyzed with a sense of loneliness.

It was mid-morning and cold. A mean wind rolled in from the west, from the river. The Brooklyn Bridge was quiet. Marjorie leaned against a wall, closed her eyes, took deep, yogalike breaths. After a second she again looked down into the lot.

She saw a chair with three legs and wadded newspaper that had turned brittle from the cold. One of the men with Ace leaned into him and said something. Ace brought his hands together, rubbing and clapping them, then stomping his feet. He threw his head back and laughed.

He turned his face up toward her window, and she smiled and waved.

Along the sidewalk, on the far side of the street, a uniformed officer was moving in the direction of the High Street Brooklyn Bridge subway station. He didn't look at Ace, or Ace's friends, or back at the gray-granite building he'd just left on Poplar Street.

Marjorie followed him with her eyes. Her thoughts racing, she stroked her neck and felt chilled.

The uniformed officer moved like a man running before a whirlwind, unsteady, quick, fleeing.

Most of the time, she thought, *it's all right, just fine. But see how it is when the loneliness comes.* "It's your choice," she said out loud, "it's always been your choice. And that's just the way you want it, no complications, no commitments, nothing to get in the way." In the way of what? "Don't know," she said, "I really don't know."

She hated this feeling, this moodiness.

A picture of Charlie's smile blended in her mind with the memory of a gray-eyed boy she'd known in her youth. He'd been like Charlie. A beautiful, warm smile. A smile that caused heat to suffuse her body and made her nipples swell. His name was Victor something or other, and lately she thought of him often. He'd pin her with those gray eyes and big grin. He never spoke, just walked on by, that sweet ass stretching his jeans. He wore a jacket with his name, Vic, written in script above three tiny golden footballs. For a full semester he had passed her by, never turning, never speaking, just pinning her for a second and grinning. Victor ruined her senior year at college.

Except for Charlie, all the men she'd met recently were lost in the loop-de-loops of midlife high jinks. It was boring.

She wasn't sure of Charlie, though; her feelings changed again and again. Strong at times, then a mood would come over her, taking her breath away, making her feel cramped, crowded, suffocated.

She could never ask him for help. Never.

And she'd made it clear. With men like Charlie you had to make it clear. A good, strong statement of fact.

She didn't need something else to worry about. It made her angry; could, if she let it, make her mean.

Thinking of Officer Kenneth Malloy, a bullet in his throat, Marjorie felt a sickness beginning in her stomach. A thought like that could make anyone sick.

"Shit!" She'd forgotten to call and wake Charlie. "Shit," she said again, then dialed.

Slowly, methodically, Marjorie took a file folder from her desk drawer. Then she looked at her watch. It was just past eleven A.M. She felt curiously anxious as she picked up the telephone and tapped out Patrolman Frank Bosco's number.

"This is Captain Butera," she said.

From the other end, a deep sigh.

"I need to see you."

A voice sounding quite distant said, "Yeah, sure, tell me where."

He'd meet her, in an hour, on the boardwalk in Rockaway Beach.

Patrolman Bosco didn't seem happy. No, not happy at all. Still, Marjorie felt a surge of optimism flood into her heart.

She got up from behind her desk, took her bag, put on her coat, and strode confidently from her office, down the hall toward the elevator.

You are what you are, she thought, *a captain from Internal Affairs, a bit of a bitch, not a bearer of good news*. And then she thought, as part of the same thought, *I hate this job. I do. Yes, indeed I do*.

"To hate this kind of work," Carow had once told her, "is the manifestation of a healthy mind."

On the street, Marjorie looked around a moment, made herself wait another moment, then quickly trudged through the slush toward her cruiser.

Ace and his friends were still warming their hands over the fire barrel. Marjorie could not resist a smile when Ace looked her way. Ace's friends laughed like kids and slapped his back. When Marjorie started her car and pulled out, Ace waved.

On her way now, Marjorie switched her radio to the five-borough frequency. In a few seconds she was at an intersection. She pulled a hard right, slowed, and watched through her rearview. Two cars were following hers. At the next corner she turned right, then she picked up speed and went right again, then once more.

She'd squared the block, feeling cool and loose. She was on a roll; no one was following. She felt sure enough of that.

Now, back to where she'd started, Marjorie hung a quick left and made for the Brooklyn Bridge.

On the ramp to the FDR Drive she slowed. Eyeing the rearview, always looking, watching for any movement behind her.

Take me on, she thought. *Just take me on, go ahead. I'm a winner; you take me on, you'll lose.*

Marjorie thumped the accelerator and moved flat out into the traffic, which was light; the entire highway was more or less open. A tailing car should be noticed. Precautions when you're off to see a field associate go with the territory. If someone tried to stay with her, on this road, at this speed, she'd pick up on it.

Suddenly she froze.

A van, a nondescript sort of van, the kind you see every day, was there, hanging back, moving easily and steadily in and out of traffic.

Marjorie floored the cruiser; several cars around her maneuvered away as she cut through and around.

The van, too, she could tell, was picking up speed. Marjorie knew that the car was following her.

It wasn't the first time she'd been tailed. A couple of nights earlier there had been lights, and once a Department car with tinted blue windows had been parked a block from her apartment. She knew, all right; her intuition picked up on that sort of thing.

As the highway rose to the Triboro Bridge, she slowed. The van was caught out, moved closer to the cruiser, to the right, then fell back.

At the toll plaza she flashed her Department plate. The highway in front of her was a straight shot. She drove fast and was doing eighty at the crest of the bridge.

Hunted, Marjorie thought. Pursued through Astoria, the land of the Greeks.

An eighth of a mile from the Hoyt Street exit, the needle bounced to a hundred. Marjorie hit the grille lights and siren. *We're on our game today; go for it.*

Fifty meters from the exit, the traffic signal held green. *All my life I've been a player*, she thought. *Play with me, you take on the best.*

A group of impatient New Yorkers moved from the sidewalk and into the street.

Marjorie went to the whooper, sailed through the intersection, and flipped off the van.

He was caught now, hung up, nowhere to go.

Marjorie looked up and saw the traffic signal go red. If the van kept coming, he would have a collision with about two dozen sons and daughters of Athens.

Marjorie disappeared into the flow of traffic, back onto the parkway, gone.

Marjorie sailed past LaGuardia Airport, feeling as close as she had been of late to ecstasy. The game with the van had raised her spirits. The light faded as the Grand Central Parkway dipped, then dived into the Van Wyck Expressway. Off to the left was South Jamaica, home of predator crack birds, Indian country.

After a few minutes of determined driving, Marjorie was airing it out on the Belt Parkway. Overhead, the sky was clear as crystal. Rockaway Beach lay dead ahead.

The character in the van was most likely a cop, Marjorie thought. She did not know, and did not care. She could feel a righteous satisfaction rising.

*   *   *

The brilliant winter sun became ocean, the Atlantic ocean, and it seemed, to Marjorie, to go on forever.

Walking briskly, she entered the boardwalk across from the Breakers Tavern at 116th Street.

Marjorie's parents had been born in Queens. Her father in Forest Hills, her mother in Rego Park. They'd moved east to Long Island just before Marjorie was born, and made their home about two hundred yards from a wharf on the Long Island Sound, in the town of Northport.

Perhaps that was it, this feeling of home when she neared the water.

An old man, bent at the waist, holding his ankles, stood in the center of the boardwalk. He did not look up as Marjorie walked by.

A gust of wind bearing sudden change blew white sand up from the beach. Marjorie looked up at the sky, which was rapidly filling with clouds and moving like a stormy river across the entire sky, out toward the horizon, heading for Europe.

Frank Bosco stood along the boardwalk rail, hands stuffed into a zippered leather jacket, a woolen scarf wrapped around his neck. He stood looking out. Marjorie hoped he was making a decision, a hard decision but a necessary one.

She approached Frank Bosco soundlessly. He turned and saw her looking at him.

"Frank, how are you?"

Frank shrugged. "Murray useta love the beach. We came here all the time."

"I was sorry to hear about Murray. I know how close you two were," she said.

Frank looked up then down the boardwalk. He seemed uneasy. "One partner for eighteen years!" Frank said. "A helluva thing on this job. One partner for eighteen years."

Marjorie gave him a sad smile. Frank Bosco stared at her, unblinking.

"I don't know if I can do what you want," he said. "I doubt I could handle it."

"Sure you can," Marjorie said.

Frank Bosco smiled. It was not a friendly smile, not meant to be.

"Ya know what I was thinking coming over here? I was thinking you could not have chosen a worse candidate to be a spy. It's not me, Captain. It's just not my kind of thing."

"You'll do fine, and do you know why?"

Frank Bosco shrugged again.

"Because you've always only done what you had to. Isn't that true? No more, no less; just what you had to do."

Frank said, "I dunno," and then, "I'm a simple cop, is all. This ain't James Bond you're looking at, lady."

"Frank," Marjorie said sternly, "I'll tell you what. You cut out the 'scuse-me-sir crap, we'll get along fine. And if we get along, you'll get your pension."

"This is all bullshit," Frank said with an uneasy chuckle.

"That's a matter of perspective," Marjorie told him.

Frank looked at her, his expression less than friendly. "And if I refuse, Captain? If I tell ya ta take a hike, what then?"

Frank Bosco's face had gone a bit red. It may have been the wind and the salt air. Marjorie assumed it was anger. The guy was getting real tense, of that she was sure.

"I'll bring charges against you, Frank," she said. "I won't like it much, considering your partner Murray was the real culprit. But I will. Frank, you hear me, I'll bring charges and specifications against you so fast, you'll be sucking wind."

Marjorie put her hand on Frank's shoulder.

"Ya know the cops call you the Dragon Lady?" he said calmly. And then he meekly pushed her hand away.

She stared straight ahead, both hands on the board-walk railing. She smiled faintly and said, "Shit."

"Trouble comes in bundles," Frank said. "Nowadays you can't trust anybody."

"Do you think that the ocean is the source of life, Frank?"

"Dunno. To tell you the truth, Captain, there ain't a whole lot that I do know."

"It's all right," Marjorie said slowly. "You're going to do something strong and noble. You and me, Frank. We're gonna nail that son of a bitch Janesky, all right—nail him just like that."

With both hands Frank Bosco waved the argument away. Then he turned and leaned on the boardwalk railing. Resting.

"My wife and daughter, they went off to Florida," Frank told her, "got a little place in Ponte Verde. I need my pension, Captain."

"Oh, I know, Frank. I know you need your pension. Work with me, help me, and you'll get it," she told him, and then she gave him the news that he was being trans-ferred to BSCO, explained to him that the place was a zoo, out of control, that the cops had gone around the bend, and that Inspector Raymond Janesky was responsi-ble. She said that this was a serious game, that he'd be her eyes and ears in the precinct.

"You know, of course," Frank said, "that asking me to be a spy in a place like that could get me hurt—killed, maybe. Making me do that kind of stuff could make me come apart. For sure I'd come apart."

"You'll do fine, Frank." She smiled. "I know it won't be easy, but you'll do just fine."

"I gotta think about it," Frank said.

"Of course," Marjorie said.

Marjorie parked the cruiser and began to walk along Central Park West. She glanced up then down the avenue. Fast. Checking everything. As she walked, she glanced again, this time more slowly.

It had been a slow drive home from her office in the early-evening traffic. When she had headed crosstown, she'd picked up the black car with its tinted blue windows. He'd stayed on her for a few blocks, then disappeared.

The discovery that she was being tailed again alarmed her, perplexed her, made her weary.

Then she got angry, a little crazy, shouting as she parked the cruiser, "Who is this jerkoff tailing me—me? Son of a bitch! I'm gonna nail this asshole, and I'm gonna do it now."

Another quick glance over her shoulder and she spotted the car, saw the headlights go dim.

She stopped beside a parked yellow cab. An Oriental man wearing a Panama sat behind the wheel drinking from a plastic cup. He smiled a mindless smile, then, as if to say, "Tough luck, lady," he gestured to the ON RADIO CALL sign, lit on the roof of the cab.

She began to walk fast, then faster. It was six-thirty, and Marjorie began to feel the sweet, rhythmical panic of the tracked animal. It did not make her happy.

Marjorie's mind tried to keep pace with her racing heart. She leaned against the building for a moment. The blue car was parked midway up the block from where she stood, waiting.

She drifted into the flow of people walking, then she began to trot. She felt a twinge that made her slightly sick.

Off the sidewalk and into the street, when she was right behind the car, Marjorie had a notion that maybe this wasn't such a great idea.

Suddenly she heard the car go into gear, the squeal of tires. She was running full out now, running, a short-barreled .38 in her hand, looking for all the world like a yo-yo, knowing she looked like a yo-yo, standing in the center of Central Park West, her arms straight up in the air, screaming, "You chickenhearted son of a bitch, get back here!"

When Marjorie entered her apartment, she saw dim candlelight, and her dining-room table was set for two. There were flowers in a vase, and a bottle of Gattinera in a bucket.

Charlie, in an apron, carrying a platter of pasta and wearing a huge grin, stood in the doorway of the glowing room.

"A tough day at the office, eh?" he said politely, then walked to the table.

He placed the platter of pasta on the table, then poured wine into two glasses.

"Yes," Marjorie said, "I had a tough day. No, I mean, it was the same ol' jazz. Ya know, a car chase, a run-in in the street, an almost shoot-out. You know, the same ol' boring shit."

Charlie nodded, then he drank the wine with his eyes closed. He began to laugh like a teenage boy.

Marjorie just shrugged.

Marjorie's first personal contact with Emi Price was when she was a freshman at Saint John's University and Emi was a sophomore. It was on a tennis court and was an extremely unpleasant experience.

Emi was a star, the number-one female player on the tennis team. Several times Marjorie watched her play. Stood around with other students and silently followed her practice sessions and looked on in awe at power, raw power from a woman with exceptional beauty and awesome athletic ability.

Young men would swarm around the gate to the courts in hopes of playing with her, meeting her. It was only young men; other women players were far too weak to give her a workout, forget a match.

Marjorie had been an all-county tennis player in high

school. A natural athlete, she never thought much about it.

Still, even then, few things gave her more pleasure than beating someone at their own game. And Emi Price, it seemed to Marjorie, was so fucking good, she had to try her.

Her plan was a simple one. She just asked the coach to arrange a match. The coach was familiar with Marjorie's high-school heroics on the tennis court.

Marjorie Butera always had courage to spare, and she was perfectly sure she'd give Emi a game. Maybe she could even win.

Her suspicion was that Emi Price was a bit heavy-footed, slow. Marjorie reasoned that if she could twist her around, use Emi's power against her, run her sideline to sideline, dink her, lob her, move her in and out, tire her out, if she could do all that, she'd win.

Marjorie had touch, a real fine touch, and no minor forehand herself.

The coach, Father Shields, smiled when he said, "She'll kick your butt."

For the spectators the match was not a great success.

It was short.

Receiving that first serve from a smiling Emi, Marjorie suspected that maybe she'd bitten off a bit more than she could chew.

She sliced the return and watched Emi streak to the net and crunch a cross-court volley, the speed of which she'd never seen before. By the end of the third game of the first set, she was embarrassed. By the end of the set, humiliated. Marjorie was also trounced in the second set, but worse than that, she'd also been toyed with.

Halfway through the second set, Emi called her to the net. Told her to relax, said she was good, real good, said that Marjorie probably should stay back more. Emi told her to play a steady baseline game and she'd do all right.

Marjorie told Emi to stuff it.

Emi laughed, and Marjorie laughed too. The match ended and a friendship began.

At that time Marjorie had no notion that her first truly close friend would remain her only woman friend for most of her life.

And now, twenty-three years later, as Emi came running across Fifty-seventh and Fifth, still bouncy and still blond, Marjorie swallowed, remembering.

She put her hands on Emi's arms, said, "Do you remember the score of our first tennis match?"

"What?"

"Our first match, the first time we played, that time at school. What was the score?"

"Christ, I can't remember if I got my period last month, and you're asking me about a tennis score twenty-three years ago?"

"C'mon," Marjorie said, "it was the very first time we played. Father What's-his-name set up the match. I can't remember if I got a game."

Emi stood calmly, smiling sadly at her. She had misty gray eyes, and Marjorie thought of her hair as a healthy blond. The day was dim, there was no sun, but still her hair had a sparkle and shine, the twinkle of the rich. Emi's haircut, Marjorie figured, cost about a hundred dollars, including tips.

"Well?"

"Marjorie, the only time I can remember that you took a game of tennis from me was when I was pregnant and had a mean case of morning sickness. We were in the Bahamas, it was about a hundred and ten in the shade, I was hung over and had a plantar's wart the size of a silver dollar that made me hop like . . . this."

Marjorie watched Emi jump backward, coming close to getting run down by a tall, bony black kid on a bike, who blasted away on a whistle and yelled, "Yo, rich bitch, watch your ass."

Life had never laid a glove on Emi; there was order in

her life. The order of a conventionally happy marriage, two children, now grown and in college. A home in Port Washington and a sense of humor that could bring Mother Teresa to her knees.

Emi had met her husband, John, during her senior year at St. John's. Emi was terrible at math but worse at French. And John was a French tutor. Sometime after her sixth lesson she became pregnant.

Emi was the product of a hard Irish working-class family and Dominican nuns, so forget abortion. She gave birth before her twenty-first birthday.

Her mother baby-sat with John, Jr., and Emi worked full-time, helping put John through law school.

During those years Emi moved around like a zombie. She had given her life to John and the raising of two boys. Emi never returned to the working world after the birth of her second son.

One night, while Marjorie was working Public Morals, sitting on a whorehouse in the East Seventies, she saw the French tutor and two buddies jump from a cab and run into the whorehouse.

She felt wounded and angry. Marjorie picked up the telephone to call Emi, but after two rings she hung up. She loved Emi and the boys as if they were her own, as if Emi were the sister she should have had. She thought about confronting John herself, thought about getting a couple of detectives she knew to bust his nose. She thought about Emi and let it die. It died, and to Marjorie, so did John.

Today Emi was in charge of plans; it was their monthly spree.

First to Tiffany's for an engraved silver teacup and spoon. A gift for John's junior partner, whose wife had just had a daughter. Marjorie loved watching Emi roll her husband's credit cards till they screamed.

A quick walk through Bendel's, then a half trot to Saks, a store in which Marjorie could spend a summer.

Marjorie bought a pair of pleated corduroy trousers

for eighty-five dollars. And Emi bought vachetta cow-hide moccasins and a cable-knit alpaca sweater.

When Marjorie said, "Why don't we go upstairs and buy something soft and frilly?" Emi screamed.

It was remarkable how their minds worked. They stood together almost nose-to-nose and simply didn't move. After a moment they spoke a cute little duet and brought all other conversations around them to a halt.

"Two beautiful women like you should buy something soft and frilly. The force of tradition demands it." A long pause, then: "Naaah, not us, but thanks, Sister, for your genuine concern."

They taxied to Tavern on the Green for lunch.

Both women could smile at anyone, confident that they'd smile back. They were smiling now, ordering drinks, sitting in a green, yellow, and blue forest. A forest in the center of Manhattan with light cast from tiny lamps in the trees outside.

Marjorie ordered an Absolut and tonic. For Emi it was a glass of champagne.

"So tell me," asked Emi, "when are you going to say shoo?"

"Excuse me?"

"When does Mr. Charlie Rose get the boot?" Emi's smile softened. "C'mon, Marjorie, you told me last month—right here, as a matter of fact—that he was making you batty."

Marjorie groaned lightly and closed her eyes.

"Did I say that? Did I really say he was making me batty?"

"You sure did, sweetheart, and it sounded as though you meant it."

Age had touched Emi only on her hands and the corners of her eyes. In the center of her cheeks was the press of a pair of smile lines. Her radiance was still in bloom, her gestures quick. "You're going to be a spin-ster," she said with enough force to turn the heads of the couple seated at a table nearby.

"Is that what you think?" Marjorie sounded ready to believe it. "So, there are worse things."

"You're not feeling very good, are you, Marjorie?"

"*Rotten*'s the word."

"Marry Charlie," Emi said in a voice as small as a worm's foot.

"He's eight years younger than I am. I think that's something I should spend some time thinking about."

"It's not the age, Marjorie. For chrissake, you know it's not the age. We both know better. It's the memory of Jeff, and that impossible job of yours."

"Please," Marjorie said in a voice heavy with sarcasm.

Two salads, two orders of salmon, and two more drinks were brought to the table. Spring peas and baby potatoes were set out.

Lovely presentation, Marjorie thought, as pretty as a photo from a magazine. Then she wondered, as part of the same thought, if Jeff's wife cooked him elegant meals. Jeff—for crying out loud, she hadn't thought about that son of a bitch in a year, well, in months, anyway.

"Damn you," Marjorie said. "Why did you have to mention Jeff? I haven't thought about that bastard in ages."

"Listen," Emi said, "no wonder you feel rotten. A five-year relationship with a married man, and a job that's a soul-killer. A job devoid of dreams. That's more than enough to spoil your weekend."

"Oh, Emi, it's not Jeff, and it certainly isn't the job. I'm just—"

"Remember what you said. You said that police work is the heart of reality, that there is no fantasy, that it's all too real. You said that you have to be hard, act hard. If you act hard, Marjorie"—Emi smiled—"you become hard. I'll never understand why you took that damn job. And as far as Jeff is concerned, it's beyond me how you could have swallowed his I'll-get-divorced-when-the-children-are-grown line for five weeks, forget five years.

Small wonder you feel rotten. Now eat your salmon before it gets cold."

It occurred to Marjorie that Emi certainly hadn't lost her gift for gab. Emi had lost none of her gifts. She considered this, pleased at the fact that she could conceal so little from Emi.

Chewing her food carefully, thinking, Emi told her, "You try to avoid pain so hard that you avoid whatever pleasure is out there."

"I don't think that's true. What I do know is that when Charlie is not around, I miss him."

Emi shook her head. "That's good enough."

"Is it?"

"Sure. What else is there?"

"Trust, I think trust is most important."

Emi finished her glass of champagne and held her glass toward Marjorie. "Marjorie, sometimes I want to scream at you. Talk about your romantic ideas. Christ, you know it's a farce to think you can find a man you could trust."

"I have my dreams."

"Your dreams are to sail the Caribbean with a man that doesn't exist."

"My dream is to be happy, to be at peace."

"I know you, sweetheart, and I love you. I suspect that to be the center of everyone's attention is as close to happiness as you're going to get."

Maybe, Marjorie thought, *you don't really know me at all.* Marjorie suddenly craved sun and warmth, the freedom of a blue, blue sea.

Chapter Four

Frank Bosco's wife and daughter had been gone from Bellrose, Queens, and settled in their new home in Ponte Verde, Florida, for a month. Lonely, he sat watching a documentary that was replaying the explosion of the space shuttle *Challenger*.

Frank slammed off the TV. He went into the bathroom and sat on the edge of his tub. He was thinking about the vicious world and the pattern of life; that tomorrow, or the day after tomorrow, or the day after that, would end, and he'd feel nothing, never-ending nothingness, an eternity of zip. Just like the seven astronauts and his partner, Murray, soon his brief life, too, would be no more than a little fart in the blizzard of time.

Fuck, he thought as he took a shaky breath, *so I'm afraid.* Everyone's afraid. Nobody wants to die. Murray didn't want to die. Murray, shrewd piece of work that he was, was the last person who wanted to die. And the astronauts . . . think they weren't pissed? Still, they died and Murray died. Not like the astronauts. Murray died flat in the middle of a stress test at his doctor's office. Murray's heart had exploded like the *Challenger*, and just like the shuttle, Murray Weiss was history. And there it was.

Frank pulled himself up from the tub and looked in the bathroom mirror. His eyes felt funny.

He dropped his pants, took out his dick, stroked the smooth cap, squeezed it hard . . . harder. He'd felt a pinch now and then, a slight burn and tickle; his kidney, or more likely his prostate. He pulled it, let it go, and watched as it sprung back, curled, and drooped. It looked old and tired. His dick was forty-six.

Frank Bosco thought about his wife, Deidra, and his daughter, Laura. A sadness landed on him, sat him back on the tub. The air was full of scents; aromas of the women in his life had lingered, or maybe the scents were rooted in his mind. It mattered not at all. The reality was that they were gone, and he, Frank Bosco, a New York City patrolman for nineteen years and six months, was left alone. No family, no partner, an asshole that itched, a prostate that tickled, and a dick that burned.

Out of the bathroom now, Frank dropped himself down on the blue living-room sectional. He brought his legs up on the sofa and closed his eyes, trying to calm himself, trying not to be afraid.

Off the sofa and back into the bathroom, he put cold water on his face. Being alone is a killer, he thought. "Being alone sucks," he said to the mirror, and meant it.

A month after Murray died, he'd finally given in and said to Deidra, "Okay, let's move to Florida."

She had bugged him for years to move south. And he'd always said, "No way, not me." And Deidra would ask, "Why not?"

"Because," he'd say. Because it was hard to think of living day in and day out without Murray.

It was impossible for him to tell Deidra that he wanted to grow old with someone who really knew him. His wife wouldn't understand. Well, should she understand? Probably not.

Murray Weiss had hated Florida. He hated the Miami Dolphins. Disney World and the Tampa Bay Buccaneers could make him woozy. Cubans and Haitians and sunshine sent him trembling. Murray was a New York guy, simple as that. And Murray was Frank's partner.

"Murray is dead," Frank said, nodding at the mirror. "I can live in Florida."

Holy shit, he thought, *I'm talking to myself.*

Deidra's plan seemed without flaw. She and Laura would set out first. They would join Deidra's mother and brother in Ponte Verde. Laura could register for college, and Deidra would look for work. A home? They could deal with that after they sold their Queens house. In ninety days Frank would put in his retirement papers, and three months later he'd join them. The genuinely remarkable thing was that Frank had never considered what it would be like to be left alone for six months.

And Deidra had been absolutely crazed about making the long drive to Florida without him. She kept on talking about flat tires and whatnot. And then there was her nightmare. Deidra could be a treasure house of weirdness. Something about a palmetto grove, a mad hitchhiker with a rope, a knife, Laura raped and killed, Deidra tied to a tree, forced to watch. Weirdness, that was Deidra.

Frank looked in the mirror again. His eyes felt shitty. If you had a really good case of depression, you could look at your tongue, see what wonders are growing there. Ahhh, he said. He moved his head from side to side. *Coated* was the word he was thinking of. Murray kept preying on his mind.

He didn't know he was going to die. Murray had pranced through life as if he were king of the hill. If he'd known, he'd have told Frank. Shit, they told each other everything, everything! For eighteen years one was the shadow of the other. Had he known, Murray would have said, "Hey, Frank, prepare yourself. It's boom time for the old ticker." But he didn't. He never said a thing. And since Murray didn't tell him, Frank found it doubly hard to believe. Even when he had looked down at him in his casket, he'd found it hard to believe.

When Murray's wife, Dorothy, mentioned that she'd like him buried in his summer police shirt, Frank had gone batty. Forgetting about her grief, he yelled, "You fuckin' nuts or what, Dot? Murray hated that uniform. Plant him in that and Murray will shoot out of the box, fly around the room, and probably piss on the rabbi there. Forget the uniform. Bury him in his goddamn Bermuda shorts if need be, anything but that ugly blue suit."

Frank told himself, pulling on his insulated long johns, that it was stupid to keep thinking about Murray.

He couldn't afford to be casual about getting dressed today. It was his first tour of duty at his new command, the first time in years that he'd be out of a police car and walking a beat. The first tour in years without Murray. Frank also knew that he'd freeze his ass off if he wasn't prepared.

Ten minutes after he arrived at BSCO, Frank sat sweating in the large, overheated muster room where a shift of uniformed cops awaiting assignments clustered against the walls. Small groups huddled—blacks with blacks, Latins with Latins, some white officers mingled, but mostly they, too, stayed together. A podium stood in the front and center of the room, and small school desks were arranged in neat rows. Four women officers sat under a ceiling light in the corner. They were black, and they joked with each other and laughed. They put Frank in mind of the Supremes, the old Supremes before Diana skipped out. Pretty.

Everywhere he looked he saw black crepe. A cop from here had been killed recently; that didn't help his mood.

The contrast among the black, white and Latins was striking. The blacks and Latins were mellow and gave each other secret messages, laughing. The whites exchanged sideways glances, nervous smiles. Although the room was overheated, there was a chill in the air, open apartheid in Brooklyn South.

Primitive, Murray would have said. This fucking command has gone native. To Frank the Latins and blacks seemed to be staging an act. It was hardly surprising; everyone deals with fear differently, he thought. But fear wasn't visible in their faces. Still, it seemed to him their stomachs must churn and dance like his. Maybe not. Nothing on their faces suggested the sickness he felt.

The desk officer began calling names, giving assignments. He halted after one or two and asked if they would take seats. No one moved. The desk officer coughed and then went on.

"Revolution," Murray would have said. "An affirmative-action revolutionary class is what we got here." And what's worse, Murray would have pointed out that nobody there could read or write, not even the desk officer, whose color was ash gray. He called Frank Basseo instead of Bosco, which made Frank run his hand through his hair and yawn.

Frank was assigned to Special Post 3, with a 10 ring and a nine P.M. meal.

Some sergeant who looked twelve years old told him that Special 3 was a tough post. The avenue was okay, but the side streets were the pits, and Frank was expected to go into those side streets. No chance—hell, he'd walk his way through this tour and forget the side streets. As long as the avenue stayed quiet and the storefront glass was safe, the tour should be a hanger. Outside, the temperature had dropped into the teens, and Frank knew that street people didn't risk frostbite.

Abruptly, almost as if the thought were shouted from somewhere deep inside him, Frank looked down. His pistol was unloaded. Then the pinching began in his penis, familiar and awful. Christ. The desk officer was shouting his head off for them to get going, to hit the street.

Well, Frank thought, *I ain't about to go out without bullets. If I was in London, maybe, but even in London nowadays cops need loaded guns*. He opened his ammo pouches, first one, then the other. A package of duck sauce hit his knee, and two bullets whose casings had gone green and slimy. About this time Murray would have been rolling around on the floor, laughing, kicking desks, tears running down that pale face of his, yelling,

"Partner, you are a genius, a certified head you are, ol' buddy." Yeah, Murray woulda gotten a kick outa this.

From the rear of the muster room Frank watched the others leave. The biggest back belonged to that gorilla Monty Adams. Rambo with his lights out, Murray would have called him. He'd have extra bullets. Probably enough to keep the contras going for a year or so.

"Inspector Janesky wants arrests, and arrests Inspector Janesky will get," the desk officer shouted. "Arrest numbers are what we need."

"Adams! Hey, Adams," Frank called, and he felt his ass tighten and his face freeze into what he thought must be a stupid grin.

"Can I speak to you for a minute, pal?" he said.

Monty Adams stood quiet and let Frank explain about his empty gun. Since Frank was an old-timer and Adams practically a rookie, there was a certain amount of deference shown—not a whole lot but some. After all, Frank thought Adams was a baby when he was out there ducking bricks. Not that Frank ever ducked many bricks; Murray saw to that. Somehow Murray was able to avoid the heavy stuff. Frank never could figure out how exactly; it was just Murray's way. Murray was a conciliator, an adjudicator, an arbitrator. That was how Murray Weiss dealt with the street. Adjudicate everything. No need for summary arrests. An arrest was always the last resort.

"I have some really terrific hollow points," Monty Adams told Frank.

"Well," Frank said, pulling at his insulated underwear, which had crawled up and was now adding to the bite and itch in his ass. Adams eyed him suspiciously.

"Frank," Adams said, "these hollow points will blow up a turdbird at fifty yards. A hundred and fifty grains that flattens out at impact to the size of a silver dollar."

"Impact," Frank said. "Impact is what we need in the street."

"Shit," Adams said. "If you don't want 'em, I got

regular Department-issue crap in my extra locker downstairs."

Adams adjusted his nightstick, which he had slung over his hand-carved pistol grip, and shrugged. His eyes were small and lackluster; they seemed odd in his huge head.

"An extra locker?" Frank asked.

"Sure, I need room for my stuff. One locker is not enough for my goodies."

"Of course you need more room."

"Well, most guys don't, but I do."

"Obviously."

"Here's my key," Adams said. "The locker is downstairs near the workout room. Take what you need, then leave the key at the desk."

Adams headed for the muster-room door. He was a big man, almost a head taller than Frank, and his height compelled Frank to look up at him. Frank grinned and said, "Thanks, Adams."

"Don't mention it," Monty Adams called back over his shoulder. Then he asked Frank if there was anything else he wanted.

Murray was what he wanted, slick Murray, rotten feet and all.

"Enough bullets to get me through the night is all I need," he told Adams. "Thanks again."

When he was on the steps that led to the basement, the air was cold and smelled of the old Police Department. That voice, the one from inside him that made him look and see his empty pistol, showed up again. This time it came, a whisper, a breath in his ear. Frank swore it was Murray's voice. He began to tingle all over, and his legs vibrated.

"Schmuck," it said. "You have a box of ammo in your summer shoes, the ones you stuck in your new locker."

Frank stood still for a moment on the steps, close to panic. He did have a box of ammo, and it was in his shoe, the ones he'd worn to the range that past August.

It was Murray's voice he'd heard! He couldn't understand it, but it made him feel good.

"Fuck it, Murray," Frank Bosco said out loud. "I'll take Rambo's."

Ohmigod, he thought. *I'm losing it, slipping right over the edge, wandering aimlessly to rubber-gun land. Murray, you are a one-way son of a bitch, bugging out on me the way you did. Wherever you are, I hope they're burning the souls of those oversize, rotten feet of yours.*

In the basement, near Adams's locker, near the workout room, he heard a snicker, then a hoarse, yet small male voice say, "You're beautiful."

I'm becoming very unstable, Frank thought. *Very loose around the edges. Talking to myself, hearing Murray, hearing sounds of love from a gym in the basement of the precinct house.*

But he had heard sounds. Undeniable sexual sounds. He peeked from behind Adams's locker. The gym was dark and the sounds soft. Low voices cooing and ooohing, teenage-style.

He thought, *I should cough, whistle, rattle the locker.* He shook his head, cleared his ears.

The listening made Frank Bosco feel a certain amount of guilt. It crawled up from between his legs, washed into his belly, and he began to sweat.

"Oh, yes! Oh, yes! Oh, yes! Oh, yes! Oh, yes!"

A chair scraped along the floor, and Frank's knees banged together. He closed his eyes and tried to think of something meaningful.

"Oh, Harry," a male voice crooned. Then Harry's name was sharply called from the darkness. Frank played hell trying to adjust his eyes; his forehead pounded. Then the man calling Harry sounded faintly stricken. Frank held his breath, but he could hold it only so long. He didn't feel good at all, and Murray's voice was screaming in his ear.

"Get the fuck out of here," it said.

Out on the street with an empty pistol, Frank tried

convincing himself it was his imagination. That's what it was, his imagination. He blinked his eyes and swallowed hard.

"I'm thinking cold, Murray," Frank whispered to himself. "I'm thinking frozen toes, ears, and nose. I'm thinking foot patrol for an old man of forty-six is nuts."

The cold, wet sidewalk froze his feet, and there was no place to go in, no place to hide. Cold can have a powerful impact on someone not used to it. Real cold can make you feel as though you've reached the very end. Real cold can make you not give a damn. It wasn't that cold on Special 3. Still, Frank felt colder than he'd ever been. He felt pathetic, and old, and a bit frightened.

Street after street, the tenements were shrouded in gray-brown gloom. And there were no people. It was as if a pestilence had arrived and now rose and spread along with the steam from the sewers. Frank felt dizzy, a little sleepy. The wind whipped his face, put tears in his eyes. He thought about Murray, then he thought about his wife, Deidra, and Laura, his daughter. They were, he hoped at this moment, warm. Frank was trembling. Murray, too, must be cold. He felt grief and loneliness.

The loving scene played in the precinct's basement had confused him, sent him running. He hadn't stopped at his locker, hadn't loaded his gun. He felt as though he were about to catch cold. Special Post 3 had some stores on the avenue. They closed at dusk. There were two bars, one at either end of the post. The Tee Pee and the Bombay, both buckets of blood, "a couple of turdbird pits," Adams had told him.

Walking the post was everything, he told himself. *Keep moving, stop thinking. High-five the sergeant when he passes in his car, then hide.* That was his plan. *This is fucking ridiculous*, he thought.

It was ten minutes past seven, ten minutes past the hour Frank had to ring in. The guy on the switchboard gave him a job, a bar fight. He didn't know the switchboard officer's name, but cops whose names he didn't know he simply called guy.

"Hey, guy," he said. "Whaddaya got for me?"

"A bar fight at the Tee Pee. I put it over the air. A car'll meet ya."

"Is it warm in the Tee Pee?" Frank asked, and the guy laughed.

As he moved down the street Frank found that if he faced into the wind, his teeth chattered so that he was forced to bend his head and hold on to his cap. He marched fast and hard. Suddenly he thought about Murray and slowed. He considered his empty gun. And the wind came hard now, spotted with snow.

Few things had given Murray more pleasure than working an entire tour and handling not one job. Being second car on a scene was Murray's genius. Oh, they'd roll on real jobs, shots fired, burglary in progress, screams for help. But on bullshit jobs—a bar fight, for example —Murray would creep along with that disgusted look in his eyes. He'd stop for traffic lights. He'd square blocks. He'd go easy, as if he were looking for an address. Murray was a genius. There'd always be a blue-and-white, sometimes two, at the scene before ol' Sector Adam arrived. There were times Frank would get angry and yell at Murray. "Move it, goddamm it," he'd yell.

"There's a brawl. They need us.

"Fuck 'em," Murray'd say. "Fuck 'em all."

A bar fight was not Murray's favorite thing.

"Let the shitheads kill each other. Let 'em wear themselves out," he'd say. "Roll in late, conserve your strength. Get in right at the end and conciliate." And he'd say it all with a terrific amount of coolness.

Good ol' Murray, Frank thought.

Still, if he had to, Murray could go. He could stand toe-to-toe with some of the best. Murray was simply the best damn cop and partner a man could have.

And could he shop! Murray loved to shop. Frank had always believed it was the main reason he'd become a cop. In eighteen years, with joyous ecstasy, Murray Weiss bent every business in the precinct. Half-of-Wholesale was Murray's middle name. Finally it got them into heavy shit. It was a Korean grocery-store owner. He got good and tired of selling Murray extra-large eggs at fifty cents a dozen. He bitched to IAD; some shy, fat little bastard that looked like the Reverend Moon dropped a dime on Murray and him. And that Butterfly bimbo captain told him in no uncertain terms, "Frank, you can't bullshit me. You're responsible for what you see, just as responsible as for what you do." He replayed their conversation in his mind. So casual and with such ease, she'd said, "You'll do fine working with me."

That was great. He was elevated from cop to field associate. Frank felt certain that that bitch of a captain would fool with his pension if he didn't go along. She was sorry about Murray, and that's all she'd said. "I'm sorry about your partner. I'll be in touch." *Well, it means I'm a spy,* he thought. *Now ain't that the numb-nuts end.*

Frank Bosco felt the full brunt of the wind as he turned onto Columbia Street. He did not think of the spinning red lights that passed him by, or the people running along the opposite side of the street, or the battle taking place in the Tee Pee bar in the middle of the block. He watched the sidewalk as it passed beneath his feet, held on to his cap, and thought about the love sounds in the basement of the precinct. This job had taken a rather bizarre turn for the worse, is what he thought.

At the Tee Pee, Officer Monty Adams stood at the end of the bar with his nightstick pressed up against the lip of a guy who looked like Mr. T. And he was telling Mr. T what he was going to do to his children after he finished running his stick through his nose and out the back of his head.

Adams had a way with words, Frank thought as he stood just inside the doorway, his body trembling from the long, cold walk. Officer Rivera, Adams's partner, held a tiny Puerto Rican by the throat. The Puerto Rican's legs were bent behind him, and he was braced against the bar on his elbow. When Frank turned, he saw his own image reflected in a shattered bar mirror. He looked old, tired, frozen, and, he had to admit, a little panicky.

Rivera shook the Puerto Rican, whose hair, which was long and straight and black, flew dramatically around his head. Then Frank realized that the man was probably an Indian, this being the Tee Pee bar and all.

The Puerto Rican's Indian features shifted. His tongue began to shoot in and out of his mouth like some kind of black demon snake.

"You sneaky little bastard," Rivera yelled. "Where's the fucking knife?"

Mr. T crumbled onto a table. The table made a ferocious crash as it hit the floor, and Adams yelled, "There it is."

Adams pointed to a shiny yellow-handled kitchen knife protruding from Mr. T's back.

For a moment there was absolute silence. Then Officer Rivera said, with a nervous sort of giggle, "Ain't that a bitch."

"The little spick stuck me," Mr. T said with a moan.

Frank called the Police Communications Bureau and told them to send an ambulance with a doctor. Told the guy he had a stabbing.

"The spick killed me," Mr. T hissed, and Adams said, "Shut the fuck up. You ain't dead."

Frank first saw the girl as she came out of the men's room wearing a peculiar smile. He thought she was cute, touching even, but a little spacey.

"Is it over now?" she said. Then she looked at each of them in turn, as if she were searching for a familiar face.

Mr. T was leaking on the floor, pissing himself. Frank could tell because steam rose through his pants around his thighs, then below his knees. He started to speak, twisted his head as if loosening his neck muscles. Rivera closed cuffs around the Puerto Rican's wrists and shoved him. He landed heavily against the bar.

Frank walked over to the girl. "Who are you? Whaddaya doing here?" he asked.

"Nobody," she said. "I'm nobody. I came in here to warm up. The fight started, everyone ran, and I ducked into the men's room."

The black women cops—the ones Frank thought of as the Supremes—arrived and moved around the Tee Pee, making birdlike sounds and clucking.

"Mr. T dead?" one asked.

"Naw, just stuck," Adams answered.

"Stuck," Rivera said.

Mr. T coughed. He was lying on his stomach, his hands folded prayerlike, childlike, against his cheek. He tried to reach a hand to get at the unseen cause of his pain. He couldn't manage. Centered, Frank thought. That little guy centered that knife.

The girl relaxed. She was small, boylike, and had short red hair. To Frank she had seemed tense, nervous, very anxious. Now she sat on a bar stool, took out a cigarette, and lit it. She flicked the match in a long, low flight that landed at the foot of the tallest of the Supremes.

"Careful, bitch," the tall Supreme said, leaving the impression that she gave but one warning.

The girl laughed. This made her seem particularly young. Frank wondered just how young she was.

"Oh, I'm sorry," the girl said, a hand covering her mouth. Then she smiled, a broad, toothy grin.

Straight on, her face was beautiful, perfectly beautiful. Her eyes were blue, a really deep, dark blue.

Frank took out his pad, tried to look serious, policeman-serious.

"Whatcha name?" he said at her.

"Ronnie."

She stared back at him and said, "Ronnie is all."

Frank laughed hollowly. "C'mon, don't be a pain in the ass. Tell me your name."

"Y-a-z-o-w," she said, spelling it.

"Yazow?" Frank asked, and instantly felt stupid.

"Yeah, yeah, Yazow. That's it, got it?"

Frank nodded, and she said with a resentful expression, "You cannot detain the innocent."

"Hey, bitch," Adams said, "just answer the officer's questions or I'll kick your Yazow ass across the street."

Mr. T struck his forehead against the floor, banged it, two, three times. Then he looked at Frank.

"Where's that fuckin' ambulance?" Rivera said with indifference.

"We're goin' back out," the tall Supreme said. "Ya want us to run the prisoner back to the house?"

"Can ya do that for us, hon?" Rivera said, smiling.

The tall Supreme nodded slightly. She was bending over from the waist, leaning over Mr. T. She spoke slowly and very softly.

"I ain't your hon, asshole," she said to Officer Rivera. "But we'll run this guy in for ya all the same."

It was a very tough moment. Frank thought there was a real good chance that Adams might go nuts, might come right out and belt the Supreme.

"Excuse me," Rivera said so softly that he had to repeat it.

Frank looked away. He watched the girl, Ronnie. She was blowing smoke rings. She looked very young. She turned and looked at him and batted her eyes, smiling.

The Supremes lifted the Indian-looking Puerto Rican by the armpits. The shorter of the two women, Frank realized, had not said a word. She continued to nod solemnly and let her aggrieved partner nag on.

"Hear him with that 'hon' shit?" The tall Supreme scoffed and wagged her head.

Frank was not going to take the collar. He could use the overtime, with his retiring and all, but he wasn't up to making an arrest. And besides, Adams wanted it. Adams loved making collars, told everyone standing around that this was his seventh of the month. Seven felonies, a good month, plenty of overtime.

"The ambulance is here," Ronnie said, pointing toward the street.

Frank noticed red and white bubbles running from Mr. T's mouth and nose. And he wasn't struggling any longer, not moving his head around. He looked limp, and his lower lip covered his upper. His teeth were clenched real tight. Frank could see the knots on his jawline. Still the bubbles dripped from the side of his mouth, stringlike things.

A cold wind rushed through the open bar door as the ambulance attendants sauntered in.

Frank began to get real nervous.

"Where the fuck did you guys come from, Hawaii?" Adams said.

Mr. T's face was distorted now, really ugly. Frank turned away from him and looked at Ronnie. She stuck her tongue out at him, moved it around, sexy-like. Frank felt on the very edge of panic. He heard Officer Rivera say, "But he wasn't dead before." And he heard the attendant answer, "Well, he is now, bro. Dead as he'll ever be."

Most cops act very cool around the dead. People die all the time around cops, and people who are alive and watching expect cops to be cool, especially older cops, who've seen scores of the dead and dying. Frank thought, *Don't look at the running nose or the drooping jaw or the spreading puddle of fluids*.

The ambulance attendants, Officers Adams and Rivera, and Ronnie, Frank thought, probably never saw an old foot cop turn white and have tears run down his face. Everyone in the bar pretended not to notice, and Frank thought it was a really good idea to go into the men's room.

He managed to make his way into the bathroom before he got sick. Leaning against a cold tile wall, he unbuttoned his collar. His legs were weak, and he wanted to sit down. When he heard the clean zip of the body bag, he began to sob.

"Oh, Murray, you prick. You should eat it, you really should eat it for leaving me alone out here."

Ronnie came in. She took his hand and said, "Mr. T was a bad weasel. It's good he's dead. Nobody should cry for that weasel."

Frank raised his hand to his head and felt his forehead. It felt warm . . . no, hot. "Great," he told himself. "I caught a fever."

Marjorie Butera stood silently, taking a long look at the two nurses who rode in the elevator with her. A matched pair who seemed happy to see her, they gave her a smile and nodded skinny little heads.

Marjorie felt distinctly ill at ease.

Her hair was mussed and she knew it; anyone would get their hair mussed running a block in the rain.

Once it had mattered to her more than anything how she looked to the world. Now, lately, it didn't seem to matter all that much. She wondered why.

Marjorie took a quick step forward, began to move down the corridor. Room 809, Officer Malloy's room, was about a hundred feet from the nurses' station.

It was just past midnight. Captain Marjorie Butera made her own visiting hours.

An orderly stood near a gurney biting his nails; he had a great barrel chest and wore a gold chain that could secure a ten-speed bike. From an open storage closet, with an upturned stainless-steel door handle, came the distinctly sweet smell of marijuana.

Marjorie glanced at the darkened closet. The orderly at his gurney smiled, then turned around.

She was fighting a wave of fatigue; still she marched in her finest captain's strut past the semidarkened nurses' station.

She'd always hated and feared hospitals; even the air seemed detached and a bit cruel. Hospitals were full of mystery and wizardry—like Mexico. To Marjorie, both places made you keenly aware of your own mortality.

Police Officer Ken Malloy lay on the hospital bed on his back, looking as though he were carved from stone. He was totally, completely, absolutely still. Except for his hands. They were at work, opening and closing.

The door had been slightly ajar, and Marjorie didn't know if she should knock or just walk in. She walked in and continued toward the bed where Malloy lay.

The hospital was old, the rooms small. Malloy was in a single room painted the same pale blue as the corridor walls. The overhead fluorescent light was off, and a small desk lamp on the night table gave the room faint light.

At the head of the bed was a small stainless-steel pole supporting an IV. Plastic tubing snaked down and entered Officer Malloy's arm. There were beads of perspiration on his forehead, and brownish material stained the bandage on his throat. Marjorie knew it was old blood.

She stood alongside his bed and thought, He's really a boy, just a boy, not nearly a man. A tide of affection and concern rose in her. She took Officer Malloy's hand and held it tightly.

"Excuse me, Captain Butera," the nurse whispered softly.

The nurse's name tag read MOLINA, and she'd been on duty every night that Marjorie had visited.

"I don't like his color," Marjorie said.

Molina stared, smiled a little. "There was a slight temperature elevation this afternoon, but now he's normal. Anyway, he's holding his own."

"His skin is blue for chrissake."

Marjorie went into the bathroom, took a towel, and ran some cool water on it. Returning, she wiped the perspiration from Officer Malloy's forehead.

Nurse Molina was still in the doorway, staring sadly at the young officer.

"Isn't it spooky," she said, "that so many young, intelligent people want to be cops? Know what I mean? With so many real jobs around . . . ya know, carrying a gun, swinging a stick. Yuck."

Just then Officer Malloy's eyes opened and he looked up at Marjorie. She grinned and said, "Hey, good looking, how you doing?"

Malloy smiled, or tried to. His eyes were closing.

"I bet when they were kids, the cops, they loved to go poking in holes and dark corners just to see what jumped out," Nurse Molina said.

Marjorie could feel her patience evaporating. She bent down and kissed Ken Malloy on the brow.

"I'm proud of you, Ken," she said. "You're some kind of hero."

Nurse Molina gave her a funny smile, a kind of mockery. "God," she said, "all this cop macho crap, it's so silly."

Marjorie looked at her with utter incomprehension.

"Maybe *silly* is the wrong word," Molina said.

Marjorie stared at her. The nurse was thirty, thirty-five, with delicate Latin features. Her arms were folded across fine, small breasts.

Marjorie said, "You down on the police? That your problem?"

"My ex-husband, he was on the job. A big Dutchman with a bigger mouth. He loved to yell and to hit; he was a prick. It's a curse of the profession. Being a prick."

Marjorie returned to the bathroom, wet the towel again.

"And a racist," Molina said. "A man without honor."

Marjorie said nothing.

"Maybe you don't know what it's like to live with a man without honor. A man that likes to beat on you. Maybe you don't know about that."

"I'll tell you what I know," Marjorie said. "You better make sure you tend to this young policeman as if he were Christ himself and you were Mary, his mother. And since you asked, if a man ever laid a hand on me, I'd cut it off. I don't like people that get off on hurting."

Marjorie looked over her shoulder at Officer Malloy.

In a low voice she said, "That policeman was doing his job when someone tried to kill him. Now, you look like you're smart as hell, Nurse Molina. I'd say you're real smart, except for your habit of blowing an occasional joint in that closet down the hall. That's not smart; it smells up your uniform!"

Nurse Molina's eyelids fluttered.

Officer Ken Malloy, a fine smile on his handsome face, was watching them. His blue eyes shone bright and clear. Police Officer Ken Malloy would be all right.

Marjorie trembled with relief.

Chapter Five

The Homicide detective was nervous because the instructions he'd received from his chief would probably piss off Inspector Janesky, and he didn't want to do anything that would piss anyone off, especially a pair of bosses, both of whom could give him the runs and ruin his weekend with a look. Smith was so nervous that when he began to say something about the cop killer's unwillingness, or inability, to speak English, he began to mumble. Inspector Janesky could hardly make out what he was saying.

Smith wished Inspector Janesky would say something.

Janesky sat in his office behind a huge oak desk. There was a flag in the corner, and plaques and framed photographs on the wall. He just sat; he'd begin to nod, stop, and listen, no expression on his face. An open bottle of beer, a glass, and a sandwich on a china plate were set out in front of him. He certainly didn't seem to be in a hurry.

Dion Smith had been a first-grade detective in Homicide for five years and had dealt with a lot of the brass on important cases. But around Inspector Janesky he suddenly couldn't think clearly, couldn't say the words he wanted to say the way he wanted to say them. All his training and experience told him that Janesky was bound to be pissed.

His partner, Fred Zito, had brought the prisoner up the stairs to the third floor, into the detective's office. Zito was probably relaxing, enjoying a cup of coffee and bullshitting about the Knicks. Zito never worried about bosses who could ruin your weekend with a look; he had too much to worry about with the Knicks, Rangers, and Giants. Zito hated the Jets since they'd let Namath go and moved to Jersey. The Giants he could forgive anything.

The inspector drank down half a bottle St. Paulie Girl Dark before he bit into his sandwich. Finally he sniffed and said, "Did your people get this character breakfast and lunch?"

Smith nodded, then shrugged.

"Where is he?" Janesky said.

"We got 'em up in the squad room; his attorney is waiting at the Homicide Bureau office. He thinks we brought the guy to Headquarters so he could stand in a lineup."

Janesky nodded. "Good."

Smith squinted, watching the inspector's eyes, looking for a signal that would allow him to relax, trying at least to catch a glimmer of what Janesky was thinking.

"Chief Hess told me to tell you, sir, that we gotta be careful. These lawyers don't like being fooled."

Janesky bent his head toward him, listened carefully, or pretended to.

"Chief Hess said you got an hour, sir," Smith added. "He was sorry, but the Chief, Chief Hess said absolutely no more than an hour. In an hour we bring 'em back, and no marks, no turban for this guy. The newspeople and the lawyer are waiting with big eyes for our man to get back. The PC is going to hold a news conference at six P.M. sharp."

Janesky didn't answer him.

"Those ain't my words, sir," Detective Smith said. "That's right from the chief. Ya know Chief Hess, he worries."

"Uh-huh," Inspector Janesky said, then he wagged his head and smiled a sad smile.

Janesky got up from the desk, walked up to him, stood face-to-face. They were less than a couple of feet apart.

Smith glanced away. "Where would you like for us to wait, sir?"

"Wherever you like. Just stay out of my hair."

Detective Smith had fifteen years on the job. He'd seen plenty of real bad-asses and knew the real thing when he saw it. He coughed and put his hand in front of his mouth to keep from saying a word. He turned away from Janesky, who now was looking at some photographs, studying them, putting them gently into an envelope.

On the stairs, heading for the detective's office, Inspector Janesky was climbing ahead of him, and Smith took note of the way he moved. For one thing, Janesky's hand never touched the banister. The inspector was in great shape. Smith watched him stride two steps at a time.

You couldn't be sure of Janesky's age, perhaps late thirties, maybe early forties. He was a lean man of medium height, but when he stood and moved, he held himself so erect that he appeared taller. There was a little gray in his neatly trimmed black hair; his eyes were large, clear, and deep blue. Forty-two, Smith thought.

On a bench in the second-floor hallway, two uniformed cops waited. They stopped talking when Janesky approached, and jumped to their feet. The big one stood ramrod-straight. He appeared ready. Ready for what, Detective Dion Smith didn't want to know. A lot of personal shit was going down here. He wanted no part of it, didn't want to be near a crew of crazy cops looking to get even.

He glanced at Janesky, then at the huge cop whose chest was covered with medals. As a matter of fact, this whole damn precinct had the smell of a Special Forces camp he'd stumbled on in 'Nam. If someone showed him a collection of skulls, it wouldn't surprise him in the least.

"Adams," Janesky said, "go down to the gym and get me three twenty-five-pound disc weights. Bring them up here and bring me the roll of lamp wire. It should be in the basement too."

Lamp wire and weights, Smith thought. Terrific. Fuckin' A. *I'd better get outa here.*

The huge cop nodded, said nothing, and left.

"You stay with me," Janesky said to the other cop.

The tag on his uniform read RIVERA, and he had worry lines all over his face. Worry lines were part of the uniform in this shop, Smith thought.

Dion Smith's nervousness made him speak without thinking.

"Can I get my partner and leave, sir?"

"You can stay or you can go," said Janesky. "You can sit on the bench here and wait, or you can come with us and watch while I talk to your prisoner. You can do whatever the hell you like, Smith. What would *you* like to do?"

Inspector Janesky found him in some way amusing, because now he was smiling. A couple of answers came to mind immediately, but Detective Dion Smith just shrugged.

"Take your partner and go," Janesky said good-naturedly.

The Homicide detective walked to the squad-room door, opened it, and called to his partner, who at first seemed to be alone. He sat at a desk sipping coffee. To his relief Smith saw their prisoner in the squad-room cage. He stood, arms folded, looking not the least bit concerned. When their eyes met, the Cuban sighed, then smiled a contemptuous smile.

"C'mon, Fred," Smith said. "These people want to talk to Luis, and they want to talk to him alone."

On the stairway, Fred Zito asked, "What the hell do you think these guys are going to say to this punk that we haven't?"

Detective Smith said, "It would take a really sick mind even to guess."

Inspector Ronald Janesky thought the Cuban prisoner in the cage looked familiar. He didn't know him; he just looked familiar.

The Cuban thrust his chin toward Janesky, pursed his lips, and kissed the air. He then threw his head back and laughed. After a moment the laughter stopped and the Cuban said something quick and sharp in Spanish to Officer Ramon Rivera.

"He wants his lawyer," Ramon said helpfully.

"Ramon," Inspector Janesky said evenly, "I want you to translate every word I say. Leave nothing out. If you have a question, if you're unsure, ask me. I want you to be certain that you get it right."

Janesky exhaled deeply and took a seat at the desk nearest the cage. There were three other desks in the office. The Cuban looked at Ramon, then at Janesky. He wore a sly smile and wagged his head.

"Ask him if he wants a cigarette," Janesky said in a dull voice.

"He said you should give the cigarette to your mother. He wants his lawyer."

Inspector Janesky took a folder he was carrying, opened it, removed photographs from an envelope inside the folder, and spread them out on the desk. He raised his head and let his eyes drift to the prisoner.

"You've made your three phone calls. You've eaten your breakfast and lunch. You've spoken to your lawyer and smiled for the TV and newspaper photographers. You've been treated like a human being. It's the American way. But now," Janesky said, turning his eyes on the Cuban, "you will be a good boy and talk to me."

The Cuban's eyes rolled and he gazed at the ceiling.

"We Americans are giants of humanity and compassion," said Janesky. "When you came here from Cuba, we didn't expect much from you. We were happy to have you. Of course, we couldn't know that you were going to kill our policemen."

"I do not want to talk to him," the Cuban said in Spanish to Officer Rivera. "I want my lawyer. I know my rights," the prisoner screamed.

Officer Monty Adams came through the squad-room door carrying three weights, seventy-five pounds, in one hand. In the other hand he held a spool of lamp wire; it was thick and beige. Adams held it with his thumb and index finger. He put the weights and the wire down on top of one of the desks, then returned to the squad-room door and bolted it. The prisoner shrugged his shoulders, staring at Rivera.

"I know you want to sit and talk with me, and you can't do it from inside that cage. So," Janesky said, "Monty, take Luis out of the cage and sit him here in front of me."

The Cuban looked Monty Adams over without looking directly at him. He started to grin, started to act cool, moving his shoulders around, spreading his legs, standing hard and macho. When Monty Adams said rudely, "C'mon, let's go," Officer Rivera didn't bother to interpret. Still Luis moved quickly to the heavy oak chair opposite Inspector Ronald Janesky.

"Use four sets of cuffs," Janesky said. "Cuff his hands and feet to the chair."

The Cuban watched Adams with intense interest as he cuffed his right and left ankles to the chair. He began to smile as Adams moved to his wrists. He had a huge grin on his face when Adams neatly clasped the last cuff.

"Sorry," Inspector Janesky said. "Sorry, but we don't want you to get up and run around. You'll certainly hurt yourself if you do."

The Cuban cleared his voice and looked away.

"These photographs I have here," Janesky began, "are simple pictures of an even simpler life."

Janesky waited for the translation from Officer Rivera. He held a photo in front of the Cuban's face.

"What you see here is Police Officer Ben Paris's family. This is a mother with her three children."

"I don't want to look at his fucking pictures, man. This man is a crazy man, crazy, crazy, crazy," the Cuban said wearily in Spanish.

"Excuse me, sir, but the prisoner said you're crazy and he don't want to look at your pictures."

"Ramon, tell him I'm beyond crazy. Tell him I'm fucking sick. Tell him he's in grave danger. Tell him he's dealing with someone who believes God is dead."

Janesky took another photo from the envelope, studied it for a moment, then scaled it across the desk, hitting the Cuban in the face.

"A father with his children," he said softly.

Rivera told the prisoner that the inspector was crazy.

"But maybe you're right, Luis. This is not the best time to look at a family photo album," Janesky said, spreading the photographs out on the desk. "If you're interested, you can glance at them while we talk."

"I don't have to talk to nobody, not crazy people, not nobody," the Cuban said with a bland smile.

"I can make him do the mambo," Monty Adams said from his perch on the edge of the desk nearest the door. "I could make him do the mambo with my little stun gun. He'd do it so good, he'd win a dance contest."

Janesky looked at Monty Adams. After a moment he said, "Monty, when I signal you, I want you to open the window. Then I want you to fling one of those weights out the open window as if it were a Frisbee. Do you think you could do that? Twenty-five pounds is a helluva lot of weight, Monty. Do you think you could do that? Scale one right out the window?"

"If you ask me to, sir, I could throw it to Court Street."

"Just into the parking lot would be far enough."

Monty Adams, looking at the Cuban, nodded.

"Okay," Janesky began, "this is what I want to know. One! Who was with you at the warehouse? Names and addresses. Two! Who fired the shots that killed Officer Paris and wounded Officer Malloy? Two simple questions that you could answer in a minute."

After Rivera translated, the Cuban looked at Janesky blankly and yawned.

Inspector Janesky took a deep breath, then slowly released it.

"You are a handsome young guy," Janesky said. "No kidding, you could be a movie star. I bet you kill the ladies, huh, man? I bet you got 'em coming and going. C'mon, tell the truth." Janesky punched his fist into his open hand. "You fuck all the time. I bet you spend your life fucking."

The Cuban opened his mouth and displayed a long tongue, wiggled it around, sexy-like.

"Faggot," Monty Adams said.

"I no faggot, man, I like pussy. You big, dumb *maricón*."

"Well, well, you do speak some English, you sneaky little devil, you," Janesky said with a chuckle.

The Cuban shrugged.

"You know we have beautiful women in New York. I'm going to tell you about our women. In the wintertime, when they're bundled up and wearing boots, you can see beautiful round asses under winter coats. If I say so myself, New York women, in the winter, look great. But, Luis, *you'll* never fuck one."

The Cuban glanced at Janesky. A smile appeared, and he began to strum his fingers on the arm of the chair.

"Still," Janesky went on with a sigh, "the springtime may be my favorite, when they first shed all those clothes, their legs appear, and their tits surge under light sweaters. The air is heavy with the sweet smell of them. Oh, yeah, in the spring, New York women bloom."

"This man really is crazy," the Cuban said in Spanish to Officer Rivera.

"And in the spring, this coming spring, when New York women, in my opinion, are at their most sexy, you'll not get to hold one. Put that proud cock of yours in one. No, sir, not you."

The Cuban raised his eyes to heaven and wagged his head, big wags.

"Summertime! Christ, summertime is absolute torture in this city. Surely you've seen our summer women. You could die from the beauty of them. In their jeans and shirts, their sandals and skirts. Tiny beads of sweat on their lips on the hot days. Summertime women make me want to work out, get ready for them, get ready to open those blouses, pull down those jeans. But this summer you'll never know what it is to have one," Janesky said vaguely, nodding his head.

The Cuban began to laugh quietly. But he stopped when he saw the fire start in Janesky's eyes.

"Now," Janesky said to Officer Adams.

Monty Adams quickly moved to the window and threw it open.

Janesky told him to take the end of the lamp wire and tie it good and tight to two of the weights.

Monty Adams suddenly smiled. He began to hum a song.

"I'm telling you, I want my lawyer. *Lawyer!*" the Cuban screamed.

Monty Adams was humming "I'm Just a Gigolo."

"It's about thirty feet to the street," Janesky said, watching as Adams stretched the wire out. "Roll out about twenty-five feet just to be on the safe side," he said thoughtfully.

The Cuban watched as Janesky took the spool of wire, measured it, then cut off the length he needed.

When Inspector Janesky folded his knife and slid it back into his pocket, he winked a conspiratorial kind of wink at the Cuban. Monty Adams was singing in full voice. Ramon Rivera did a sort of bolero.

"The names and addresses. It'll be our secret. You can tell your friend Officer Rivera; you don't even have to tell me," said Janesky.

"I don't know what you're talking about," the Cuban howled.

Janesky smiled and said, "I've been talking about women. How many have you fucked in your young life? One hundred, two hundred? Shit, I couldn't even guess, as good-looking as you are. Three hundred, maybe?"

Ray Rivera did a neat pirouette, and Monty Adams said, "He's just a gigolo."

A cold wind rolled in through the open window, and though he was sweating, the Cuban twitched and shuddered.

"The seasons of women. That's what we were talking about," Janesky said aloud to himself.

"Pull down his designer pants and shorts," Janesky said.

The Cuban closed his eyes for a moment, then opened them.

Officer Rivera danced over to where the Cuban was sitting. He undid the prisoner's belt, then lifted him by the waist.

The Cuban squirmed and struggled. Adams tugged at the pants. In one deft motion, down came the Cuban's trousers and shorts. All the while Monty Adams sang impressively.

Janesky turned to Monty Adams, told him to check the parking lot. "Make sure no one is out there," he said. "Be certain."

Then Inspector Janesky told Monty Adams to scale one of the weights out the window. With little more than a flick of the wrist, Monty Adams fired the weight through the open window.

"See how far this strong young man can throw that weight," Janesky said, leaning forward and grabbing the Cuban by the arm.

Then quickly, with an impressive move, Inspector Janesky made a slipknot with the other end of the wire.

"Now," he said calmly, "you will understand why all the conversation about women. You will at last get the point," Janesky said with a look of triumph.

"Luis," Janesky told him, "understand that if you don't answer my questions, all the beautiful women in the world will not matter one bit to you anymore. And do you know why?"

The Cuban sank back into his chair and looked at Janesky as if he were insane.

"You'll never fuck another one," Janesky whispered, "because, Luis, you filthy, cop-killing scumbag, I'm going to tear off your cock."

The Cuban mumbled something inaudible.

"Monty," Janesky said, "slip this wire over his balls, and be sure to pull it tight. At my signal you'll throw those weights out the window. When the balls go, maybe we should all back up. There could be a terrible mess in here."

Monty Adams nodded, wide-eyed. "Yeah," he said. "This fucker is gonna do the mambo all over the room."

"Ramon," Janesky said thoughtfully, "you tell Luis that if he doesn't answer my questions, the worst moment of his life will arrive in about ten seconds."

As Officer Rivera spoke, Monty Adams slipped the knot over the prisoner's balls. He pulled it tight, humming as he set about his work.

Though Inspector Janesky snipped the wire about ten feet from the fifty pounds of weight, the Cuban didn't notice. He couldn't notice, not with his eyes rolling back into his head. And when Monty Adams pulled the wire tight, the Cuban let out a howl of fear and pain.

"Names and addresses," Ramon shouted.

The Cuban screamed in a language that even Officer Rivera couldn't understand. And when Monty Adams picked up the steel discs to fling them through the window, a black Latin fire lit the Cuban's eyes, and names and addresses flowed from him like a man with a Ph.D. degree in fast talk.

In a hallway across the street from the precinct parking lot, Officer Frank Bosco stood station-house patrol. His job was to make absolutely certain that no cars parked in the lot. He stood in the hallway and looked up at the open precinct window.

Frank Bosco moved his head from side to side. Strange sounds were coming from that window. The parking lot and the street in front of the parking lot were deserted.

When he saw the first disc slam into the parking lot pavement, he thought, What the fuck?

As hard as he could, he tried to make out the words mixed with the screams that came from the open precinct window.

The next thing he saw were two more weights, trailed by what appeared to be a cord. Frank Bosco stopped thinking and moved quickly two steps left, then two steps right. He didn't know where the hell to go.

The weights hit the ground with a thunderous boom, and the cord followed them to the earth, falling flat nicely and settling on the pavement.

Somebody was yelling; Frank could hear it, but he was too far away to make out the words. Besides, the words were coming fast and in Spanish. And Frank Bosco, being an experienced policeman, was not about to get any closer to any building where steel weights were flying from the windows.

While Frank Bosco sat on the curb near the precinct parking lot biting on the bill of his cap, believing with all his heart and soul that he'd finally made it, that at long last he'd crossed the great divide to rubber-gun land, Chief Inspector Raymond Janesky told Sergeant Jim Casey that when he wasn't looking, somehow the world had tilted and all the subhuman scumbags had slid into his precinct.

"Where do we find these shitheads?" Janesky asked. "How come they all find peace and happiness here in my precinct?"

The hallway in front of Janesky's office was heavy with traffic. Cops coming and going, an unceasing rain of feet heading for the streets of Red Hook.

Casey sat erect in a chair, near the window that looked out onto the street. He sat with his legs crossed at the knee; sunlight lit his face.

"You'll be six-o'clock news," Casey said. "You broke the case, solved the killing. You did it."

Janesky looked at him good-humoredly. "Nothing to it," he said, then going on, not pausing, "Ya know, these Cubans really value their dicks."

A sector car, its siren blasting, took off, followed by another, then another.

Casey looked around in disgust. "This place never slows. Man, the shit never stops rollin' around here."

"Everywhere, it's everywhere!" Janesky shouted. "The city is out of control." Inspector Janesky was up now, taking long strides around his office, moving from wall to wall. "The scumbags and douchebags have taken over, Jim. You know that, but it's my duty and my right to kick ass, and let me tell you, that's what the people want. The good people want serious ass kicking."

"You're the best we got," Casey said softly, hoping the inspector would lower his voice.

"The nigger lovers, the fags, and the Jews. They'll try to stop me, get in my way."

"Shiiit," said Casey. And he said it with a mean little grin.

"No shit, Jim," said Janesky. "I told you what they told me. That guy from downtown, the one that pulled my coat, warned me about that bitch from IAD. She wants my head, that Lesbian bitch. Only she don't know that if she fucks with me, she's counting back from ten."

"Counting back from ten," said Casey. "Captain Butterfly is counting back from ten. I like that."

Janesky smiled, and Casey smiled too.

"She hates good cops," Casey offered. "Always has. I tol' you. When I worked PMD with her, she worried more about the hookers than she did about her fellow officers. Oh, yeah, she hates you, Chief. Ain't no doubt about it. The broad's sick."

Janesky whirled, his blue eyes narrowing, "Oh, yeah, oh, yeah," he said. "Well, you stay on her, Jim. We'll fix her ass. Would you like a beer?"

"No thanks, boss."

Chief Raymond Janesky smiled a melancholy smile, said, "We know these humps for what they are, don't we, Jimbo?"

Charlie had called at six. Left a message on her machine in his soft Humphrey Bogart voice.

"Got us a table at Losito's. The reservation's for seven-thirty. But I'll wait till spring for you, sweetness."

At just after six-thirty Marjorie walked over to "picturesque" Amsterdam Avenue. A mental deficient driving a red Jeep jumped a light and almost put her on her butt at Seventy-first Street. Marjorie put her hand across her eyes and memorized the license-plate number.

She'd been a cop for nineteen years and knew how to get even.

Marjorie wasn't one to indulge in sudden flights of self-examination. Still, as she stood on the corner, with the lights of cars, trucks, and buses rushing toward her, she felt a horrible shiver. No matter how she tried to rationalize it, she owned the soul of a fanatic, and she knew it.

Face facts, she told herself. This obsession about Inspector Janesky, this thing that didn't allow her to give a damn about anything else, was starting to control her life. There were other cases, stacks of them, and they were piling up. No time—no time, she told herself. First Janesky, then everything else.

Her relationship with Charlie, like the deafening hum of the city, was always there. She'd outsmarted herself this time. The affair had movement and weight; it slid on its own. And it was slipping into a place she doubted she wanted to be. Still, the loneliness frightened her, the boredom of a Sunday morning alone, the death-in-life of living just for a job—

"Oh, boy," she said to herself as she started toward the restaurant. "This is all there is, just this job, and a going-nowhere relationship with a younger man. The rest is silence. Oh, boy," she said again.

Charlie was standing at the bar, laughing and chatting with a man who wore boots of some reptile's skin. The scales glowed blue-black in the bar's yellow light.

New York men who wore cowboy boots always made Marjorie's mood darken. And his jeans were so tight that she was sure his balls must be caught in a vault of pain.

Charlie was happy to see her and, giving her a wide grin, said, "Terry Messina, meet the love of my life."

Messina spoke in the low voice of the cool, West Side, powdered-nose set.

"Lemme tell ya, this man's in love," said Terry Messina. "I stand a very good chance of losing the best, all-night, club-bouncing buddy I got."

His long, straight hair was combed flat back, with a cute little ponytail that stuck to the back of his head like a dart. His wispy voice annoyed Marjorie.

He asked Marjorie if she'd like a seat at the bar. "No thanks," Marjorie told him. "I haven't eaten all day, and I'd very much like to."

Marjorie thought that she detected perfume, and he had a thin mouth, the kind she always associated with cruelty.

"Our table won't be ready for a few minutes," Charlie said with a nervous smile, glancing at Terry Messina. Then he gazed around the bar, smiling, shaking his head. Calling the bartender over, he ordered a Campari and soda on the rocks with a twist for Marjorie.

Marjorie said, "Give us a kiss, sweetheart." And Charlie complied.

Terry Messina eyed them both. Marjorie noticed that he wore a tiny diamond in his earlobe.

A waiter, a plump young man, said their table was ready.

Terry Messina took the opportunity to slip away.

"Feeling a bit less than friendly tonight, aren't we?" Charlie said. "Poor ol' Terry Messina looked like he needed a hole to jump into."

"Is Messina your friend, Charlie? How come I've never met him?"

"Not a friend, really, just someone I've known for a while."

"I'd like some wine," Marjorie said, then, "Your buddy Terry is a putz."

"He very well may be."

"Okay, I just wanted to get that straight."

"He owns this place."

"He does? Impressive. He's still a putz."

"You have a mean streak, you know that, Marjorie? How can I cure you?"

"Too late for that."

Charlie looked at her blankly.

"Oh, well, since he's your friend, I'll try to think well of him." Then, after a moment, she whispered, "Can your *friend* get us a waiter? I'm starving."

"You know," said Charlie, "we've been together for a year. We don't talk about us anymore."

Marjorie sighed.

"I'm sorry, but one of the things I was thinking about," Charlie said, "was that we should get married."

"For chrissake!" Marjorie shouted, and Terry Messina, who was in quiet conversation with the pudgy waiter, cleared his throat. Lowering her voice, she added, "Marriage is not a topic I want to discuss."

"Oh, shit, now you're mad at me," Charlie said.

"I'm not mad at you, Charlie."

"But you refuse to encourage me, don't you?"

"It would be nice if you'd think of my needs once in a while."

"Why do you keep pushing me away? You hide behind your work and we never talk about us, our future. I want to be married. Is that so strange? And I want to marry *you*. What's so terrible about that?"

"I made a choice a long time ago, Charlie, between a career, which you'll admit I'm good at, and marriage. I'm a skilled survivor, Charlie. I've always done better alone."

"Then I came along."

Marjorie laughed.

"You think it's funny. It's my life, it's not funny."

The waiter brought pasta with pesto, opened a bottle of a good, cool Italian white from Piedmont.

"Charlie," Marjorie said, "you're right. We've been together for a year. And I'm the first to admit that it's been good, great at times."

"So?"

"You're eight years younger than I am, Charlie. Eight years is a long time."

There was something in Charlie's eyes, bright and full of pride. He reached out for her hands; one, then the other.

"I'm not going to let you hit me with that again. I'm not."

"Well, I think it's something worth considering, don't you?"

"No," Charlie said sharply, then, "I'd make you happy. C'mon, you tell me why I couldn't make you happy."

Marjorie didn't answer. A rush of love, or something like love, eased into her. And then that other mood descended on her, the feel of it, clear and sharp and painful. A swirling in her stomach. *A loner, that's me,* she thought. "Maybe I could use some therapy," she offered lightly.

"Bullshit," Charlie said.

He shook his head slowly and poured them more wine.

Marjorie watched him, wondering if she really could be in love with him. Wondering if she knew the feeling. Of course, she thought, it's not hard; it's a helpless feeling. When you're truly in love, you feel fucking helpless. It's not flowers and music and bells, it's helplessness. And to Marjorie helplessness was goddamn painful. She'd felt it once, long ago.

She remembered how Jeff had stood there passively, indifferently, in the clear morning light of her kitchen telling her no, no, it was no good, he'd never leave, not while the kids were young. He just couldn't. Somehow he'd forgotten what he was, who he was. Somehow, for five years, they'd lived a lie. He'd spoken slowly, staring at her, telling her, maybe when the kids were older, maybe then. Her mind filled with the memory of it, the pain. And she'd sworn then that if she'd had a knife, she'd cut it out, the helplessness, the pain. "Never again" was the oath she'd taken.

An hour and a half later she stood naked before Charlie in her darkened bedroom. She stood in silence while Charlie touched her and spoke in whispers, telling her how much he loved her, how beautiful she was, and how much, oh how much, he wanted her.

They stood together, and she felt his hands, his arms, their breath joining, then parting. And Charlie moved slowly to give her pleasure. He urged her down onto the bed, and it seemed to Marjorie like forever before he quietly slipped into her. She tossed her head with pleasure and thought of golden light creeping up mountainsides. And of incredible blue water, a white beach, and waving palms. And at her center, she thought, *Oh, please, Charlie, please let your dream be the same as mine.*

Later a rain, hard and steady, drilling against the bedroom window, woke her. Marjorie caught sight of herself in her dresser mirror. Her body, like a stranger's, fine, almost perfect, lay across the bed, her head on Charlie's chest.

She lay there resting, not moving. Charlie's head was in the pillow. In the mirror Marjorie could not see his face.

Suddenly the telephone rang, loud, shattering, unnerving. She jumped up to grab it.

"Sorry to call so late," Carow said, "but I tried earlier and got your machine and hung up. Listen," he said, "we need to be downtown by nine. The chief of ops wants to see us."

"Do you know why?" Marjorie asked.

"Naw, but it can't be a big deal. If it were, I'da heard something."

When she returned the phone to its cradle, Charlie, awake and stretching, asked, "So what's up?"

"Nothing's up, Charlie," she said. She looked at his body, smiled a playful sort of grin, and said, "Maybe my baby needs a bit of help."

She kissed his thighs, used her tongue a bit.

Charlie kissed her head, pulled her up and over, on top of him.

"Show me," he said. "Show me how you can help."

Chapter Six

Marjorie knew that when you drove over the Brooklyn Bridge into Manhattan, if the weather was clear, you'd find yourself looking at the windows of the new Police Headquarters. And if you concentrated, you could easily believe that there were people looking out from those windows, tense and angry people looking out of those black windows, maybe a dozen or more people with brass and braid and lacquered bills on their caps, all thinking about what they were going to do to you, say to you, to ruin your day.

Marjorie sat slouched in the front passenger seat with one knee resting up against the dash, her elbow on the armrest, her chin in her hand.

Carow, who was driving, asked, "What are you thinking about?"

When Marjorie shrugged, he went on, "Your eyes just got small and beady. Will you stop worrying, for chrissake?"

"Easy for you to say. I'm a captain. If these people get good and pissed at me, I'll stay a captain. You know that, Andrew."

"No, wait, listen. So the chief of operations wants to see us. That's no big deal."

Marjorie nodded. "Sure," she said.

Carow smiled, then he tapped her shoulder with his fist. "You'll eat him up. It's the women that make history, Captain, you know that."

Marjorie looked over at his watery brown eyes. "Why is it," she said, "that when you try to reassure me, it makes me even more nervous? I guess it's because I know you, know your rap, know when you're totally full of shit! Headquarters people want my head. I can feel it, Andrew, I can smell it. It's all around me."

"C'mon," Carow said. "That is something you really don't know."

For a brief second Marjorie felt furious, then, realizing that her anger was not directed at Carow, she offered a little sigh to the windshield.

"Just stay calm, don't loose your cool," Carow said. "Please, please relax. This is a Headquarters bullshit meeting, that's all it is."

There was a brief, tense silence. Marjorie broke it by saying, "Wait, wasn't it you who told me that if Janesky found out I was coming after him, he wouldn't exactly be tickled?"

"Oh, yeah, that's true. The guy doesn't take a joke well. I'll tell ya, Margie, I've met Janesky a few times, and I've looked in his eyes. Ya know what I've seen there?"

Marjorie didn't answer.

"Nothing. That's what I saw in his eyes, nothing. You haven't seen anything till you've seen Janesky's eyes."

"Wouldn't be a bad idea if we changed the subject," Marjorie said.

A bright day, sunny, warm, a hint of early spring in the City in March. She gazed out of the cruiser's window, looked down at the East River. There was a stiff wind, and as far as she could see, whitecaps whipped across the water.

It had been a week since the pier shooting, and she'd sensed something was up. If she could feel or sense anything at all, she could tell when something spooky was coming down. If you spent your life in police work, you'd better know when spooks were flying.

You'd better watch your ass, Marjorie told herself. She heard the horns of cars in line on the bridge, and a boat whistle rose up from the river.

She watched Carow's long fingers push his hair back, his other hand holding tightly to the wheel. He felt it, too, the menace in the air.

Carow said, "Manhattan on a day like this has got to be the most beautiful city in the world."

After a moment Marjorie laughed and said, "Manhattan's not a city. Besides, how many cities have you seen, Andrew?"

Sitting up straight behind the wheel of the cruiser, his eyes darting around for fear some yahoo was about to run into him, Carow said, "I've never been interested in seeing another city."

Marjorie said, "I know."

"Say what you will, you live in New York all your life, there's no need to see another city."

"Uh-huh," Marjorie said, and looked at Carow from the corner of her eye.

They crawled along, Carow peering through the glass at all the Chinatown activity.

"Chinamen in cars make me very nervous. Not one of 'em knows how to drive," he said. "Not a one."

After a few more blocks, during which there were several hair-raising near misses, Carow rolled the cruiser into the subterranean garage at Headquarters.

Stopping, turning in his seat with a huge grunt and a terrible amount of agitation on his face, Carow backed into a spot. He ran down two yellow-and-black traffic cones, and Marjorie wanted to shout in his ear, "If this is the way you drive, why the hell do you always insist on driving?"

But it was not important. They were already parked, and Carow wouldn't listen, anyway.

Carow locked the cruiser door. Then they walked over to the security office.

The two on-duty security cops nodded when she and Carow went into the office. Marjorie knew most of the cops working security by sight, and they all knew her.

A very pale, thin officer was seated at the front desk.

There was a folded newspaper and an open paperback book by Ken Kesey on the desk.

She thought, The cop that's reading *this* book is at least still conscious.

The seated cop was explaining to the other policeman standing stiffly at his side what he could and could not eat.

On the wall there was a Rambo poster with the mayor's face superimposed over Stallone's.

"Once you get over the lousy break," the seated officer said, "you can get usta living with a heart condition. There are worse things. Ya know what I mean?"

"Good afternoon, Captain," the standing officer said. He wore the combat cross. He looked at their faces, nodded, smiled, and for effect, checked their IDs.

The tag on his shirt read R. MARTINEZ, and he walked with a cane.

The seated officer was hunched over so that his face almost touched the logbook. He sat discussing something with himself.

"Can I have the book?" Marjorie said, pointing with her finger.

The officer pushed his chair back and slid her the log. He looked solemn, concerned.

"I'll sign for the inspector too."

"Fine, that's fine. You can sign," Officer Martinez offered quickly, nodding his head. "As long as you're in the book, that's great, we're all set. By the way, I love your shoes, Captain, they're real sharp."

He's the one reading the book, she thought. Then she said, "Thanks."

Martinez closed his eyes and nodded. "Is it snowing in Brooklyn, Captain?"

"It's beautiful outside," whispered Marjorie.

Martinez seemed flustered.

She patted his shoulder, saying, "Officer, please push your little buzzer and open the door for us."

The door that led from the garage to the elevators of Headquarters swung open.

As Carow took hold of her arm he said, "Margie, this could turn out to be a long day."

Marjorie waited until the elevator door slid closed, then she turned and faced Carow.

"Listen," she said, "I've decided that I'm not taking any shit from these people." Which was not what she had meant to say. She was going to say that if they stuck together, presented their case intelligently, they'd listen.

She decided not to correct herself, then turned back toward the door and sighed.

"I don't think we're here to get jumped on, Margie. They wouldn't have to call us to Headquarters to cut our legs off. That they could do with a telephone call. Think about it," Carow said, tapping the side of his head. "Let's not be hasty," he said. "They probably need information for a report to the mayor or some such thing."

"You're wonderful, Andrew," said Marjorie.

"No, really," he said, "think about it."

She drew herself up and studied the elevator ceiling.

Forget that it was the middle of the afternoon when the call came. Forget that the word was all over the Department that Janesky had broken the police homicide and was a hero again. Forget that she had sent two confidential memos to the three-star chief, John Riddle, requesting a psychological profile on Janesky. Forget that the mayor was singing Janesky's praises all over the damn city. Marjorie tried very hard to believe that the summoning to Headquarters could be explained reasonably enough. She tried very hard. But it wasn't easy. She'd been with the Department for nineteen years, worked a whole lot of small-potato cases, and every so often a big one. But she had never been called to Headquarters before. And forget that it was Friday afternoon, late Friday afternoon, when every piece of braid and brass was normally long gone.

Inspector Carow leaned in close and whispered in her ear, "Remember, this is just some kinda Headquarters bullshit. That's all this is, Margie, just some kind of bullshit."

Marjorie nodded.

Marjorie had felt reasonably composed all afternoon, but as she walked from the elevator onto the fourteenth floor, she felt a thin stream of sweat snake from under her arm, and her legs were having a little trouble supporting her. This meeting could shatter her career if it were to go wrong.

Captain Litke, the chief of operations' aide, came across the hallway in his white uniform shirt and his finely creased blue trousers trimmed with navy piping. He was a small, frail-looking man who sprayed his hair so that he looked as if he were wearing a helmet. Reaching out, Litke shook Carow's hand and nodded to Marjorie. Marjorie looked at him and thought that one of the benefits of working at Headquarters was that you learned how to look worried with little or no effort.

"I'm glad you're not late," he said, wagging his head and glancing at his watch. "For a meeting like this, there really is no excuse for tardiness."

Captain Litke continued to talk as they moved down the hallway, through the reception area, then stood at the closed door to the office of the chief of operations.

Litke glanced at his watch, announced that it was precisely four P.M., threw back his head, and tapped on the door.

Marjorie paused at the now-open door, not sure of the procedure, wondering if she should let Inspector Carow enter the office first. She decided that she should go in cockily, but catching a glimpse of the brass and braid inside, she was suddenly terrified.

Carow, standing behind her, calmly said, "Margie?"

The chief of operations was seated at a table that butted up against a desk. Hanging above that desk was a series of framed photographs: the mayor, the police commissioner, and a flock of five-star super chiefs, one of whom she recognized. The table was long, perhaps twelve feet, and, with the desk, formed a neat *T* of fine mahogany.

"Chief," Captain Litke announced, "this is Captain Butera and—"

"C'mon, c'mon, I don't have all fucking day, Litke. This ain't the Roman Senate. Cut the bullshit and go chase that cop you wanna grab smoking in the security shack. Go ahead, Litke, beat it."

"Sir," Litke shouted, then he sort of bowed, spun on his heel, and left.

As Marjorie and Carow stood by, the chief of ops began nodding with enthusiasm. "Would you believe that strutting putz is a two-star general in the Army Reserve? You don't think this country's got problems? Well, c'mon in and take a seat."

This is the highest-ranking uniformed officer of the Department—this guy with the little face, blue eyes, blond, short-cut hair, and hardly any neck at all, Marjorie thought. Fascinated, she couldn't stop staring at him.

The chief of ops got right to it by saying, "You have something to tell me about Chief Janesky? You got maybe fifteen minutes. Use 'em."

He said this in a deadpan sort of way, which Marjorie thought was probably natural for him, a lot of nodding, pretending to listen.

"Yes, certainly," she said calmly, and opened the case folder marked JANESKY/BSCO.

Carow had taken a seat beside her; his hands were out of sight. Marjorie could not escape the thought that they were trembling.

The chief of ops said, "I take it you have facts in there. It's important that I get some facts. I really don't want to hear rumors, gossip, or any kind of unsubstantiated crap."

Then he smiled a small smile and turned to Carow. "You understand that, don't you, Andrew?"

Carow sighed.

Thoughtful, squinting slightly, the chief of ops watched Marjorie open her briefcase, and as she reached into it she became convinced of two things: one, Andrew Tony Carow was about ready to jump through his skin; and two, this was going to be a heavyweight meeting, no bullshit.

She cleared her throat, tried a smile. No, she couldn't do it. She heard the chief of ops tapping his fingertips impatiently on his desk.

"Well, Chief," she started, taking the folder and a pad from her briefcase, opening the pad, laying it on the table in front of her, putting her fine-point pen atop it, showing this big-time Headquarters guy that she wouldn't panic, that she was ready. "We have a precinct, an entire command, that's out of control."

"Bullshit," said the chief of operations. "What you got, probably, is an isolated incident involving a cop or two. Don't talk about an entire command, Captain. It makes me real edgy. Be specific."

Looking straight into the chief of ops' eyes, she said, "The whole command, the entire precinct, has gone over the edge. And the CO of that command, Chief Inspector Ronald Janesky, is responsible."

The chief of ops squinted at her, causing creases to form in his cheeks. Marjorie waited, but there was only silence from across the table. Finally he said, "An entire command gone crazy?" He was mimicking her, overdoing it, making her bite down.

She shot a glance toward Carow to see how he was doing.

"Chief," she said, "I've been looking at Janesky and BSCO for over six months now. Many of the arrests in that precinct have been tainted." Marjorie's gaze moved from her notes to the face of the chief of ops. She could see his jaw tighten, his eyes narrow.

He lifted his hand and pointed his index finger as if aiming a gun. His hands were large, his fingers as long and thick as a nightstick, his nails well kept and cared for. He sighted in on Carow and said: "You knew about this, Andrew?"

Carow smiled vaguely, as though he were involved in some abstract thought.

"I've been kept up-to-date from the beginning. There have been some fairly serious allegations."

"Allegations," the chief of ops said. He was silent a moment. "You're investigating a command—an entire command, mind you—and a full inspector for six months based on some . . . some *allegations*? Is that what you're telling me?"

Carow tried to grin, but Marjorie could see pain and fear coming together in his face.

Picking his words with a certain strategic care, Inspector Andrew Tony Carow whispered, "Captain Butera has a number of reports from a field associate." He spoke so low, Marjorie had trouble hearing him.

The chief of ops grinned, a mean, unpleasant grin.

Well, Marjorie thought. Well, now, you are a slick bastard. "Chief, I have quite a long series of specific incidents that indicate a pattern."

"Oh, shit," said the chief of ops. "A pattern, eh?"

"That's right, a pattern of abuse of prisoners, illegal arrests, a total lack of supervision, a breakdown of control and command. The thing is, Chief," she said, looking straight at him, "we have a man out there making policy decisions for the Department, a man that has absolutely no concept what our policy is or should be."

The chief of ops made a funny twitching motion with his shoulders.

"Tell me more about this field associate. Is he reliable? C'mon, tell me where you're getting these allegations."

"He's wounded," Carow said. "Shot at the pier last week. He's in stable, but serious, condition."

"Officer Kenneth Malloy?" said the chief. "I saw him at the hospital. He looked a little weird to me. Maybe his wound, a bullet in the throat, had something to do with it. Anyway, he looked like . . . his eyes . . . anyway, he looked weird, like a troublemaker. I hate the entire concept of field associates. They're all fucking weirdos. Anybody who'd spy on their fellow officers—"

Marjorie cleared her throat.

"Listen," the chief said. "I've heard some of this stuff about Janesky before. And his command too. I've heard some of the rumors."

Then he settled back in his chair and closed his eyes like a man who had heard enough.

"Look," Marjorie said, raising her eyes toward the chief, "I think—"

"I know what you think, Captain," he said, half rising to his feet. "But do you have one allegation that directly implicates Chief Janesky?"

"Yes."

"Well, then, tell me." He waited three seconds, then said, "If you have something substantial, tell."

"Janesky and two other officers tortured the prisoner that was involved in the pier shooting."

"Really?" The chief of ops sounded impressed.

"I have a new F/A working the precinct, and he saw steel weights attached to electrical wire, and those weights were apparently thrown from the detectives' squad-room window, the place where Chief Janesky was holding his personal interrogation."

"He," the chief of ops asked softly, "saw Janesky torture the prisoner?"

"No. He wasn't in the room, but—"

"Ya see, ya see, you're doing it again, Captain. Now listen!" he shouted. "The police commissioner and the mayor are going to give Janesky another medal. We're gonna promote Chief Janesky real soon. The man broke the homicide of the policeman; he identified the others, the shooter and two others. FBI and DEA agents arrested the three in Clearwater, Florida, this very morning. Malloy and his partner, Paris, those cops didn't come on a bunch of burglars. They stumbled into a delivery of three hundred kilograms of Colombian cocaine." The chief of ops gave her a wink. "Everyone sees the man as a hero, and you're here trying to vilify the guy."

Marjorie looked at Carow to see if what the chief of ops was saying made sense to him. Carow shrugged.

"Now," the chief of ops said, "I'm going to try to do something for you."

Marjorie had to smile.

"Forget this Janesky thing. It's a dead issue."

Marjorie bit her lip and looked at him.

"Well—?"

"Okay," she said, "but I'm delivering a warning. If we allow to continue what is presently taking place at BSCO, this Department and the City are in big trouble."

Carow was looking at her, wide-eyed, fearful.

"That damn precinct is going to go; they're really going to mix it up there. Sooner or later you're going to hear one helluva bang outa Brooklyn. But it's your call. If you want me to drop the investigation, I will. I'll just forget it and move on to other things."

"Christ," the chief of ops said. "Obsessive, that's what you are. You're obsessed with this."

"Of course," Marjorie said. "How else do you do this job?" She could feel herself starting to lose control. Tension, sadness, and anger were coming together, forming an acidic mix in her stomach.

"Janesky is a terrific commander, an experienced supervisor, Captain," the chief of ops told her.

"The only thing Janesky supervises is his own career," Marjorie said, glancing at Carow, who she knew was about to slide under the table.

The chief stared at her. "Please," he said, as if playing to an audience. Suddenly he seemed to lack the energy to go on. "Look, Captain," he said. "Cut the shit. You have bubkes on Janesky. Sure you have some notions, but notions are not going to move me."

Marjorie didn't answer.

"Are you sure you want to continue with this? Maybe not?"

Marjorie didn't answer. She was seriously tempted to let it out. To tell this big-time Headquarters guy just what she was thinking. Except he looked like the type that wouldn't take it well. So she just sat and stared, giving it all she had, looking at him and letting him know what she thought with her eyes.

"All right, then go ahead, finish it." He turned to Carow. "No one will interfere with her investigation. We know who her boyfriend is. Oh, yeah, we know. Everyone knows. That reporter who goes off on all that liberal crap; makes him feel big. He's one of those wind-up bullshitters. I read him once in awhile."

"Excuse me?" Marjorie said.

The chief of ops took a quick glance at her, then went back to Carow. "I read that story he did about her. That Captain Butterfly bullshit. We know he'd love to hear we covered up an investigation. But we're not!"

Carow tried to make himself smaller.

Marjorie loved being talked about as if she weren't there. She was getting tired and very angry. Still, she said nothing and stared hard.

"All right, then, you'll stay with this investigation for sixty days, not a minute more. Then you'll close it." The chief of ops said softly, "There is nothing there, Captain." And he was grinning when he said it.

Marjorie sat wondering, steaming, thinking that the sickness here was stupidity, that there hadn't been a doctor born who could cure that.

"First of all, Chief," she said, "I'm a little old for *boy*friends."

Carow coughed.

"I have *men* friends. Secondly, it strikes me that in a city that's always a bit lopsided, we don't need a psycho precinct commander running wild. But then, maybe I'm wrong."

Carow closed his eyes.

The chief of ops stopped smiling, then said, "You have two months, sixty days, to come up with something specific involving Inspector Janesky. In sixty days I want this investigation concluded."

"Fine," she said. Pausing a moment, she saw Carow hunch over the table. "Anybody can see that sixty days will be more than enough."

The chief of ops said, "Sure, anybody can see that."

When they left the office to walk to the elevator, Carow nodded to people in the hallway. One or two called to him from inside offices, and he waved. But they all seemed to be staring hostilely at Marjorie.

Carow said, "You did just great. He listened to you. You made me proud."

"That's bull, Andrew. Let's get out of here. This place is making me ill."

Carow didn't answer.

"The bullshitters come from every direction around here. I feel like I'm knee-deep in assholes," Marjorie said out loud.

"Easy," Carow said, then he moved quickly, walking in front of her now. After a second he stopped, waited, then said, "I disappointed you, didn't I? Let you down? Margie, these people frighten me, scare the hell out of me. I can't explain it, 'cept that I've always been that way around the top guys."

Marjorie didn't answer.

They stood by the bank of elevators near the fourteenth-floor security desk, Carow with his hands in his pockets, Marjorie holding her briefcase.

Down the hallway, Captain Litke was talking to a man Marjorie thought she should recognize but didn't.

She asked Carow, "Who is that man with Litke?"

"The tall guy in the gray suit?"

"Not so tall, Andrew, but he's the only one talking to Litke."

"That's Chief Thomas. You know him, don't you?"

"Right," Marjorie said. "The chief of detectives."

Litke was walking toward them now, and not, Marjorie was sure, by chance. He gave them a big, phony grin and said, "Chief Thomas would like to talk to you, Captain. Do you have a minute?"

"Well, we can talk to one more, huh, Andrew?" She nodded.

Carow surprised her by saying, "He wants to talk to you, Marjorie. If it was both of us, he would have said so."

Litke was saying now, "The chief said he only wants a minute of your time. Follow me and I'll take you to his office."

Carow pushed the elevator button, saying, "I'll wait in the garage. Okay? I'll pull the car out."

Marjorie nodded at Carow, then at Litke, then looked down the hallway.

"Lead on, Litke," she said.

Turning, moving quickly down the hallway, Litke checked his reflection in the office's glass partitions as he went. Finally he turned to her and gave her what must have been his best evil look.

"Second office on the right," Litke said with a triumphant sort of grin.

The chief of detectives had once been in good shape. There was a time in the not-so-distant past that he had muscles. Now a bit of flab showed here and there, but it was all redeemable. A few workouts, a couple of months of Nautilus and free weights and he'd firm again. But his eyes were quick, his smile bright.

You could tell, the man was a born politician. Marjorie was sure he gave out doughnuts the day Reagan was elected president.

He sat at his desk, and unlike the chief of ops, who seemed to look through you, Chief Thomas made a quick study, and Marjorie could tell he liked what he saw.

It occurred to her that the man was a major-league mover. So what was he up to? And she began to wonder, *Why me? Why these eerie images?* Auras and things unfriendly around people? Her intuition told her he was there to bait her, taunt her.

Chief Thomas stood when she entered, saying, "The chief of ops is impressive, isn't he?"

Marjorie shrugged and smiled, wanting to please. "May I sit?" she asked.

"Of course. Go ahead, sit down. I know how those meetings go. You must be exhausted."

The windows in his office looked south, past the Brooklyn Bridge, toward the Battery. A great New York view.

"Chief," said Marjorie, "can I say something, and please believe me, I don't mean to be disrespectful."

"Ohh, yes, you do," he said, smiling. Going on, without a pause, he touched his fingers to his lips, rolled his eyes, and said, "I saw you walk into that office, and I thought, Christ, how is she going to handle this?"

Marjorie looked at him.

He went on. "I wondered if you were as sharp as everyone seems to think. Would you listen, be still and hear, maybe learn something? Or would you behave like my ol' buddy Tony Carow said you would?"

Marjorie looked into his face and shook her head.

"Your ol' buddy? Tony Carow? Tell me, Chief, how did Carow say I'd behave?"

She watched him as he looked at her, as he walked to one corner of the room, as he crossed his arms. And she wondered, *What are we playing here?*

"He said that you have one of the best brains in the Department, but you have some trouble controlling your mouth. He said you give him fits. He said you're not likely to back away from anyone, not the chief of ops, not even me. He said, Captain, that you're not a team player."

"Well, that's just great," said Marjorie. "That's terrific. You need a scorecard around here to match the players with the team. You have to join sides, right?"

Thomas walked over to his desk and flipped open a manila folder, saying, "On the sergeant's test you scored in the top ten percent, the same for lieutenant. And for captain, you came in second. But let me tell you, Captain, that's it. There're no more tests. All your promotions from now on are appointments made by the PC."

"What are you telling me?"

"I'm telling you that there are no independents above the rank of captain, Captain. And that's my lesson for the day."

"Okay, Chief," she said, "I'm a quick study. So tell me, whose side is Janesky on?"

"He's the number-one seed, everyone's top choice to go all the way."

"He's an asshole," Marjorie said with a small smile.

Thomas stared at her for a moment without answering, then smiled.

"Take a look around you, dammit. You think that really matters here?"

Marjorie cleared her throat and stood up. "Maybe if one of the super chiefs, someone like yourself, just maybe if one of you would say something, they'd listen."

Chief of Detectives Thomas said, "Who? Who'd listen?"

"The well-intentioned people around here, that's who. There must be a few around this place, a few people that care a little. There must be a few people that give a shit!" She hadn't intended it, but Marjorie's voice had risen a bit.

Chief Thomas's body revolved slowly as he looked around. Raising manicured fingers, joining his hands prayerlike, he said, "There are two ways to go here, and let me tell you, your way leads fucking nowhere. The other—"

Marjorie cut him off, giving him her serious look, telling him, "Janesky's a certifiable wacko, and he's gone as far as he's going to get in this job, if I have anything to say about it. The son of a bitch is going to damage us all, and I'm going to pull the plug."

Smoothing back his perfectly trimmed hair, Chief Thomas leaned his tanned face forward to say, "*Damage* is a good word. You'd be wise to remember it."

She looked at him for a long moment, then looked right past him at the postcard view of lower Manhattan.

"You know," she said, "this is a great city. Why does

such a great city have so many weak bastards running it?"

"Beautiful." Chief Thomas sniffed. "I'm not disappointed. You are exactly what I was told you would be."

Marjorie considered her answer for a long time. "I'm not trying to fool anyone," Marjorie said. "I mean, I'm just trying to do my job. Aren't we, all of us, simply cops here to do a job?"

"Sure," Chief of Detectives Thomas said. "Yeah, that's it. Civil servants, that's us, trying to do a job in this jewel of a city."

In the cruiser again with Carow, driving across the Brooklyn Bridge, Marjorie said, "Someone's been following me."

"C'mon, you don't really believe that," Carow said. "You're getting paranoid."

There was a long pause before she said, "Andrew, I know it. Someone has been following me for several days."

Carow said, "Whaddaya gonna do?"

"You know, this shit is crazy. Really, this is dangerous and crazy."

"Margie, I've been trying to tell you that for months."

"They've made a big mistake, Andrew." Marjorie paused. "I can be a mean, miserable woman! It's not smart to piss me off."

Chapter Seven

Frank Bosco heard the window shatter as he was fussing with the driver of a black Chevy. A second later he looked up and saw a bundle of pink tumbling through the air.

"My God," somebody screamed.

"Motherfucker," somebody else shouted.

What the fuck's going on, Officer Frank Bosco thought. Then he saw the bundle smash onto the roof of a Gypsy cab, and blood exploded from the pink blanket, streaking the car. Then a bouncing baby girl tumbled onto the street.

But that was later. First a black Chevy backed through a crosswalk, mounted the curb, then slammed into a no-parking sign.

Frank tried to remain calm. He told the driver to get out of the car. Then he told him to get the car off the sidewalk. The car backed up quickly and smashed into a trash can, making the street come alive with shouting people trying to escape across the sidewalk, fleeing from an out-of-control car.

"There, see what I mean, Murray? This place is a zoo."

Frank said this out loud. And for an instant his eyes met with a huge black lady's who was wearing a green vinyl coat and was staring menacingly at him.

The black lady in green shouted, "Ossifer, ya oughta git yoself a sanity hearing like mah ol' man, den dey can ship ya ass off to Bellevue like he was."

A small, thin man who seemed to be wearing red paisley pajamas scrambled from the car. He stood next to the no-parking sign, pivoted, then threw a ferocious kick at the Chevy.

"Hey, asshole, easy," Frank Bosco said, closing his eyes. *Murray, Murray, Murray,* he said to himself.

"Chew know," the man in pajamas shouted. "I put de bucking ding in first and de motherfucker jump back."

"License," Frank said. "License and registration." Then he glanced up to the sky.

March sun; the day was warm for March, artificially warm.

That's it, Frank thought, there's a wrongness in the air. He felt uneasy. He couldn't quite place it, but a familiar stench was all around him. Then he saw the girl Ronnie, from the Tee Pee Bar. She stood on the sidewalk eating a Big Mac and making sexy faces at him. Whenever he saw her, which was often during the week, she made sexy faces at him.

Frank smiled, gave her a wave, then reached for his summons book. He was gonna stick it to the sucker in the Chevy till he got writer's cramp.

Frank settled himself against the no-parking sign. Then he opened his personal summons book. Then he tried to read the registration of the car, tried to make out the name on the driver's license, tried to make some sense out of a classic Spanish mystery.

The driver's license belonged to a Mr. Ponce Vega Cruz. The Chevy was registered to a Vega Cruz Ponce.

The insurance card said insurance had been issued to Cruz Vega.

He reread them again. Carefully.

Then he put his pen in his mouth and held it there.

Then he heard the crash of the window and saw something so strange, so remarkable, someone actually flung a baby through a window.

Things are out of control again!

Everything has gone haywire again!

They threw a baby out a *fucking window*!
For chrissake, Murray, how can they expect my brain to handle this? I'm just a simple cop. . . .

Frank Bosco tried hard to figure a way out, because now everyone in the street was pointing at him.

Screaming, *"The baby! The baby! The baby!"*

As if he hadn't noticed. As if he'd been too busy writing a summons to notice a baby sail through the air and splatter off the roof of a Gypsy cab.

Later Ronnie told him that the guy had done it before, tossed the baby out the window before. But the last time a teenager had caught it.

Everyone knew it. It made all the papers, all the local TV news shows. They took the guy away, kept him in the hospital for a few months. He promised them he wouldn't do it again, swore to God he wouldn't drink and do it again. So they let him go, sent him home. And the dumb-looking crazy fucker did it again.

People huddled over the baby now, touching it, trying to put the pink blanket over it. And Frank got more scared, because they were yelling at him to pick up the baby and put it in a car or a taxi or something, anything, just rush it to the hospital. But remembering what he'd been taught, he didn't want to touch it, to move it. Someone had called the ambulance. The ambulance was on its way. But the crowd was going crazy, pushing him, pulling at his coat. And that familiar stench was all around him, making him dizzy. He couldn't help it; he was dizzy and feeling sick. Then he heard the sirens and whoopers in the distance, too far away to do him any good. People were raising fists in his face, and he kept getting dizzier and more frightened.

Fifty people or more were screaming that the cop had killed the baby.

And that's how it happened; that's how the riot started on Gene Street.

The crowd made room for the ambulance and they put

the baby in, the attendant saying, "Jesus, good Jesus, good Jesus."

The ambulance took the baby away.

Shaking now, his back up against the black Chevy, Frank Bosco saw the crowd move. Saw the blue-and-white on two wheels, riding the curb, chasing the crowd off. The thin man in the pajamas was pressing him, forcing him to turn his face, screaming at him, "Bucking killer, bucking baby killer." Frank couldn't stop shaking.

The fat black lady in the green vinyl coat was on top of him. And the guy from the Chevy continued his attack, calling him "Bucking baby killer."

He was on the ground. He didn't remember getting knocked down, but he was down and looking up into a fat lady's face. A big, round moon face with a gold tooth and a black mustache. She was on top of him, had him pinned; he couldn't move, couldn't budge her.

The baby was dead.

The little thing in the pink blanket was among the dead, with Murray.

Whonk! That's the sound the nightstick made as it ricocheted off the fat lady's head. *Whonk!* That's the sound it made off Ponce Vega Cruz's elbow as he tried to zig right but ran left into a thunderous backhand, no hitch in the swing, a clean follow-through stroke delivered by a giggling Monty Adams.

Officer Eddie Banks helped him up.

"Okay?"

"Sure, great."

Banks led him to his patrol car, opened the back door for him, told him to get in, saying, "You look like shit, man. You'd better get in and take a blow."

"Sure."

Alone in the backseat of the blue-and-white, Frank tried to sort out what had happened. He tried to explain himself to himself.

Something hurt. His leg hurt like hell.

As he prepared to get up, to get up and move, he

noticed that his right pant leg had been torn. It was shredded at the knee and he was bleeding.

There are a whole lot of ball-shriveling moments in a cop's life, and Frank told himself, *You're living one of those special moments. Now get off your ass and help.* But as he looked out through the patrol-car window he was filled with terror. The crowd had backed the six cops up against the Chevy.

Frank, praying "Please, God," tried to open the door of the patrol car. But he had no idea in the world just how to do it. There was no door handle on either of the backseat doors. Then he tried to picture what the cops would say if he didn't get out there. Right away he knew he'd better hit the street, and fast. He made himself reach over the seat to the front door. Tried it. Tried real hard. Then he tried to find his nightstick. It'd gone under the seat. Finally he rolled over the seat and grabbed the front door handle and pulled. He thought a moment, watching the door open. *What am I gonna do when I get out there?* He had a feeling he wouldn't do much. Just join that tiny circle of cops who were surrounded now, and ducking as tons of all kinds of shit was being thrown at them. It was a terrible feeling. Your nerves can really do a number on you if you let them, he told himself.

"Throw up your hands, you motherfuckers. You're all under arrest." That's what he wanted to yell when he stepped out of the car and looked at the situation. Instead he jumped back into the front seat of the car, picked up the radio, and screamed at Central. "Central," he yelled, "there's about a million fucking Zulus down here at Gene and Water Streets, and they're 'bout ready to eat us."

Frank felt relief when he heard the sirens; it sounded like a thousand of 'em coming. Every car in Brooklyn South was rolling.

He tensed up again when he saw the fat, moon-faced lady in green vinyl. Her head was leaking blood, and she was running, her mouth open and her tongue flapping.

Adams and his partner, Ramon Rivera, were laughing like kids, watching her go. Police cars were coming up both ways along Gene Street. With a 10:13 assist patrolman, you get the full treatment; there were cops everywhere.

It was almost four o'clock by the time they rounded up the worst cases and left.

Don't stay mad, Frank thought, think of it as one of those special cop days and let it go at that. Four o'clock was the end of the tour, and it would be nice to sit with a tall drink and think about the fact that you'd made it through one of those days. More than anything he could think of, Frank Bosco wanted to relax and think of nothing. But then all of a sudden, as Frank edged his way along the still crowded street, he saw the girl Ronnie, and she was running toward him, sort of skipping.

"Kindhearted cop," she said. "You're my hero."

She wore tight-fitting jeans tucked into gray boots, and a black sweater. A leather shoulder bag hung over her arm, and she had a big smile on her face.

"Correct me if I'm wrong," Frank said, "but ain't you and me the only white people on this street? I mean, if you don't include some of the cops. They're gone now, so that leaves you and me."

"Soooo."

"Whaddaya mean, 'so'? Don't you feel a bit out of place?"

"Whaddaya mean, 'out of place'? I live here, been living here all my life."

They were walking along together now, Ronnie saying, "You're the nicest cop I ever seen, talking to everybody, smiling a lot. And you're cute. You're the cutest. Wasn't that awful, that baby and all? The baby's dead, isn't she? She gotta be dead, a fall like that."

Whoops, Frank thought. Think about it—only a nutty white person would live around here.

He asked, "Why do you follow me around? I see you.

Fact is, I see you way the hell too much. How come I see you so much?"

She was giving him a funny look, wanting to tell him something.

Finally she said, "I like you. I liked you the minute I saw you at the Tee Pee. And when you went into the bathroom and cried over that lowlife Mr. T, I thought, 'This is the nicest man I've ever seen, and I'd like to do it with him.' "

"Do what?"

"It."

"It?"

Around this time Frank's leg began to hurt again. He took a chance and bent over, patting it lightly. Yup, he was bleeding. "Ow," he said.

"Wow," she said. "Your leg's bleeding, pooorrr thing."

He said to her, "Ronnie, I finish up in a half hour. I shudda gone back to the precinct with the others. I think what I'm gonna do is call in and have a car come and get me."

She said, "Don't you wanna do it first?"

It amazed him that he was fairly calm.

"Maybe sometime," he said. "How's that sound to you? Maybe sometime soon we'll do it."

Later, at the precinct, sitting on the bowl in the john, after dabbing some peroxide on his knee, Frank took hold of his dick and looked at it.

There was gray hair all around it. He hadn't noticed *that* before, hadn't seen gray hair near his dick or on his balls before. "How'd you like to do it with that cute little dizzy blonde?" he asked his dick.

"Oh, that's good," Murray's voice told him. "That's great, just you and Khadaffi talk to your pricks. Just you two and about two hundred people at Bellevue. Keep this shit up and I'm leaving. You're not gonna hear from me again."

"Eat it, Murray," Frank said aloud.

"You say something, Frank?" Police Officer Lazzari asked from the next booth.

He couldn't tell Phil Lazzari he'd been talking to Murray.

Actually, Frank decided there wasn't anyone he could tell that to.

"Naw, Phil," he called out. "I didn't say anything. You must be hearing things."

"Figures," Officer Phil Lazzari announced. "Don't surprise me none. You work here long enough, Frank, you'll begin hearing things too."

Frank had real pain in his stomach, and gas like you wouldn't believe. The telephone message the desk sergeant gave him didn't relieve it any: "Your cousin Mary called, said you should meet her in the bar of the River Café."

The desk sergeant had given him the message with a great big grin, certain he was delivering good news.

"My cousin?" said Frank.

"Said she was. I got the message right here. Your cousin Mary will meet you at six o'clock in the bar of the River Café. That's what it says right here on my pad."

Frank smiled and nodded his head, not letting on. The sergeant's look let him know that the cousin line had been used once or twice before.

"I wish I had a cousin that sounded like that," the desk sergeant said. "What's her name, Frank, Mary what?"

Frank just stood there with a real dumb smile on his face. For the moment he couldn't remember his own name. He shrugged.

"Amnesia," the desk sergeant said. "It happens to a lot of cops in this precinct. It's the food or something."

Frank moaned. Probably the last person he wanted to see today was Captain Marjorie Butera of IAD. Who would feel like shooting the breeze with that tough bitch on a day like this? *The River Café? I don't go to the River Café. I don't know any cop that'll go to the River Café. I guess that's why that Captain Butterfly, with her movie-star legs and her know-it-all grin, chose the joint.*

Frank walked out of the precinct shaking his head, wondering why life had turned out so crummy.

Because you pulled the plug, Murray, that's why. God-damn you, you hadda prove you're smarter than me. So you've proved it, Murray. So I can't get along without you. Great. Now what, you bastard?"

Frank Bosco had his exhausted, it's-been-one-helluva-day look ready. He figured that since Captain Butera had been a cop once, she would understand, maybe cut him a little slack, maybe postpone the meet for some other day. And so, when he sat on the bar stool next to her, he faked a yawn.

But she didn't seem to notice. Seemed happy to see him and gave him a smile.

She said, "Hi, Frank, how are you?"

"Beat," he said, wagging his head. "Am I beat. Let me tell ya, Captain, I've been in the job, what, nineteen, nineteen and a half years? I've never had a tour like today's."

Marjorie hesitated. About to take a drink, she stared over the rim of a Black Russian for a moment, then said, "Well, you've avoided work for a helluva long time. A couple of months of real police work will do wonders for you. Increase your scope, so to speak."

Frank felt a terrible churning in his stomach. He dropped his hands into his lap, joined his fingers together, and glanced around the room.

Marjorie finished her drink, then neatly returned the glass to the bar.

"Somebody threw a baby out a window on my post today. It landed with a hideous plop on the roof of a Gypsy cab, almost right in front of me."

"How terrible for you."

"Worse for the baby," Frank said quietly.

"She never felt a thing. It's over for her. For you it'll be more tricky than that."

"How'd you know it was a baby girl? Was it on the radio or something?"

"It's always a girl," Marjorie said. "I pay attention to that sort of thing. Whenever someone throws a baby out a window, it's always a girl."

Whew, Murray, Frank thought, this is one snake-hearted bitch.

He said, "I can't take working in this precinct."

"Sure you can," Marjorie said, raising her chin toward the bartender. "Would you like a drink? Frank, you look like you could use a drink. C'mon, have one on the City."

Frank was another type entirely from Ken Malloy. Still, Marjorie saw him as a basically good man.

He's a cop, she thought, a man, just an ordinary man, trying to stay afloat in some deep shit.

In fact, it would be painful to come down on him. But if need be, she would. She'd come down on him and jam him up good and proper. Carow's got it right, she thought. To like this kind of work is for sure the manifestation of a none-too-healthy mind.

Outside, what had been a springlike day was frosting up into one of those cold, crystal-clear March nights. Through the glass, lower Manhattan looked majestic, showing its best nighttime face.

Frank said, "What do they have on tap?"

Marjorie called to the bartender, who was in quiet conversation with a couple of dudes who spoke English with heavy Spanish accents and had done-up hair and knuckle-sized rings.

Frank made it easy and ordered a bottle of Beck's Light.

"Ya know," Frank said, "I'd really like ta ask you something, but I'm a little tense, you know, you being a captain and all?"

"Timidity will get us exactly nowhere. Ask."

"Ya wanna tell me what's so important about dropping this Inspector Janesky? So far as I can see, all the guy does is talk a lot of crap about the crack of doom landing on the City. Ya know, the bad guys takin' over, the kind of crap I've been hearing for twenty years. He's funny, puts all sorts of silly memos on the board and shit. Maybe you should just laugh at him and he'll go away."

"A lot of people were laughing at Hitler, Frank. They stopped laughing when he danced into Paris."

"Yeah, well," Frank said, "I gotta hand it to ya—ya gotta lot of heart takin' on one of the big guys. If ya know what I mean? You're talkin' some bad shit about this guy, and ya gotta know, it ain't making his friends happy."

"Hey, Frank, when people are afraid to speak what's on their mind, when they're willing to swallow a whole lot of bullshit, we end up with assholes, thieves, and tyrants for leaders."

"Yeah, but Jesus," Frank said, "this really isn't my kind of thing."

He glanced over his shoulder at the room, filling now with some of New York's more beautiful people.

"And let me tell ya," he said, "this here sure isn't my kind of place."

A young man at the piano struck up a soulful rendition of "Mandy."

"I'm not any good as a spy, ya know."

"Sure you are."

He just shook his head.

"Hey, it's exciting," Marjorie said. "You're a real cop for a change."

Frank Bosco gave her a long, cool look, studying her, looking her over. He felt a wave of anger rising in his chest, but he overcame it and laughed politely.

Marjorie grinned at him with a sideways glance. And Frank cleared his throat, then turned away from her.

Marjorie tapped his shoulder, said, "Remember something, Frank—I chose you, and I chose you for two pretty good reasons."

"Yeah, what's that?"

"I know that you just went along with Murray. That you probably never initiated anything. You were just there. Your partner was a thief, but you—you were just there. And two, I know you're bright. I know you understand that you have an enormous vested interest here. You can lose your pension, Frank, half your pay for the rest of your life. Be honest with yourself," she said, taking her time. "You haven't done real police work in years. You and Murray stole your salaries, and God knows what else. Now you have an opportunity to clean the slate, start over, earn your keep. And when you get your pension, you will have earned it."

Frank swallowed a little of the beer and took a breath. A stream of visions, flashes from his day, filled his head. He wanted to scream, then belt this smiling bitch sitting next to him. The coolness in Marjorie's eyes was so total that he had trouble looking at her, but he did, saying, "You think you're so damn smart, Captain, don't you? What's your problem? I know—don't tell me. People been telling you all your life you look like Jane Fonda, and you play her for all it's worth."

She reached to the bar, picked up her glass, and finished her drink.

"Easy, Frank," she said. "Go easy."

"Easy, hah! I'm not some asshole, Captain, and Murray, he was no thief. Murray Weiss was the best patrol cop I'd ever seen, the very best. He could walk into a situation with twenty screaming wackos and have 'em all laughing in two minutes. On a real job he never let anyone down. He had heart, Captain, real heart. You have no right to talk about him that way, no right at all, Captain!"

"I know just what Murray Weiss's story was. I know what he did; I know how he conducted himself."

"And from what you think you know, you make judgments about a man's life, a man's career. You bother to read the papers, Captain? The politicians in this city are walking off with everything but the mayor's desk, and that'll probably go soon. And you throw dirt on my partner because some grocery-store owner tells you he gave Murray a dozen eggs for fifty cents. I think it's a bunch of shit, Captain."

"I'm not concerned with politicians, Frank. My concern is the police. And it wasn't a dozen eggs. Aw, Frank, c'mon, a dozen eggs, and a dozen steaks, and a suit of clothes, and a mechanics bill, and theater tickets, and, and . . . I could go on. And you—good, loyal, righteous friend—shared in all that. If you didn't, you sure as hell knew what was going down. And there it is. Case closed. Your ass is mine."

Frank shook his head and sort of moaned.

"Listen, Frank, I like you, and I really hope you do the right thing. I think you will."

Frank Bosco said, "You are something, Captain, you really are."

"I have to go to the ladies' room," she told him pleasantly. "When I get back, we'll discuss just what it is I want you to do for me and for yourself. The bottom line, Frank, all this hoopla aside, you're the one in the hopper. You alone make the decision. You should think of this as the first night of a whole new life."

"Shit, Captain, c'mon." He sounded tired. "I'm no new kid on the block. This is bullshit."

"You think so?"

Frank Bosco suddenly became aware of the bartender watching him, glancing at him from the corner of his eye. He seemed real interested, his eyes moving from Marjorie to Frank, then back again.

"Don't fret," Marjorie said. "You're going to make a terrific spy."

"Terrific," he said, and nodded.

"You're a natural," said Marjorie, getting up and patting his hand.

"What the hell am I gonna do?" Frank asked.

"What's right, Frank. You're gonna do what is right." Frank didn't answer. After a moment he said, "And you're gonna tell me just what right is, I suppose?"

"Right," said Marjorie.

An hour later, the night had turned a bit warmer, and Frank was cruising to Red Hook in his beat-up Toyota, feeling no pain and looking for the girl.

The meeting with Captain Butera had set him off, locked his jaw, made him feel mean.

Worse, horny *and* mean.

Each time he thought about the things she'd said, the way she'd said them, with that dead stare in her eyes, he'd pop another beer and throw the empty in the backseat.

He drove through streets of torn-down or boarded-up buildings, thinking, *I have a serious problem here.* Then: *I don't want to be alone tonight.*

To Frank Bosco, being alone was crazy-making, Murray talking in his head of babies flying through empty spaces. Being alone on this night was nearer the end than he ever wanted to be.

Frank was drifting. His eyelids itched, and he knew that sleep would be no good tonight.

So he set out to find Ronnie Yazow, the little red-headed cutie who'd been following him around, asking him if he'd like to do it and smiling that smile. *Go for it,* he told himself. *Forget this day, forget Captain Butterfly, be clever, and have a party.*

"Schmuck," Murray's voice said as Frank wheeled the Toyota across Water Street against a red light. "You're thinking with your prick. Go home! Clear your head and go home!"

"Idiot!" Murray's voice shouted as the Toyota rolled through dark Red Hook streets. "That Captain catches you prowling your own precinct, she'll put your nuts in a vise."

"Frank," Murray's voice warned, "you're no good at this."

"Leave me be, Murray," Frank said, not even starting to think about the trouble he could be letting himself in for. He was depressed, disgusted, drunk, and horny. Mostly he was horny.

Policemen get horny a lot—most of them, anyway. Especially after a day like today. Especially after six beers and one of those days.

It was unbelievable that Captain Butera didn't know that he and Murray had shared plenty of those lunatic tours. Hell, way back then, he and Murray had more than their share of rotten tours. Tours when he'd bite into his lower lip and rock back and forth on the patrol-car seat, thinking, The world sucks, people suck, most people in the world suck.

"You and me, Frank," Murray used to say, "we got a handle on things, we know 'em for what they are."

And it was then that they stopped doing the job right. When they stopped believing.

Murray had said he'd never believed anyway. Not since the day he could read, not since the time he was able to read and understand.

In the beginning they would sit for hours, not speaking, watching all the large and small sufferings people threw at one another.

"It's no great loss," Murray had said. "The loss of belief is easy in the fucking street. Because strickly speaking, if ya just take a gander around ya, whaddaya see?"

That wasn't something Frank could answer, so he'd never say anything. Then Murray would say, "Right, Frankie boy, there's nothing more to say."

Still, Frank had missed it.

For days he'd mourned the loss of belief.

Then one day Murray made him feel better, telling him not to worry, they'd build their own things to believe in.

Now Murray was gone, and here was Captain Butera asking him to believe all over again.

Taking him for a fool.

Frank moved the Toyota smoothly and slowly through the late-night streets.

A clear night, no wind.

Broads on the corners, and junkies too.

In these streets there's always action, Frank thought, always a party. In these streets you can't hide from the truth.

Frank had felt the first surge as he watched Captain Butera walk off toward her Department car. Under that fancy raincoat she wore was the most gorgeous ass he'd seen in a while. That's when he felt his heart beating in his throat and he decided to go and find Ronnie. Not sure if it'd help, but certain it'd beat hell out of going home and not sleeping, or dreaming weird wide-awake dreams.

He parked the car in a bus stop halfway up the street from the Bombay Bar. He sat for a long time looking out the window, across the street over at the bar. Then he got out of the car, sat on the fender, and looked some more.

Christ, the street was a sleaze pit. Ten o'clock at night and there were skels everywhere.

Murray had called street people skels. Fact was, most of the old-time cops called street people skels. It was a good word, and he used it too.

On the sidewalk in front of the Bombay, a group of them stood against the building. A drunk surged through the door, bounced off one skel, then another, stood for a moment, did a little dance number, and moved off down the street.

Two skels fell into step behind him. The drunk moved around the corner, looked back, then kept going, wary but too far gone to run.

He could hear music coming from the bar.

Music followed the skels following the drunk.

Pretty soon he'd go. Couldn't sit there all night. He felt a first-rate throb between his legs and heard Murray's voice whisper, "You're disappointing me."

He pushed down on the swelling between his legs with the heel of his hand, then froze. He suddenly felt he was being watched.

A figure moved out of the darkness, out of an alleyway. When he passed, he was sucking on his teeth. Frank's already considerable nervousness increased. The figure began to say something, a greeting, something cool. Then he thought better of it and turned away.

From where Frank stood, he could see a few taillights pulling in and out near the bar. Across Water Street, closer to the docks, the street was in darkness. A huge dog trailing a rope loped into the intersection, stopped, barked at the night, then ran toward the pier. The dog sprinted after the skels, who were making sounds loud enough for only him to hear, dancing on the drunk.

Frank Bosco patted the pocket of the windbreaker he wore. The feel of his off-duty pistol comforted him. For the first time in a long time Frank felt like a tough guy. He headed for the bar.

Two men stood silently in the entranceway. Frank gave them a small smile. "Evening, skels," he said, walking past them.

He could smell fat frying in the bar's kitchen; it mingled with the odor of disinfectant. And there was the stink of cheap wine.

Crazy things were going on.

There was an instant when the laughing people along the bar seemed to freeze and stare at him. Taking a quick look, he saw trouble everywhere and wondered, *What the hell am I doing in here?*

Suddenly there was an explosion of rock music and strobe lights. He looked down, blinked his eyes, tried to protect himself. The green tile floor beneath his feet was peeling. When he looked up there were brown eyes and angry voices all around him.

This was a place where people got hurt, often. . . .

But Frank didn't think about that. The momentum had him, carried him; nothing could stop him now. Certainly not the hand from the sturdy arm of the man in the yellow fedora who moved unsteadily from the bar rail and grabbed his shoulder, saying, "Whoa! Hey! Whadda-fuck?"

He pushed the man off and kept looking around him. He felt solid and firm on his feet.

Officer Frank Bosco felt that if he had to, he could kick some ass.

When he saw Ronnie, she was sitting next to a small black man with a Chinese face who was wearing a St. Louis Cardinals baseball cap.

"Hey," she called, spreading her arms out in welcome. Chinese face looked at him quickly, then looked away.

"C'mon, c'mere, sit down," she said.

Frank took a moment. Things began to clear. He was somewhat surprised at just how good he felt finding her.

She did have those blue eyes, and when he let his gaze drop to her breasts, which were pointed up nicely against the cowboy shirt she wore, she smiled a nice-ain't-they? smile. Proud.

Sitting in a booth across from her, Frank began to feel a little queasy. Suddenly he knew just how drunk he was, because he felt a churning in his gut and knew he'd better scoot to the men's room.

"Now where you goin'?" Ronnie asked, watching him stand, looking at him looking at her, glancing at the bulge in his pants, smiling.

"To pee," he said cheerily, and the small black man with the Chinese face doffed his cap, saying, "Take one for me, will ya, man? I can't move."

People let him by, and he moved down a short corridor and through a door marked GENTS.

The bathroom was tiny, barely room for two grown men.

Frank tried not to touch anything.

The dude from the bar with the yellow fedora stood in front of the mirror and played with his nose. He saw Frank come in and said, "Yo! You, gotta be da man or crazy, uh-huh."

He was frowning and made a little sign with his hands to indicate surrender.

Frank had to think about that one.

Then the man said, "Ya gonna give me some cash so I can get a little taste, aintcha?"

Frank glanced around before saying, "A bathroom is no place to die," and he looked hard at the guy in the yellow fedora, who then turned straight for the door.

Back in the booth, he asked Ronnie what had happened to the guy with the baseball cap.

"He went to get me something," Ronnie said.

"What?" Frank asked, then he said, "Never mind, don't tell me."

Rock music thundered at Frank as he tried to use a little charm. He was a handsome man—striking, a friend of his wife once said. Still, casual charm was not his strong suit.

"Here's the thing," Frank said quickly. "I'm in the mood right now. Whaddaya think?"

Frank was concerned that the Chinese-looking guy with the baseball cap would be back any second and ruin his chance to be charming. So he spoke quickly, more quickly than he wanted to.

Silence from Ronnie across the booth.

"Well?" he said, lowering his voice.

Frank had to take a moment. This was not working out the way he'd hoped.

Nothing ever did.

"You wanna leave here with me? Go with me somewhere, someplace where we could be alone?" he asked.

This was bad, awful; he could have put it in a different

way. A simple "Would you like to go and screw?" probably would have been fine.

She sat silently for a long moment, thoughtful.

Ronnie was still in her jeans, and her jeans were still tucked into gray boots. Suddenly one of her boots moved gently up between his legs.

A nice sort of surprise, it made Frank grin.

The toe of her boot did a little soft-shoe between his legs, making him come alive. The six beers he'd had kicking in made him feel cool and loose. All part of the rhythm at the Bombay, the music of a night that offered some adventure.

Ronnie got up from the booth slowly, her hands on her waist, her strawberry-blond head cocking more to one side than the other.

She said, "Can you tell me what we're doing here, sweet thing? Geez, we could be sliding down to my place." She looked up at the ceiling for effect. "We're wasting time, and I hate to waste one little drop of time. I never waste one little drop."

Out on the street, taking his arm, leading him along the sidewalks, Ronnie asked him if he was lonely.

"Not all the time. But sometimes, yeah, I guess I'm lonely," said Frank, feeling like a trick.

Ronnie said that Pennyweight, the Chinese-looking black guy, had gone off to get her a little coke.

Now, to Frank Bosco, anyone who smoked a joint was a junkie, pure and simple. It wasn't a complicated question for Frank, no gray area there. Dope was dope.

"Coke," Frank said, pulling his arm free. "Whaddaya mean, 'coke?' "

His breath was coming hard, and he tried to hide it, asking, "What the hell do you need dope for? Do you need to be stoned to sleep with me?"

"Geez, I thought a little be-nice. Ya know, just a bit."

Jesus Christ, she at least could have asked him first.

"Okay," he said, putting his arm across her shoulder,

pulling her in close. "But that Pennyweight comes near me, I'm gonna bust his ass." He said this like he meant it, giving it all he had, making sure she understood.

"Don't get so excited. It's just a little coke."

Pennyweight was moving toward them from across the street. He had his baseball cap in his hand and was waving it. He wore tennis shoes, and man, was he quick.

"Look at that asshole," Frank whispered. "There could be people watching him."

Ronnie looked at him, unimpressed.

"I can't stand here waiting for some pusher to drop some coke on me. I'm a cop, for chrissake."

"Frank," Ronnie said calmly, "everybody around here does coke. I mean, even the cops do some."

Frank said "Shit," and stepped toward Pennyweight, who stood directly in front of them on the sidewalk and stared at Ronnie as if he'd never seen her before.

"You come near me," Frank shouted, "say a word, and so help me, I'll drop ya where ya stand."

It was amazing, Frank thought, how fast the guy could move. Even when he'd been young and new in the job, he couldn't get near a guy who moved like that.

Pennyweight gone, Ronnie stood with her arms folded, pouting.

"Ya know," she said, "some people should get to know about things before they get crazy over things they don't understand."

A skel passed them on the sidewalk, a skinny little guy about thirty. He pointed at Frank with his chin, then looked at Ronnie. Ronnie smiled and shrugged, then wagged her head.

The skel moved on, and Frank said, "How far to your place?"

"Just a block or two. Just down the street and around the corner."

He let her take his arm, let her lead him.

"I think this is gonna be fun," said Ronnie.

*   *   *

Marjorie paced across her kitchen floor, stirring honey into a cup of tea and holding the telephone with her shoulder and chin.

She had changed into jogging pants, a Springsteen T-shirt, white leg warmers, and tennis shoes. Her long brown hair was pulled back in a ponytail, cheeks glowing from an intense twenty-minute workout.

"You called me, Andrew," she said patiently.

"Well," Inspector Andrew Tony Carow said, slurring his words, "I did have something important to ask you, but it seems to have slipped my mind."

"I'll be here all night, soon as you remember why you called. Call me back, okay?"

"Tell you what, Margie," he mumbled, "soon as I remember why I called, I'll call you back."

"I'll keep the telephone near the bed," she said with a great amount of control.

Climbing the stairs to her apartment, Ronnie talked and Frank listened.

As they moved from stairway to landing, he peered into the dark spaces and saw trash, bottle caps, and bits of bloodstained cotton. There were soda bottles half filled with water, and tiny glassine envelopes scattered everywhere.

Ronnie's apartment was in a building that was a veritable shooting gallery. Junkie ghosts hanging in the corners, arms crossed, heads bowed. Their quick eyes followed Frank as he climbed the stairs. And their breath came in sour puffs, making Frank's skin crawl.

There was little doubt in Frank's mind that the end was near. It hadn't happened yet, but he felt a great unhappiness.

He considered Captain Butera's words: "Serve me or I flush you away. You have no options."

Suddenly Frank felt wide-awake. He put his hand into his jacket pocket and felt the cool comfort of his pistol. At that moment he understood what is a great truth for all policemen. Chaos can drop you only so far. Inescapable pain need only be endured by the brave and reckless. There is a way out, an escape route provided by an old and familiar friend. An old buddy—a partner, really—carried for years on the hip or in the small of the back. All his fears began to fade, and a pleasant peace came over him.

"Hello! Hi! Hey, you with me?" Ronnie asked.

Frank nodded his head, taking his time.

Ronnie watched him, fascinated, as Frank tried to get a smile to stay.

They could hear the panicked wail of a siren heading east on Water Street.

Frank whispered, "Ain't this romantic?"

"Look," Ronnie said, "I told you this was gonna be fun. Give it a chance, will ya!"

"I'm lonely," Frank said. "Fuck'm I supposed to do?"

"Careerwise, or tonight?" Ronnie asked, and wagged her head. "I know how you feel, Frank. I understand. But, sweet thing, I can fix it. If there's anything I can cure, it's loneliness," she said while opening her bag, taking out her keys, and giving him her professional look.

They walked into the apartment silently.

Ronnie flicked a switch, and two small lamps on either side of a sofa lit, giving the room a warm glow.

Frank looked around. It was nothing like he'd expected. When he turned toward Ronnie, she was close enough to touch.

"Did you think I'd live in a hole or something?" she asked. "This is my home. No one comes here 'less I want 'em to. Clean, ain't it?"

Frank followed her like a sleepwalker, his eyes barely in focus. "Yes," he said with a smile.

He felt her hand between his legs, and he felt her squeeze him, her head shaking, her eyes closed.

"Hmm," she said. "I've been looking at this a long time."

She undid his fly, and her hand went inside his trousers. "You like this?" she said. "I do."

"It's been a while," said Frank, closing his eyes.

When he opened them a moment later, she was wearing a wide grin, and those big blue eyes were bright with pride.

She took hold of his hand, then looked at her watch. "C'mon," she said. "I want you in my bed."

Marjorie took a bottle of brandy down from the kitchen cabinet, poured a hefty shot into her tea, and stared at the phone. Her instinct was to leave it to the luck of the draw. Carow or Charlie or Emi would call. She thought she'd read for a while. Follow Mailer around Provincetown a bit, drink some tea, and try to relax.

Her mood was good, the exercise had helped, and in her mail she found theater tickets she had ordered for a new musical. Charlie liked musicals; he loved the theater.

She sat at the kitchen table, drank a full half of her drink, thought about Charlie, thought a little about Jeff. Decided that Jeff was something she'd better stop thinking about.

She missed Charlie, wouldn't mind seeing him. Maybe he'd call, ask to come by. She smiled. Maybe he'd get lucky.

Carow had phoned earlier and left a message. He sounded blitzed. In his day the man had been quite a cop, an inspiration. During the time when everyone's hand was out, Carow had stood practically alone, clean, apart from all that. Now guys that couldn't carry his stick in the old days made dirty jokes about him. Carow had lost it, lost the edge, and when you lost that spark, people could tell.

Police life had always been a rush for Marjorie. Nineteen years and never bored. No small thing in a life—amazing, really. To her the Department was real, a living thing. Something fine, separate, and apart from those sleezy Headquarters characters.

When she first joined the force, friends would squeeze her hand and smile indulgently at her as if she were simply a foolish young girl out playing boys' games. Emi tried to be understanding, but even she kept wondering what had gone wrong, thinking Marjorie had lost it. An enthusiastic young rookie, Marjorie spent time telling Emi of her days, her nights, the pure adventure of it all. Tried to explain the rush. But Emi would look at her from behind a pile of photos of her kids and husband, sitting in her big house, with clean floors, and say "Hmm."

Marjorie went back to her book. Mailer got to her, angered her. She began to read quickly, as quickly as she could. Then she thought of Frank Bosco and closed the book. She polished off the tea, wondering what Officer Frank Bosco would decide, when the telephone rang.

It was Charlie.

"I need to talk to you," he said.

"So?"

"Tonight. It's important, it's about Janesky."

He sounded anxious. Charlie anxious?

And the sound of him, just like Mailer, made her angry.

"Marjorie?"

"Yes?"

"C'mon, whaddaya say?"

"Charlie?"

"Yeah?"

"I don't like this. What are you up to?"

Ronnie settled on the far end of the bed and looked at him. She was pulling at her boots, smiling that smile, telling him that someday, if he wanted, she would leave the boots on and they could do it standing up, or doggie-style. But that night, she said, her legs felt crampy and her feet were cold. So, if he wouldn't mind, she'd like to take off her boots, get under the covers, and they could do it there. Then she turned on him suddenly with a very sexy look and described about a dozen different ways she'd like to do it—once her feet were warm and her legs weren't crampy.

Her voice reminded Frank of his daughter's when she teased him, promising him things. Sweet promises made at the moment, promises from the bottom of her heart.

Frank had removed his shoes, and he lay on the bed still wearing his slacks and sweater. His windbreaker, with his pistol in the pocket, was draped over a chair in the corner. Ronnie looked at him with those great blue eyes. Her smile made him lonely.

She stretched across the bed and kissed him; her lipstick tasted of strawberries. "Nice," Frank said. "Your lipstick tastes like berries."

"I'm not wearing lipstick."

She laughed, then he laughed. "Frank, I think you're stoned."

"I had a few beers, but I'm not stoned. And I don't like that word."

"What word?"

"You know."

"What? Stoned?"

"Stoned is what you get when you do drugs. I just had a few beers. I'm slightly blasted, but I'm not stoned."

She sat up, supporting herself on her elbow. Frank reached over and undid the top two buttons of her cowboy shirt.

"Go on, stud," she said. "Open them."

When he finished, she took off the shirt, and he decided that hers were the most beautiful tits he had ever seen.

Ronnie put her hand, and not too gently, around the back of his neck. She pulled him to her. But he held her away, wanting to see her. She understood, crossed her legs, and sat back. She joined her hands behind her head and held her breath and stretched, putting on a little show.

Shaking a bit, he touched her breast.

Ronnie ran her hand along his arm, and that calmed him, made him feel strong.

The room was lit with candles, and he eased her into the light, wanting to see her blondness, her blue eyes. His hand traveled from her breasts to her shoulders, along the back of her arm, over her elbow. In the crease of her forearm he felt a tiny bump, a little nub, something small and hard.

For the moment he paid it no mind and took hold of her fingers, bringing them to his pants, kissing her, his tongue stroking her lips, tasting the berries. She grabbed hold of his slacks and pulled at him.

"Help me, Frank," she said gently.

He undid his belt, twisted free of his pants, then kicked them to the floor.

Her jeans bit at his skin. "C'mon," he said, "get 'em off." And she did, quickly, then she bent forward, hooking her fingers in his briefs, sliding them over his waist, tossing them onto the chair in the corner, alongside his windbreaker and pistol.

Frank heard footsteps outside in the hallway, then several soft taps on the door.

"Who's that?" he whispered, shooting bolt-upright.

Ronnie hesitated before she said, "Probably Pennyweight. It'll just take me a second, but I gotta see him." He could hear nervousness in her voice. He wanted to stop her, but she had already rolled from the bed and was out of the bedroom in a flash.

Frank lay back, his legs and arms trembling. "I can't do this," he said to the empty room.

He heard the door open and close. Heard the bolt drop, thought *You'd better get the hell out of here.*

Frank Bosco felt a cold breeze creep in from under the door, and a shiver ran through him the likes of which he'd never felt before.

He saw Ronnie's shadow pass the doorway, heard the bathroom door open, saw the light go on, heard water run.

Frank thought about what was going on, watching the light under the bathroom door.

He heard Murray's voice nagging him, telling him: "Weirdness is going on. What the hell do you think is going on?"

The water off and the light out, Ronnie returned to the bedroom.

"Oh, man," she said sadly. "I'm sorry, but I hadda tell Pennyweight somethin', give him an important message. You understand, don't ya?"

Frank shrugged without answering. Ronnie's hands went to his cheeks, pulling his head, his mouth to her. For a moment Frank worried that he would choke on her tongue. It was coarse and dry, and she plunged it into him in such a way that it made Frank grab hold of the sheet. He tried to make himself believe that this would be the best sex ever.

"Lay back," she said, and he did.

"Be still," she said, and he was.

"I'm gonna fuck your brains out," she said with a snort, and Frank's dick began to go limp. When she took hold of his nipple and bit into it, he yelped.

She was all over him, breathing hard. The candles flickered, casting shadows on the wall.

A wave of fear and excitement roared through him like a current.

Ronnie moved quickly in the semidarkness, rolling him onto his back, opening his legs, pushing her face inside his thighs, putting her mouth to his prick.

Almost immediately he was hard. Surprised and not a little delighted, he moved and grabbed her shoulder, rolled to his side, folded his knees, and drew her to him.

Frank Bosco was gonna give it his best shot.

He shifted position and brought her breasts—one, then the other—to his mouth. She stroked him slowly with both hands, no talk. Frank yielded to the sensation and quickly, much too quickly, felt himself spurt.

"That's okay," she said. "That's all right." Her voice was small and innocent, like a child's.

For a moment Frank worried that he would be through, finished. It always happened that way, just when the best was coming, just when he wanted to go on . . . spurt.

Ronnie tightened the grip on his prick, forced just a few drops of semen to flow, and with them she stroked her breasts till they were wet and shone in the light of the candles.

He heard a soft moan, and Frank, wanting to do better, joined Ronnie's legs together, put one hand behind her calves, and lifted. He put his thumb in her cunt, his index finger in her ass, then he moved his hand to the rhythm of the sounds of her breathing, which was coming fast and hard.

He could do it, he'd show her, he could do it good.

Ronnie arched her back, spread her legs wide, loosing him for a moment, then she dropped both legs over his shoulders. Her palms went to his temples, and she drew him to her, telling him to lick her, easy, easy, gently, just at the very top.

Suddenly she spun off him, changed positions, and in a instant she let herself down on his prick.

Frank looked up at her now. Her eyes were half closed and she purred a satisfied moan.

Getting into it, Frank raised his buttocks, pushing for more of her.

She shouted, "I'm gonna come. Oh, Frank, I'm gonna come." She seemed surprised.

Frank Bosco felt proud, then suddenly a huge groan escaped him, and fear returned to his chest. It froze his heart, made him shudder.

Looking up at Ronnie, his hands on her waist, her palms now on his shoulders, he noticed a point, just a tiny spot of dried blood. It lay within the fold of her forearm, atop the tiny nub he'd felt earlier.

Oh, shit, he thought, she's a junkie, a fucking junkie skel is what she is.

*   *   *

Even though it had only been five minutes since Charlie's call, Marjorie wasn't the least bit surprised to hear the doorbell. Charlie often called from a pay phone only a block away.

She unlocked the door, wondering what Charlie could have found out about Janesky. Her investigation, she knew, had been kept totally confidential, completely in house. Still, Charlie was a hotshot journalist. He could have stumbled onto something.

She stepped aside to let him in, and in her hand she held a snifter of brandy. She handed it to him as she came through the door.

Charlie took the drink and walked straight to the window, the one that looked out over Central Park, his expression serious.

She sat on the sofa, her eyes not leaving him. "You're making me nervous, Charlie. What the hell is going on?"

"It's all over town," said Charlie, not turning around, talking straight at the window. "The Department is in for a major shake-up. Janesky's moving, and the direction he's moving is up."

"He'll fail," she said evenly.

"Good Christ, Marjorie, the only thing Janesky will fail at is going away."

"Why all of a sudden this panicked interest in Janesky?"

"My editor called me, asked me to meet him for a drink. He told me he wants me to do the story."

"What story?"

"That's a good question," Charlie said. He turned toward her, smiled, and shrugged. "We both know what the story is, don't we?"

"Do we?"

"C'mon."

"No, Charlie. No, c'mon. What's the story? Is it another puff piece about the promotion of a hero, or something else again? Because, Charlie, if it's something else again, then all you know is what you've learned from me. And you'd better not even think of doing *that* story."

"Why not?"

"Because my career is on the line. My life. You do the story about Janesky and his command, they'll know it came from me. And I'm finished."

"Marjorie, I was sitting right there when my editor called the publisher. They'll back you all the way."

Oh, boy, Marjorie thought, *are we in trouble*. Her face was beginning to feel hot.

"Are you telling me . . . I hope you're not telling me that you discussed my investigation with both your editor and publisher?"

"Marjorie, Marjorie, listen," Charlie said.

But she was no longer in the listening mood. "Damn you, Charlie, you're so fucking smart. Did it ever occur to you that your publisher is a friend of the mayor's? He'll tell him, and the mayor is going to put his hand over his ass and run to the PC, and the PC, who won't want to get fucked himself, will go to Janesky. Did that ever occur to you?"

"C'mon, Marjorie, these are journalists. They know how to keep quiet. And they'll protect you. If you really want to get Janesky, this is the only way to do it."

Marjorie leaned back on the sofa and stared at the ceiling, then at the wall across from where she sat, which was covered with photos of family and friends.

"We can get him. The magazine can bring Janesky down."

She did not answer him.

"You, you'll never get him," Charlie said with a sad smile. "But I have the tools to take him apart. You're shouting at the moon, and what's worse, you know it."

She thought very carefully before she answered him, and when she spoke, she spoke with great deliberation.

"Charlie, that is total bullshit. All you can do is embarrass the Department, and at best maybe ruin Janesky's weekend. They'll ride it out, and your publisher will sell a lot of magazines. And that'll be it. Left alone, I can make a solid case against Janesky. And it'll be a police case, made by the Department, no cover-up. Given the time, I'll drop him."

"Aw, shit, they're laughing at you. You went to Headquarters and what happened? You went to give 'em hell, took on the palace guard with a popgun, and gave them an afternoon laugh. A little humorous break at Police Plaza. I can blow them right out of the fucking water, and I want to do it."

Walking to the window, she looked down at the park. She blew softly on the glass, watched the moisture form a neat circle.

A siren wailed on Central Park West.

Charlie said, "Marjorie?"

"You're just another one of those bastards," she said disgustedly. "Just another reporter who doesn't care who you use or how you use 'em. You could ruin my career, Charlie, and not do a damn thing about Janesky," she said, not turning, just staring out the window.

"Hell, I thought I was the careerest," she said. "Self-involved, not considering other people. You're worse than I am."

She looked at her reflection in the window. *And you think you love him, want to be with him?*

A cure for the loneliness.

He reached out and touched her shoulder, stroked her arm.

She began to shiver, feeling the knot grow tight in her stomach. "Goddamn journalist, sticking your nose where it doesn't belong, thinking all the while you're doing it, I'm making a better world. Smug asshole."

"Bullshit."

"Yeah, right."

"You'll see, Marjorie. C'mon, you've been around long enough. You're going to dance to their music; you'll hear the beat and you'll have to follow. Sooner or later you'll be doing a tango right around Headquarters. That's what's going to happen, unless you let me do this story."

She whirled around, away from him. "I don't want your help. I don't need it and I don't want it. I'm always fucking alone, anyway. I know how it goes, and it goes just fine. And let me tell you something else, hotshot. I don't dance for you or anybody else. I make my own music."

"Is that the way you see it, Marjorie?" he said.

"That is exactly the way I see it."

"Isn't it something! Don't you find it rather amazing that you're always right?"

Charlie sighed, and Marjorie moved toward him, saying, "I think you'd better go. Go, Charlie, before I really do get angry."

He held her stare. Then he turned, said, "Call me if you need anything."

Marjorie controlled her tone, made it even and smooth. "Don't stand on your goddamn head near the phone."

Listening to his footsteps retreat, she thought, *It's time to take a long walk.* Marjorie took a whole lot of long, cold walks after Jeff and before Charlie. Then she thought, as part of the same thought, *Maybe tomorrow I'll get my hair cut.*

Just before daybreak, Frank heard the water running in the bathroom . . . again.

As silently as he could, he rolled from the bed and moved to the closed bathroom door. He listened with his eyes closed. Not a sound, just water running.

His knees trembled. She was in there. He knew that Ronnie was in the bathroom.

He braced himself on the door frame and pressed his cheek to the cold wood. He heard Ronnie's small voice.

"Okay, okay, okay. Right . . . that's right . . . that's righteous . . ."

"Ronnie," he whispered, "are you okay?"

"Hey, Frank," said Ronnie, "Look, why'nt ya make some coffee or something?"

"Coffee?" he said. He was thinking, *I'm gonna ask her to open the door. If she don't, I'm gonna bust it in. I'm gonna kick the fucking thing down.*

"Open the door, Ronnie," he said, "I wanna come in."

"You can't come in here," she told him.

"Oh, yeah?" he said. Frank braced himself, took a deep breath, and smashed the door with his shoulder.

He could not believe how easily it flew from its hinges. Bang—one shot. He watched Ronnie cross her hands in front of her face.

"What in the fuck," he shouted, "are you doing in here?"

"You are so fucking crazy," Ronnie told Frank. "Shit, the door was open. All you hadda do was turn the knob."

"You're shooting dope in here!" he screamed. "Christ, you're gonna kill me. You're gonna give me AIDS!"

"Frank," Ronnie said, sitting on the john, her hands folded neatly in her lap. "I know you mean well, being a cop and all. But for whatever it's worth, I was in here reading a magazine, letting you sleep, just sitting on the john . . . You paranoid kook."

"Bullshit!" Frank said.

"Fuck, you knocked off my bathroom fucking door, almost killed me with it, screaming something about AIDS and shit. . . . You're kooky, Frank—that's what you are, kooky."

He kept his eyes on her and began to think about the noise they were making. It occurred to Frank that someone just might call the police, and then where would he be?

He lowered his voice to ask, "What magazine?" then said, "Who you kidding? I've been a cop for nineteen years. Don't you think I know a junkie when I see one?"

She thought a moment, then in a deadpan sort of way

she pointed with her chin to a copy of *Playgirl*, wedged in the corner near the fractured door.

He nodded and asked, "And what's that track on your arm? Whaddaya gonna tell me about that? Don't tell me, I know—you gave blood yesterday."

She threw her arm across her forehead and sighed. "Oh, what can I tell you, Frank? Everybody's got ta do something."

She said this with a real smartass grin.

Frank kicked the door.

Ronnie looked unhappy. She pulled up her panties and sauntered past him, thumb on her nose.

"If ya like, Frank, I'll turn ya on, give ya wings. How'd ya like that, Mr. Pooooliceman?"

Frank looked at Ronnie quickly. She was about to make another smartass remark, her eyes wide and shining.

"How would *you* like me to kick your ass all over this room?" Frank said, standing immovable with his hands on his hips.

Ronnie Yazow jumped up onto the bed, crossed her legs, and folded her arms.

"Frank," she said, "you have no sense of humor."

"I got news for you. There ain't nothing funny about you, 'cept maybe the way you're gonna die."

She leaned back on the pillows, blew him a kiss, and said, "Go home, Frank."

Frank waited, kept looking at her eyes, sad and lonely and a little crazy. He waited, taking his time, making a decision.

The telephone rang in Marjorie's bedroom around two A.M. It was Carow, and he seemed wide-awake, clear-headed, in charge.

"Listen, Margie, I want you to call that cop you have the beef on. What's his name, Adams, right?"

"Call him?"

"Bring him in. Bring him and his partner in. You have the complaint and it's time you questioned them. Do that number we talked about. You know, get one to turn on the other."

"Yeah, sure, I can do that. I'll send a message to BSCO tomorrow, get them in on their next set of day tours."

"I already did that. I called BSCO and left a telephone message with the desk officer. They start days next Tuesday. What I want you to do is to call and break them up. Bring in one, then the other. Don't bring them in on the same day."

"Andrew," Marjorie asked, "are you okay?"

Andrew Tony Carow said, "Okay? Oh, yeah, I'm okay. Ya know what the desk officer told me? He said he'd try, try to get Adams the message tomorrow. But it would be tough, because the guy has a court appearance or something."

Carow's voice grew loud in remembered anger. "I told the desk officer that I'd left him an official telephone message. Tomorrow! That's what I said, Margie. I said he'd better fuckin'-A get that message. Whaddaya think?"

"I think you did good, Andrew."

Marjorie waited, hearing Carow laugh.

Charlie was gone. And she hadn't been sleeping well to begin with. Now this peculiar call, this odd laughter from Carow; it could turn into a very long night.

Charlie! She hadn't told him about the theater tickets for the new musical.

What in the hell was she thinking? She had thrown him out.

And he had left her so easily. Left.

Carow said, "Margie, I've had about enough of this shit. Let me tell ya, I've had enough."

"I'm happy for you, Andrew," she said, trying to get him off the phone, wanting to get some sleep.

Things could start to go badly now. She thought of the pension form she had filled out on Monday. Spouse, none—children, none.

"There's no doubt in my mind that we'll nail Janesky.

You and me, Margie. Like the ol' days. We're gonna do it. Well, what can they do to me?"

"What can who do to you, Andrew?" she asked.

And Andrew Tony Carow said, "I dunno, I guess the insider crowd at Headquarters."

Marjorie said, "Oh, them. You mean those people."

"I don't understand how you can do that every day of your life," Frank said, watching Ronnie's eyelids flick open, then half close, then open again, little twitches.

"I mean, to stick a needle in your vein, punch holes in yourself every day of your life. Christ, ya know what I mean?"

"You still here? Aww, shiit, whaddaya still doing here?" Ronnie looked at him, squinting.

Earlier, as he'd sat and watched her sleep, he'd given a lot of thought to leaving.

Get moving, he'd told himself, get out of this apartment.

"This is not your world," he'd heard Murray's voice say in his head. Then Murray had said, "Let her be, let her lay in this shit and die. That's what she's doing, Frank," Murray said, "she's dying ta die. Like all the skels in the world, she's lookin' for a place to fall over and die."

When she was in a deep sleep, all curled up on the pillows of the bed, he had touched her skin, her eyes, her hair. Though she didn't know it, Ronnie was a true beauty. Such white skin, luminous in the light of the candles. In her sleep Ronnie seemed to be a virgin, all pure, all innocent.

In the bathroom cabinet he found a bottle of liquid makeup, and taking a cotton swab, he touched up the purple-and-red nub in the crease of her forearm.

Standing over the bed now, Frank told Ronnie to be still and rest. He would make her something to eat.

"Oh, fuck," she said. "There ain't nothin' to eat here."

Frank had gone out earlier and bought eggs, bacon,

some milk, an onion, a fresh loaf of good Spanish bread, some coffee and butter.

The kitchen had a gas range. Frank liked that; he liked to cook.

He lit a fire under a pan and filled the coffeepot. Then he chopped the onion, diced the bacon, and when the pan was medium-hot, he dropped in a bit of butter, then the onions and bacon.

Frank beat two eggs, holding a bowl, using a fork, feeling good, inhaling a fine Saturday morning. As he folded the eggs in the pan the coffeepot began to perk. He heard Ronnie squeal from the bedroom, "Geez, that smells great."

He said, "Where would you like to eat?"

"Here. I'd like to eat here in bed."

Frank sliced the bread, buttered it, then stuffed the bread with the omelet. He poured two cups of coffee, placed everything on the one large platter Ronnie owned, and carried it into the bedroom.

"That sure looks good."

"You need to eat a decent breakfast."

"I'm happy you stayed," she said, smiling.

She let him set the plate out in front of her. When she raised the coffee cup to drink, he saw that she was staring at the track in her arm, the track he'd painted. She rubbed it with the palm of her hand, spit into her palm, and rubbed it real hard.

Ronnie turned away. He touched her chin with his finger, turned her head. "C'mon, eat your breakfast, drink your coffee, you'll feel better."

She was holding her arm out in front of her, inspecting it.

Ronnie looked at her arm as if it didn't belong to her, as if it were a thing she hadn't seen before.

Finally she laughed, and he smiled, ashamed that he had painted her arm.

"I don't know why I did that," he said. "I didn't like looking at it, I guess."

There was a silence in the room that seemed to Frank to go on for a very long time.

Finally Ronnie broke it, saying, "Everybody's crazy."

She said it in her little-girl voice, her blue eyes wide, her head falling back on the pillows of the bed.

He watched Ronnie's eyes close, her hand holding tight to the sandwich, her blond hair now being caught by the morning sun, the light touching her cheek.

"It's gonna be okay," said Frank. "I'm gonna take care of you."

Ronnie wept.

Waking, Marjorie woke to morning sun lying in bed next to her. She would have preferred to find Charlie.

She heard music that she guessed was Bach, caught the scent of brewing coffee, and realized that Charlie *was* there.

He came into the bedroom carrying a silver tray with a fresh bagel sliced in half, smeared with cream cheese and fine Swiss strawberry preserves; and coffee and freshly squeezed orange juice. He'd tucked a dozen roses, wrapped in yellow tissue paper, under his arm.

Marjorie had to smile.

"Bastard," she said.

"A smug bastard," said Charlie, looking at her out of those cool gray eyes, "but I think you've earned this. You've earned this because you're kind, and wise, and did not ask for your key back! I could do this for you every morning, morning after morning. Let no one say I don't love you, need you. Let no one dare."

He put the tray on the bed and climbed in with her.

"I didn't invite you into my bed, lover. I'm not ready for old times, Charlie. I'm still not happy with you."

He was all softness and affection, fluffing her pillow, smoothing the covers. His eyes were bright, his lips smiling.

She looked at Charlie, then away. Quickly, she rose from the bed and went to the window.

"That's it," Charlie said. "No more police stories for

me. Last night I called my editor. I said, 'Hey, no more fucking police stories. I'm not going to lose the most fabulous woman I've ever known for a goddamn story.' "

Marjorie was able to master a small laugh. She nodded. She thought about Jeff. Charlie was an entirely different sort of man from Jeff.

Jeff the Eagle Scout, the churchgoing Eagle Scout who wore expensive Ivy League gray suits and probably was never more than in the middle of his class but worked like hell to excel.

Thinking of Jeff made her dizzy. There was no joy in it.

Jeff had been a war vet. He'd arrived in Vietnam a second lieutenant and come home a twice-wounded, highly decorated major.

When she met Jeff, he was the deputy director of the New York office of the FBI. He was married with three children, and he proved to her that she knew nothing about men.

He charmed her into a room at the Warwick—and out of her clothes—on their second meeting.

She smiled, remembering how the air burned between them.

She thought Jeff was the man she'd always looked for. Married or not, she had wanted him.

Charlie walked from the bedroom to the living room, and was going through her record cabinet looking for his favorite tape.

Through her bedroom window Central Park showed her a hint of green in the morning sun.

She was so glad Charlie was here to keep her from being alone. "Charlie," she called, "I'm glad you're back. I missed you."

"I didn't sleep much last night myself," he replied. "I don't like fighting with you."

Music, the sounds of guitars and mandolins, came from the living room.

Early on Jeff had told her that he'd discovered the

Doors in 'Nam and played their tapes. And he loved the old Bruce Springsteen. But Jeff also listened to Haydn, Vivaldi, and the hits of 1712 on his car stereo. Thoughts of him, his music, the way he looked, suddenly seemed unbearably painful to Marjorie, and on impulse she called out to Charlie. But he'd gone into the kitchen and couldn't hear her.

On the street Jeff turned women's heads, no big deal. But men turned, too; he could take your breath away.

And how he swore he loved her.

His marriage, Jeff told her, was a long time dead, a long time gone. He stayed for the children, and the Bureau. Soon, he vowed, they'd buy that sailboat and go where they could drop anchor off a black-sand beach and spend days and nights lost in a blur of happiness, eating from cooking pots and fucking to the sounds of creaking canvas.

The lying sack of shit. What an idiot she was.

Bill Jefferson, Jeff to his friends, was so much like her that Marjorie was sure he would understand her.

Then Jeff was transferred to San Francisco, and the praying and lying stopped. Just the pain remained. Sure, there were a few phone calls. Talk of a trip east or west or of meeting somewhere in between.

She had come close, like a child on a merry-go-round, the ring just out of reach. She shivered and thought, The hell with him, that lying son of a bitch.

Charlie played Edith Piaf's *No Regrets* tape on the stereo. "The perfect choice," she said out loud.

Marjorie found her way back to the bed, and breakfast.

Charlie smiled when he returned to the bedroom and found her naked. He stood alongside the bed, staring down at her. He looked at her for a long time. When she reached a hand to him, he took it.

She lay back and pulled him with her so that he ended up leaning over her. She went after his clothes with a certain ferocity. It became very basic very quickly. They tried to perform a series of delaying moves with light touches and kisses. But when Charlie put his right hand in the cleft of her buttocks and pulled her to him, they joined with such intensity that the only sound she heard was his small, disembodied voice telling her he loved her, only her. It touched her deeply. Charlie, she believed, could conceal nothing.

She loved it when he came because he stayed hard inside her. Soon she felt the muscles of her body tense. Then from somewhere deep came indiscreet cries of joy as she rode her climax in Charlie's arms.

Finally she heard the sounds of soft splashing on a creaking deck and smelled the smooth salt air of a tropical rain.

Later they moved to the living room. Charlie stretched out on the floor, and Marjorie went to the sofa, put her feet up, and lay back.

She had wrapped herself in a blue silk robe, and Charlie had put on one of her T-shirts, which stopped an inch or two above his navel. From navel to toes he was bare.

The stereo hummed in rewind.

Charlie spoke first, in the quietest voice he knew. "My sole purpose today is to make up for last night."

Marjorie nodded with a great glowing grin.

"You'll get no complaint from me. Certainly the beginning deserves some applause, maybe even a curtain call."

For a moment they were silent; the tape in the stereo reversed itself, and Streisand's *Classical* album came softly and slowly into the room.

"No more police stories, eh?" Marjorie said finally.

"You know it's a rare thing for me to walk away from a big story," he explained.

"I know you pretty well by now. Last night you were a stranger. I couldn't handle it. The thought that you'd use me, hurt me, knowing all the while how much I trusted you."

Charlie did a quick, low crawl across the floor and put his head in her lap.

"Sometimes, I guess," he said, "my ambition is limitless, and I go for it without shame."

She caressed his head but was not at all sure if she was ready for love. She looked away and wondered if it were possible to be free and singular and still be together as one. She could feel the emotional currents getting stronger. When you are in love, she thought, there is no sense of proportion, everything goes, helplessness sets up shop in your life.

"Ah, Marjorie," Charlie said softly, "I could have made you a star."

"I imagine myself a star sometimes, Charlie. Is that wrong?"

Charlie did his Rod Steiger imitation. "I coudda made you a *real* star, baby. I coudda given you *power*."

He gave her a sly look, a kind of over-the-shoulder half smile and a little shrug. "With me in your corner you'd knuckle under to nobody."

"Most stars are pompous and blind, Charlie," she said. "Personally I'd prefer an afternoon with you in the sack."

That's what she said, but she was thinking about all the police brass paranoia she'd been witness to over the years. There was a genuine fear of the media. All the upper-echelon braid talked constantly about the depth of media misunderstanding. Or worse yet, the press understanding, knowing, then pointing a crooked finger.

Chief Janesky had been able to use and control enough of the media so that he could wave a flag and write his own ticket. It was a simple drill, really; journalists get used all the time, like women, Marjorie thought.

Chapter Eight

"All right," Frank Bosco said. "I thought this whole thing out and I'm gonna do it. I don't like it much, Captain, but I'm gonna do it."

"Frank," Marjorie said, "I never had any doubt that you'd eventually do the right thing."

Silence from Frank.

"Are you at home?"

"No."

"Were you home over the weekend?"

"I visited a friend. Why?"

"Well, it's a mean world, Frank, and I was worried about you. I tried reaching you on Saturday, then again on Sunday night. I just wanted to reassure you that I'll stand with you through this. I wanted you to know that."

"Hang on a minute will ya, Captain?"

She heard Frank turn away from the phone. He was shouting at someone, telling them it was *his* car and that he would move it in a second. There was a sharp crack as the phone swung free and slammed against the glass of the booth. Frank yelled louder. "Will you get the hell outa here, you skel son of a bitch."

Finally heavy breathing, and then Frank's voice.

"Sorry, Cap, but I stuck my car in a bus stop. A meter maid was gonna write me, then some wino started spitting on my window. Geez, what a pit this place is."

"Where are you?"

Frank didn't answer.

"Are you okay, Frank?"

"Sure, Cap, I'm fine, never felt better. When am I gonna see ya?"

"I don't think it's too good an idea to see each other too much. Are you going back to work, today, tomorrow, when?"

There was a very long pause on Frank's end.

"Frank?"

"I start four-to-twelves tomorrow. Listen," he said, "I have something for you."

"What?"

"Big-time drug dealers. Two of them up from Miami. They're operating out of the Golden Door. That's a motel on the upper end of the precinct."

"I know the Golden Door. But listen, Frank, that's something for the Narcotics Unit."

"I should just report it to Narcotics, huh?"

Marjorie thought about it. She felt Frank just might have something here. "No, wait." Then, going on without a pause, she said, "Report it directly to your command. Let's see what happens. You're sure this information is good?"

"Yeah, Captain, I think it's real good," Frank said.

"Report it, Frank. Let's see how Janesky handles it."

"Sure."

"And, Frank," she said, "I want to get you a body recorder."

"Okay, Captain, okay. How do I get it? Where do you want to meet me?"

"Say the parking lot of the River Café. Around six. And Frank?"

"Yeah."

"Are you all right?"

"What . . . sure, I'm fine, never been better. Around six, you said?"

"I'll bring the recorder. You be careful."

"Don't worry about me, Captain. I'm fine, just a little sleepy."

*   *   *

Frank Bosco was in a wonderful mood. He was tired; a little groggy, sure; his gums burned, yeah; his ass itched, and his gut rumbled. But that, he told himself, was all just nerves.

Everything was gonna work out, of that he was sure. Things were gonna be just fine. Except for the numbness in his fingertips. That worried him.

He banged his hand on the steering wheel as he drove.

Man, could he use a serious sleep. In a big bed with fresh sheets and a feather comforter; in a sunny room with huge windows, one open. Make him feel good all over, that's what it'd do; a serious sleep would make him feel real good.

Frank was a solid eight-hour man. The past weekend he had been lucky to grab a measly six out of forty-eight.

He was screwing up big time, that much he knew. Sleepy or not, he knew he was throwing a whole lot of crap in the game. He certainly didn't need Murray's voice coming at him the way it was to know that.

That goddamn voice wouldn't quit.

And this downtown Brooklyn traffic—that wouldn't quit, either.

He parked the Toyota in a lot on Schermerhorn Street, walked down to Smith, scooted past the courthouse, then ran across Atlantic Avenue.

The Greek's was on the corner of Smith and Atlantic.

He stopped and studied the place. It was his favorite kind of coffee shop. Steamed windows, huge urns of coffee, fresh bagels, and stacked hard rolls with real butter. A buck and a quarter for three eggs, any way you want 'em, plus coffee and a roll. A cop's breakfast nook.

Sitting in the last booth, as if he owned the place, Detective Jerry Brooks seemed lost in thought, eyes lowered, both his hands around a cup of coffee.

Brooks and Murray had grown up together in the West Bronx. They'd come on the job together and were tight. Not like Frank and Murray; they weren't partners, just real good friends.

Brooks was studying his watch as Frank walked into the café. There was no one at the counter, but there were four people in another booth: two couples, all cops, none of whom looked more than sixteen to Frank. Only one looked like he could fight.

"It's a good thing I'm on the bottom of every calendar in the courthouse," Jerry said, putting down the cup, smiling at Frank.

Jerry was a narcotics detective, one of the best. Hell, he should be; he'd been doing it for sixteen years.

Frank had met him a few times over the years. The guy never aged; looked like he was twenty, for chrissake.

Frank said, "Good morning, Jerry, thanks for coming."

"You wanna tell me, Frank, what you're doing calling me at six o'clock in the morning, talking that shit on the telephone, on the *telephone*, no less?"

Jerry stopped talking, turned around, then looked back.

"I have no way to tell, Frank, but it sounds to me like you've gone and lost your fucking mind."

"Did ya bring it for me?"

"Ya know Frank, in my time on the job the one thing I learned to count on is that you can't count on anything, especially people. Now, who in hell would've figured you? Mr. Gloomy. That's what Murray useta call ya. Ya know that Mr. Gloomy, that's my partner, Frank. That's what he useta say. Now, who'da figure you'd be calling me at six o'clock in the morning, asking me if I could get ya Dolophine. And you didn't say Dolophine, you said dollies, just like you knew what the hell you were talking about."

"Did ya bring 'em?"

"You asked me, didn't ya? Plus you said it was a matter of life and death. So, asking did I bring 'em is a silly question. Of course I brought 'em."

Jerry grinned at Frank.

"Thanks, Jerry. Thanks a lot."

"I got exactly what you asked for. Twenty-five dollies, ten milligrams each."

"Hah?" said Frank.

Jerry put down the coffee cup. "Whaddaya mean, hah?"

"Nothing," Frank said, "Nothing. Jerry, if I needed more, could you get 'em?"

"Fuck, no. Whaddaya think these things are, aspirin?"

"My question was, can you get me more if I need 'em? I know what they are. If I didn't really need 'em, I wouldn't ask, Jerry. Believe me, I wouldn't ask ya."

"Sure," Jerry said, then sighed. "Sure, I guess I could. You wanna tell me what you need methadone for? *You* trying to kick a habit?"

"Nah, not for me. All I can tell ya right now is that I need them badly."

"Yeah, I guess you must."

"Someday," Frank promised, "I'll tell ya why I needed them, and you'll understand."

"Like hell I will," Jerry said flatly. "Frank, you were Murray's partner for what, fifteen years? That's good enough for me."

Jerry grinned across the table at him. He said, "Anybody who could live with Half-of-Wholesale Murray Weiss for fifteen years has got to be one helluva guy."

"Murray had his faults, but he was a good partner, Jerry. The best."

"It was the three packs of cigarettes—*three packs*—and the gallon of coffee a day that wacked him out." Jerry Brooks said this while lighting a Merit 100, from the tip of the one he was already smoking.

"I see you're still banging away at 'em," Frank said.

"Yeah." Jerry sighed. "They'll put me away, too, if some freaked-out Colombian Indian don't beat 'em to it."

Jerry wore a zippered leather jacket with a hand-knit white woolen scarf draped over his shoulders. His leg stuck way out from the booth, and Frank could see his jeans and cowboy boots.

Jerry Brooks looked like a narc. And he kept running the palm of his hand around his nose and sniffing. It was the sniffing that made Frank twitch. The sniffing was really getting on his nerves, which were shot to hell, anyway.

Jerry reached into his jacket pocket and handed him a vial of white tablets, saying, "You don't want to take this up at your time of life, Frankie. You be careful with 'em; these things will kill ya a whole lot faster than cigarettes."

"Thanks," said Frank, "but they're not for me. You know that, don't ya?"

"I don't *know* anything."

Jerry Brooks smirked, gave a few quick sniffs, then asked Frank if he'd wanna give the Greek's coffee a try.

Frank said, "Thanks, anyway, but I'd better get goin'."

Jerry reached across the booth. He tugged on Frank's jacket, whispering, "Murray doesn't need any company. Careful with that shit." Then he winked, cool, like a narc.

Waving good-bye, Frank left the Greek's, walked to the corner of Smith and Schermerhorn, and waited.

I don't for one minute regret not making a whole lot of arrests, he thought. *Look around, look at 'em all coming.*

Cops from all over Brooklyn were descending on the courthouse, unhappy to be there, but they had no say in the matter. And with them, the sun at their backs, came lawyers in pin-striped suits, and swaggering defendants, walking that stiff-legged, I'm-pissed-off-and-bad walk, followed by victims and more victims, and judges, and prosecutors, and courthouse groupies.

They all streamed along Schermerhorn, hustled along Smith Street.

"Why'nt ya all just forget it?" Frank wanted to yell. "Fuck it, go home, have a tailgate party. The game's been called off." A rage rose in his throat, and Frank Bosco did yell; he shouted at a black uniformed cop who stood at the intersection with his eyes closed, waiting out a long red light.

"Go home," Frank yelled. "Wake the fuck up and go the hell home."

The cop's eyes opened and fixed Frank with a crazy-little-mother look.

"Don't ya know there ain't nothing happening here?" said Frank.

"Why is that?" the cop asked.

"Anybody living in this city that's gotta ask is brain-dead. You're brain-dead," Frank said evenly.

He kept on walking, heading for the parking lot. It was ten o'clock, and all the robes, Frank knew, would just now be taking their seats.

Frank started running. His heart was exploding in his chest. He didn't know why he was running; there was no real need to, he just felt like running.

There was sun, a lot of sun this morning, and he ran toward the light, out of the shade of the courthouse.

A trio of police officers gabbing with Sergeant Peterson were making a great deal of noise, but the talking and laughing stopped as Marjorie walked past. She thought she heard a timid "Morning, Captain" from Peterson and raised her hand. The air was redolent with the smell of freshly brewed coffee.

Marjorie sat at her desk, picked up the telephone, and called the clerical office.

Sergeant Peterson answered the phone.

"Mike," she said softly, "you've been jawing all morning with those old ladies in the clerical office. I hope the interrogation room is ready."

"I set it up an hour ago, and everything's ready," Peterson replied, and asked if she needed him for the interview.

"Only if you're not too busy," Marjorie said sharply. Then she apologized, saying, "Sorry, Mike, I'm a little tense this morning. Yes, I'll need you. But it'll be a short interview. It won't take more than ten, fifteen minutes."

Marjorie couldn't get the telephone conversation with Frank Bosco off her mind. The man sounded as if he'd lost it. Maybe it was the early hour. Maybe it was the problem he was having with his car. Maybe it was because she had expected to find him home over the weekend but hadn't. If she were as tough as everybody thought she was, she wouldn't give a damn about a middle-aged cop that got himself into trouble. But she knew something was going down with Frank, and she worried.

The interview was at eleven. Officer Ramon Rivera was already waiting, looking confident.

"Captain," she heard Peterson say over the intercom, "we're about ready to go. The PBA delegate and the lawyer are here now."

"Get them coffee or something. I'll be right there."

When she stood, Marjorie could see her reflection in the glass of her office partition. Her hands crept across her shoulders, down her sides, and over her waist. She pulled down her suit jacket.

"Lookin' good," Carow said from the doorway.

Marjorie said, "Christ, you do sneak up on people, don't you."

"In and out with Rivera, right, Margie? Like we talked about, nothing specific, make him wonder why in the hell we called him here."

Carow was grinning. For the first time in a long time, Andrew Tony Carow looked like a man of importance, a man in charge.

"I've done this once or twice before," Marjorie said with a small smile.

"Sorry, Margie. I know."

"You're the boss, Andrew. There's nothing for you to be sorry about."

"Listen," he said, "I never again want to feel the way I did last week at Headquarters."

Marjorie looked at him.

"Uh-huh, they've seen the last of the wimp side of Tony Carow, you'll see, you'll see. And so will they."

Was he serious? Marjorie wasn't sure. But she liked what she heard.

Sergeant Peterson appeared to announce that the PBA lawyer and the delegate were getting antsy.

Marjorie said, "I'll be there in a second."

Carow said, "Let 'em fuckin' wait."

No one noticed Frank come in the hallway, busy as they were unfolding rolled-up money, sticking little bags of heroin in their socks. They didn't notice that he had walked the length of the hallway and was now watching their little festival. They did hear the hammer of his Colt Detective Special click. That they heard, and there was considerable screaming and yelling as all four of them tried to get through the door into the rear yard.

Frank announced that he was gonna kill every one of them.

Pennyweight was jammed in the doorway, a customer on either side of him. A dope-pusher sandwich.

"You're gone, motherfucker," Frank said, leveling the gun.

Pennyweight's bladder gave out, and he fainted. The two customers fled.

Frank turned from the prostrate Pennyweight and headed for the stairs.

Ronnie's apartment was on the fourth floor of a five-story walk-up. He took the stairs two at a time. At the third floor he realized that the gun in his pocket was still cocked. Breathing hard, he removed the gun cautiously and lowered the hammer.

A Puerto Rican with sandy brown hair came out of an apartment wearing a gold polo shirt. He looked at Frank, looked at the gun in his hand, and said, "Woooo, nice."

Frank stuffed the pistol into his slacks.

"Just keep going," Frank said.

Frank moved quickly from the third to the fourth floor. He wasn't out of breath at all, and that made him feel good. It made him feel strong.

On each landing he heard voices coming from the apartments. He couldn't understand the words, but their tone made him think about fear and desperation and loneliness.

On the landings and in the hallways there was always coldness.

On the landings, in the corners, sometimes street gorillas waited.

Whenever Frank Bosco thought about the tenements of Red Hook, he thought first about the gorillas. But next, as part of the same thought, he thought about the people. The people who lived in the tenements. Desperate people who had to make it past gorillas to get to the street. Every day. And in the street were the skels. The skels were not as bad as the gorillas. But they were bad enough.

He knew Ronnie would still be in her apartment.

To keep her from disappearing while he met Jerry Brooks, Frank had handcuffed Ronnie to the bed in as gentle a way as he could manage. She hadn't objected— well, not really objected. Of course, at the time she was pretty high. He put kitchen sponges over her wrists so that the cuffs wouldn't cut her, and so she would understand that he did not want to see her in pain. When he told her that he would be right back with some medicine, she had smiled and told him to please hurry, because she was bound to be real sick, real soon.

He flew up the last flight of stairs, used Ronnie's key for the door.

He thought about his wife and daughter in the Florida sun. He hadn't spoken to them in over a week.

They were over a thousand miles away, happy without him. Busy with their daily whatever, they hadn't called or sent a card recently. No one cared that he was alone.

But to Ronnie he mattered. With Ronnie there was real human contact. He would make her fine again, make her well.

When she's well, then what? Frank didn't like thinking about that. He only thought that there had to be a better life for Ronnie than this confusion.

Into the apartment he went, hoping that he was smart enough and strong enough to save Ronnie. It was a life he was saving, a human life. He said, "Now that's something worth believing in, isn't it? The possibility that you could save one human life."

Inside, the apartment was dead silent. He could hear the hum of the clock radio on the refrigerator in the kitchen and nothing more.

"Ronnie, I'm back," he called out.

And he ran down the hallway, through the apartment to the bedroom door.

He opened the door quickly and went inside.

The room smelled of candles and Ronnie's sweat.

"We gotta get outa here. They're snakes all over this building," Frank said, unlocking the cuffs, rubbing Ronnie's wrists.

Ronnie was trembling so much that when she spoke, Frank had trouble understanding her. And her breathing—little whistles of breath coming hard—seemed to take all her energy.

"I'm gonna die," she managed. "You kook, you're gonna kill me."

He wrapped a blanket around her and held her. She looked very tired, very sick. Her blue eyes were rimmed with red, and she was sweating, sweating more than he had ever seen anyone sweat. Her sweat was cold, and she trembled.

"I'm taking you home," he said. "We're getting the hell outa here. I got the medicine. You'll be okay."

Ronnie smiled when she heard him.

"Do I look like I'm gonna be okay?"

"Yeah, but now I have the medicine."

"What medicine? I'm dying, for chrissake."

"The fuck, you are. You're not dying, you're getting well."

"You don't know shit, Frank. You're a kook! A kook! You handcuffed me to the bed and left me to die, you son of a bitch."

Somewhere in the building a door slammed, a quick exit, someone running downstairs.

"Take what you need," he told her. "You won't need much."

Ronnie grabbed him with her little fingers, nails chewed off. She held his cheeks in her palms and kissed him, whispering, "Frank, I need a cure. C'mon, you can understand that, can't ya? I'll go, I'll go anywhere ya want me to, but first let me get a cure."

"I got it," Frank said, feeling a little sick as a stream of liquid rolled from Ronnie's nose, across her lips, over her chin, and onto the bed.

"Jesus," he said. "My God, I've gotta get you outa here. I got the medicine, you'll be okay."

"This ain't the fucking movies," Ronnie said with a moan. "You can't tie me up for a few days, watch me puke and shake, then I get well. It don't work like that, Frank."

Frank went into the bathroom and returned with a wet cloth. He wiped Ronnie's face, saying, "I have all the medicine you'll need."

Ronnie threw her arms out, palms up, disbelief on her face, tears in her eyes.

Frank watched as Ronnie lay back down on the bed.

He reached into his jacket, took out the vial of tablets, and shook them.

He thought of asking her why she wanted to just lay there and die. But then he thought of a better question.

"Won't these do it for you? Won't these pills make you better?"

Ronnie glanced at the vial and wagged her head.

"Dollies, Frank, you got me dollies?"

She began to shake.

"Enough to make you well."

"Where did you get these?" Now, more interested: "How many did you get?"

"I got 'em, is all. I got 'em and they're gonna help

make you well. Twenty-five ten-milligrams. That should do it, don't you think?"

Ronnie began shaking again, then she laughed, explaining that twenty-five ten-milligram Dolophines would last her, at the most, a day, a day and a half.

"Okay, let's go," he said. "We're leaving."

"What're you talking about, we're leaving?"

Ronnie put her hands up toward Frank's shoulders, "Don't touch me," she said. "You touch me, I'm gonna scream like hell. The cops'll come and you'll be in heavy shit."

"Ronnie," Frank said, "you screamed all weekend. You screamed when you told me about the big connections at the Golden Door Motel. You screamed when you asked me to get ya some Dolophine. You screamed when I put the cuffs on ya. The only time you stopped screaming was when I put the bandage across your mouth. You don't remember talking to me, Ronnie, and you don't remember screaming your damn ass off, but you did. You talked to me, told me things between screams. Now you're goin' ta Queens. If I gotta cuff ya and tape your mouth and put you in a burlap bag, you're goin'."

Ronnie stood with difficulty, then she sat back down facing Frank. Both of them on the bed.

"Why you doing this? Why not just leave me alone?"

Frank got up from the bed and began pacing. He hadn't had much sleep in the past two days, and he knew that if he didn't move, he'd crash.

"I became a cop nineteen and a half years ago. When people asked me why, why did I take this silly job, ya know, walking around in a blue suit, swinging a stick, working around the clock, working on Christmas and New Year's, looking like a dummy, carrying a gun, I tol' everybody I needed the work, and it was steady, ya know, no layoffs, good retirement, plenty of vacation time, good benefits."

He opened Ronnie's closet door, found an overnight bag, and threw it on the bed.

"But that's not why I took the job, Ronnie. That's just what I tol' people. I was embarrassed to tell people the truth, embarrassed to say I believed, that I was a believer."

He began going through Ronnie's drawers, found a pair of warm socks, a sweater.

"What are you doing, Frank? I told you, I ain't goin' anywhere."

"Yes, you are," Frank told her wearily.

"I'm not, you kook, I'm staying right here."

Frank took Ronnie's jeans off the chair in the corner of the room. "A fuckin' believer, that's what I was. I always believed that I could help people. Do something in this life, ya know, be worthwhile."

He threw her the jeans.

"Get dressed," he said. "We're leaving."

Once, out of curiosity, Marjorie had paced off the distance from her desk to the interrogation room: thirteen steps. From her office you could look down the hall to the room. It was a quick walk, an evil number of steps.

Officer Ramon Rivera, dressed in full uniform, stood in the narrow hallway and did not move as she went past him.

Marjorie smiled a good-morning.

"Come in," she said.

Rivera advanced slowly, giving her a resentful, close-mouthed look.

In the interrogation room she found the lawyer, Tom Butler, sitting hunched on the edge of his chair. He looked across to Rivera, then looked up at her.

Butler was a retired sergeant. He was stealing just a little more money now, as a lawyer, than he once stole as a vice cop, but just a little.

He started to rise as Marjorie came into the room but apparently thought better of it and sat back down.

"Good morning," she said.

Butler scratched the top of his nose and looked at her

as if she were someone from outer space, an alien, probably dangerous.

"We're not gonna be long, are we, Captain?" Butler asked, moving around in his chair, glancing at his Rolex, bored.

"As long as it takes," said Marjorie, smiling.

Butler had a thin, arrogant face. He managed a twisted smile and shook his head.

Officer Ramon Rivera sat down next to him at the table.

The interrogation room was small and full of sunlight. Two large windows without shades allowed the sun to warm the whole room. There was a table and four chairs; a Tandberg reel-to-reel tape recorder was in the center of the table. There was no telephone.

Sitting erect and still at the head of the table, Marjorie sipped coffee and squinted at Sergeant Peterson, who was tapping a pen vigorously on a legal pad.

"Okay, are we ready?" Marjorie asked.

Peterson nodded, Butler shrugged, and Rivera cleared his throat.

Marjorie switched on the tape recorder, saying, "This is Captain Marjorie Butera, Internal Affairs Division. Present with me is Sergeant Michael Peterson, Internal Affairs Division. We are about to interview Officer Ramon Rivera, of Brooklyn South Command Office, in connection with an incident that occurred on December 5, 1988, at 1402 Gene Street in Brooklyn. This is a test—end of test."

She took another sip of coffee as Peterson rewound the tape. When he pushed the play button, her voice, sounding weird, edged with authority, filled the room.

Butler took a cigarette from his pocket.

Marjorie told him to put it away.

She pointed over her shoulder to the no-smoking sign.

Butler said, "C'mon."

Marjorie said, "Please, there are no open windows. This is a small room. If you want to smoke, go outside."

Butler held the cigarette in his hand for a long time, looking at her, nodding.

"When *I* was in the job," Butler said, "there were no women above the rank of sergeant."

Marjorie tried to look even more bored than Tom Butler when she said, "No kidding, that's really interesting."

"I have a feeling you're putting me on," Butler said.

Sergeant Peterson pushed the record button on the machine. Butler put his cigarette away, and Rivera gave him a look that said he'd be very happy if he never had to see this horse's ass of a lawyer again.

"Officer"—Marjorie nodded at Rivera—"will you please state your name, rank, shield, and command for the purpose of voice identification?"

"Officer Ramon Rivera, shield 2908, Brooklyn South Command Office."

"And present with you is . . ." she said, and pointed to Butler.

"Tom Butler of Butler, Mooney, and Wolfson, 500 Court Street, Brooklyn."

"This is an official Department investigation," she said evenly. "It is my duty to inform you that you are required to answer questions directed to you by a superior officer, truthfully and to the best of your knowledge."

Rivera nodded his head, weary.

She gave him her cold look, then said, "Are you familiar with Patrol Guide Procedure 118-9?"

"That's the same as G.O. 15. He is familiar, and I have explained it to him," Butler answered with annoyance.

"Are you satisfied with your representation?" she asked. Marjorie watched Officer Rivera sigh, then nod his head.

"Speak," said Marjorie.

Ray Rivera hadn't been spoken to sharply by a woman since the nuns in grade school.

The corners of his mouth turned down, he said, "Yes, sir."

Marjorie said, "What?"

"I'm satisfied with Mr. Butler here."

Butler winked at Rivera.

"Okay," Marjorie said, "let's go on. At this time, Officer, I want to tell you that you are present as a subject of this investigation. The allegations against you are as follows: On December 5, 1988, you and another member of Brooklyn South Command Office used a ruse to enter the premises at 1402 Gene Street in Brooklyn, the residence of one Felix Falco, also known as Felix Colon and Felix Puta. That once inside the aforementioned apartment you struck Mr. Falco with a blackjack and broke his nose and his jaw."

Marjorie said this flatly, and Officer Rivera said, "Mmmm," and nodded slowly.

"The allegations continue," she went on, "that you and Officer Adams of BSCO placed a fully loaded Beretta 9-millimeter automatic pistol on the kitchen table, along with a small quantity of cocaine, and falsely arrested Mr. Falco for the contraband."

Officer Ramon Rivera gave a short, ugly laugh and looked over at Tom Butler, who had edged forward to rest his elbows on the table.

Butler was all eyes as he stared at Marjorie.

"Okay, Officer, I want you to know that you will be asked questions specifically directed and narrowly related to the performance of your official duties. You are entitled to all rights and privileges guaranteed by the law of the State of New York, the Constitution of this state, the Constitution of the United States, including the right to have legal counsel present with you at each and every stage of this investigation. I further wish to advise you that if you refuse to testify or to answer questions relating to the performance of your official duties, you will be subject to Departmental charges, which could result in your dismissal from the Police Department. If you do answer, neither your statements nor any information or evidence that is gathered by reason of such statements can be used against you at any subsequent criminal proceeding. However, these statements may be used against you in relation to subsequent Departmental charges."

Marjorie said all this without raising her voice, without taking her eyes from Officer Rivera's face. She said it from memory, and no one interrupted her.

"Do you understand all of what I just said?"

Butler looked at her, began to say something. Marjorie raised her hand, spread her fingers. It was Rivera's face she wanted to see, his eyes. This was the interrogation game, and it was being played on her field, by her rules.

Rivera said, "Yes, sir . . . ma'am. I understand all of it."

"I'm a Captain, not a ma'am."

"Sorry."

"How long have you been a member of the Police Department?"

"I'll have ten years next month."

"Do you enjoy the work?"

Marjorie watched Rivera's face as he looked over at Tom Butler. It was a question he need not answer, and she knew it.

Butler shrugged.

Rivera said, "You bet. I like it just fine."

Marjorie spoke in a soft, little purr.

"Good," she said. "That'll be all for today."

"What the hell?" said Butler.

"That's it?" Rivera asked.

"I do have one more question."

Officer Rivera cocked his head, smiling.

"Do you trust Officer Monty Adams?" she said in her most pleasant voice. "What I mean is, do you think the guy is playing with a full deck?"

"Whoa, Captain," Tom Butler said. "Ain't no way Officer Rivera is going to answer that question. What are you trying to pull here?"

Marjorie shut off the recorder, then closed her folder. She said, "I'm simply curious if Officer Rivera trusts his partner's words. If Officer Monty Adams told him some-thing, would he ever question it, or just accept it as gospel?"

Marjorie watched as Officer Rivera stood. She looked him in the eye, smiled an open smile when he moved his shoulders in a macho gesture.

"Police Officer Monty Adams is one thousand percent. I'd trust him with my life. I wouldn't doubt his word for a second," Rivera answered Marjorie, wagged his head, and gave her a pleased sort of smile.

"Good," Marjorie said. "That's good, that's impres-sive. There aren't too many people I know that I could say that about."

"You don't know Monty Adams, Captain," Rivera said. "Adams is a thousand-percenter, the best."

Tom Butler was trying to appear casual, but he knew he was out of the game.

Marjorie picked up the folder and walked to the door. Turning, she said in a quiet, calm voice, "So it would make sense that if Officer Monty Adams told me some-thing about you, I should believe it?"

Rivera's eyes grew opaque. His expression told her that he had suddenly felt a little ache in his macho stomach.

She paused. She nodded. There was nothing more to say.

"What the hell's goin' on here?" Tom Butler asked.

"Ask your client," Marjorie said, leaving the room and walking the thirteen steps back to her office.

Frank's plan was to get Ronnie out of her apartment and into his car. Then he would drive her to Queens, to his house, and there he would keep her until she was well.

"We're gonna have us some high ol' time at your house, huh, Frank?" Ronnie said when Frank opened the Toyota's door to let her in.

"Ya think yer wife will get a kick outa this? Huh, you

kook? Ya think yer neighbors will come over and we can have us a little tête-á-tête, a little friendly chatter, about how the neighborhood is goin' ta hell?"

"Shut up," Frank said. "Just shut up, Ronnie."

He put the key in the ignition, and the Toyota roared off, the streets of Red Hook disappearing behind them. Frank Bosco tried to concentrate on the road, but it wasn't easy. Ronnie was making a loud hissing noise through her teeth.

"You're a bomb," she shouted. "You're gonna go *bang*."

They drove past the docks, where the street was full of tractor trailers. A burned-out Buick sat on the center divider. Four boys were lined up at the corner, near the flashing light on Hamilton Avenue. They had bottles of water, and rags and sticks edged with rubber to clean windows.

Frank scooted through the light, past the boys. Once he hit the parkway, he turned the radio on.

"All I'm saying is that I want to give it a try," he said. "Ya got the medication, you'll be away from the neighborhood. Just give it a shot."

"Okay, if it'll make you happy. I'll try."

"No kidding?"

"I said I'll try."

Frank stepped on the accelerator.

"You'll do it," he said. "You're gonna make it work."

"Shut up, Frank," Ronnie said, laying her head first back against the seat's headrest, then against Frank's shoulder. They hit the Belt Parkway and were just passing the exit to Emmons Avenue when she put her head in his lap.

"That's what friends are for," Frank said, "to help out when things are getting real shitty."

"Hmm," said Ronnie.

He had never had a feeling like this before in his life.

She was with him, she needed him, and this place, this time, was the center of the world.

Frank began to hum "Somewhere Beyond the Sea." It was one of the four or five melodies he knew. He had loved Bobby Darin's arrangement of it.

He felt something reach into his body and twist.

"He's dead," Frank said to the road. "Bobby Darin is dead."

When Marjorie returned to her office, Sergeant Peterson gave her a slip that said she should meet Carow in the second-floor conference room. Marjorie took the message from Peterson, paying no attention to the look of nervous bewilderment that covered his face. Mike Peterson, after all, was a career IAD man; nervous bewilderment was his uniform.

In the conference room she found Chief of Detectives Thomas, but no Carow. And that explained Mike Peterson's reactions.

Chief Thomas started off in one direction, then moved the other way. His irritation was extreme.

"Well," Marjorie said, "the chief of detectives at Internal Affairs. Should I be frightened?"

"I listened to that interview on the receiver in Carow's office. I have to tell you, Captain, I wouldn't want you on my case. You're a tough lady."

Marjorie took that as a compliment. "It's my job," she said, "and I do it. I hardly ever like it. I try to be moral but sometimes end up being cruel."

Chief Thomas didn't answer her.

"What can I do for you, Chief?" Marjorie asked after a while.

"We have a big problem," he said.

Marjorie took a seat in the heavy oak chair in the corner. She chose the one with wide armrests, crossed her legs, dropped her hands into her lap, and asked, "What have I done?"

His gaze flicked past her and back. "You haven't done anything."

The chief of detectives stood with his hands shoved

deep in his pants pockets. "So much bullshit," he said. "You know bullshit and more bullshit." Chief Thomas tapped his skull. "There are lunatics running this city. Incompetents directing the Police Department."

Marjorie said, "So what else is new?"

"Carow will be here in a second. I want him here when we discuss this, this—madness."

What madness? Marjorie thought. What does he mean?

Chief Thomas wore a gray, pin-striped, finely tailored suit, Marjorie noticed, and she wondered where he carried his gun, or if he carried a gun at all. He looked like a stockbroker, or maybe a TV news commentator. He had a calm, in-charge quality about him, a man sure of himself, sure of his command. His eyes moved over her, studying her, but Marjorie didn't feel it as an intrusion. Like his voice, it was almost . . . soothing.

When Carow entered the room, Thomas said, "They're going to promote Janesky."

"That's not news. I've heard he's getting another star," she said.

"No! To chief of operations. They're going to make him chief of the Department."

"Christ," said Marjorie, then she asked, "But what about Chief Reardon?"

"Reardon's going to First Dep," Carow said, and shook his head in disgust.

Thomas stared at Marjorie, letting her know, without saying a word, that this was the worst news possible.

Her stomach was not taking this conversation well. She didn't know what to say. Thomas asked, "Do you know what happens next?"

Marjorie said, "No."

"If we don't get on board real quick, they'll harpoon us. That's what happens next. We gotta march in their band, dance to their tune, because if we don't, it's put-in-your-papers time for me and Andrew here. For you, Marjorie, you'll be a captain till you're a grandmother."

"They don't have that kind of power," she said.

Chief Thomas smiled thinly.

"The hell they don't. Who do you think runs this Police Department? Not the PC, sweetheart. He's a politician. He'll just go on doing what he's doing. And that's doing lunch with the mayor, and bullshitting every pressure group in the city. That man couldn't run a band of school crossing guards, and the mayor knows it. The first deputy police commissioner and the chief of ops run this job, and that's the hard truth."

Marjorie thought about it. Thought about the music makers, the bandleaders.

"Andrew," she said.

Carow shrugged. So much for his newfound courage, Marjorie thought, with images of bandleaders and dancers going around in her head.

"But look," Thomas said testily, "we've got one shot here. We nail Janesky, embarrass the bastard, embarrass the PC and the mayor for giving him this promotion, and they'll clean house, they'll drop Janesky and Reardon like the plague."

Marjorie felt herself tense.

"Tell me," she said. "When is all this coming down?"

"Days, a month, soon."

Marjorie turned to Carow. "I can get him, Andrew. Janesky is dumb; he's going to do something stupid. Trust me, I know I can drop this guy."

Carow only shrugged and looked more unhappy.

She walked over to Thomas. "And when I get him," she said calmly, "then what?"

"Whaddaya talking about?" Carow asked.

Chief of Detectives Thomas smiled.

She turned to Carow, her expression composed, said, "When I nail Janesky, and nail him I will, what happens then? Who will they promote to chief of operations?"

Carow almost shouted, "Margie."

"No, no," said Thomas, "let her go on."

Marjorie nodded, almost to herself.

"If Janesky's out, they'll promote you to chief of ops, isn't that right?"

Thomas didn't answer her, just folded his arms. His grin faded.

"Well, good," she said, giving Thomas her best smile.

"I want to be a full inspector," said Marjorie.

"That's a three-grade jump, Captain," said Thomas.

Marjorie said, "Uh-huh."

Andrew Tony Carow said, "Jesus Christ."

Chief of Detectives Thomas said, "You got it. Nail Janesky and you're the highest-ranking woman ever in the NYPD. How's that sound?"

"Pretty good."

Thomas shook his head. "I wouldn't want to think about what will happen if Janesky becomes chief of operations."

"That's not going to happen," Marjorie said. "Trust me."

Sunlight warmed Ronnie's face and neck as she gazed through the windshield of the Toyota at the row houses of Rego Park in Queens. Neat, modest homes with curtains in the windows and plants that seemed to grow from the sills where the sun shined. In her apartment everything died.

"All right," Frank called out happily. "Here we are."

"A nice goddamn house," said Ronnie.

"It is, isn't it?" Frank said. He loved this house. He had caulked the windows and painted the whole thing himself during the past summer. It was a small house, six tiny rooms and a finished basement. But it was well built, brick and wood, and attached on one side so that the heating bills were low. And, hell, he had paid the mortgage off six years ago. It was his house, his own house, worth ten times what he'd paid for it. In his backyard, his favorite place, there was a long picnic table under a red maple, and the gas grill from Sears, where Murray used to barbecue those steaks just the way Frank liked them.

Summer days with the Mets on the portable; winter, knee-deep in snow, he'd stand there, good ol' Murray, grilling a beautiful sirloin, medium rare, sipping his Miller from a frosted mug, telling him, "Frankie, boy, it don't get any better than this." Then telling him the steaks were gonna taste sooo good because the price was half of wholesale, the price was right.

"It was those magazines," Frank said, "those glitzy brochures, those dumb letters from her sister, filled my wife's head with Florida. A paradise—whadda bunch of bullshit."

Ronnie said, "Florida's nice," standing in the kitchen, the sun streaming through the window onto the floor, warming her.

"How the hell you know Florida's nice?"

Ronnie shrugged. "Shit, man, I can read," she said, following Frank now as he took the stairs to his daughter Laura's room. She said, "I seen it on TV, Mickey Mouse and them other dudes, them fish jumping up in the air and shit. Hey, Frank"—she smiled—"ain't we gonna sleep together?"

Frank looked at her. "You gotta be kidding," he said. "This is my house." But when he saw Ronnie turn red, and watched the way she bit the inside of her mouth, he felt terrible and whispered, "Geez, I'm sorry. I didn't mean to hurt your feelings, but I just couldn't do that. Ya know, in my own house and all."

Ronnie shrugged and nodded, then asked, "Would ya like me ta suck your little thing in the kitchen? Ya know, while you're lookin' out the window in that weird way you do. It'd be like a religious experience for ya, sweetness."

"Geez, cut it out, will ya, Ronnie?" Frank was embarrassed. "Hey," he said. "How come you're not so sick anymore?"

She smiled, held out her hands. "See," she said, "the shakes stayed in Red Hook. Them dollies, Frank, they'll do it every time. Twenty milligrams of that stuff will block anything I could get in the street."

"Ya mean in a day or two you could be better? Well, I don't mean all better, but better?"

"Oh, sure, Frank," Ronnie said with the sweetest smile he'd ever seen. "In a day, maybe two, I'll be just fine." And then she swallowed another ten milligrams of the Dolophine, no water, saying, "Now I'm gonna get me some sleep, so if you'll excuse me . . ."

Frank was feeling pretty fatherly just then, so he said, " 'S all right. You sleep, Ronnie, get some rest."

On his way down the stairs he thought about what Murray would have said seeing Ronnie in his daughter's bedroom. The thought annoyed him, left him feeling pretty pissed, because he was no dummy, just a thoughtful sort of guy. Not a rock heart like Murray.

"Everything is under control," he told himself. "I know what I'm doing."

Frank said this aloud while staring out the kitchen window, watching the sun fade, looking at the picnic table, seeing that it could use a new coat of stain.

"You say something, Frank?" Ronnie shouted from the second-floor bedroom.

"I said that I have to be going now, but I'll be back real soon."

And Frank Bosco thought, Don't die on me, Ronnie. Don't die and be gone like everyone else.

Michael Peterson had been a top-flight tech man for IAD before his promotion, so Marjorie brought him along to explain the gimmicks to Frank Bosco.

But Peterson and his chain-smoking made her shiver. She wondered if anyone ever believed what they saw on TV or read in the newspapers about cigarettes.

"Does anyone take a warning seriously, or does everyone have to be hit between the eyes with a hammer before they wake up?" Marjorie said soberly. "Does anyone ever listen to any damn thing?"

Mike Peterson said, "What?"

They were sitting in the cruiser parked in the lot of the River Café. Lines of people bound for good times, soft chatter, and great food went past them, unseeing.

Suddenly angry, she turned on him, saying, "Why in the hell do you smoke so much?"

"What?"

"Do you enjoy smoking?"

"Yes, and I see it as a kind of neat way to commit suicide. You know what I mean, Captain? Life being what it is," he said slowly.

"Do you know what I just decided?" Marjorie said. "No sane person should do this kind of work."

"Ya got a point there, Captain," said Peterson, then he said, pointing toward the street, "Here comes a red Toyota. That's your guy, ain't it?"

Marjorie stared at Frank Bosco, who gave her a look in return as he nosed the Toyota alongside the cruiser.

For no reason she could identify, Marjorie felt a sudden rush of affection for the middle-aged cop as he flopped onto the backseat of her car.

"Hi, guys," Frank said. "How ya doin'?"

Sergeant Peterson stretched his arm into the backseat, took Frank's hand. "Mike Peterson," he said. "I know who you are." He smiled.

They could hear traffic above them, rolling over the Brooklyn Bridge, the trucks making the largest, most grating sounds. Marjorie could make out the steady *wap-wap-wap* of a helicopter going north above the river.

She turned around and faced Frank directly; she smiled, then he smiled. "Nice coat," he said.

"Nice of you to notice."

Marjorie was wearing her Burberry's, without the liner.

"Frank," Mike Peterson said, "we're gonna show you a couple of devices. You'll use them when *you* best feel, but they should be used."

"You make the decision, Frank." Marjorie said this looking right at him. Frank, leaning back on the seat, staring at her with no expression on his face, made her feel uncomfortable.

"You still want to go through with this? You haven't changed your mind?" she asked.

Frank made her wait a minute before he said, "I'll do what I can, but when it's done, I want out of this job. I want my pension, no strings attached."

Frank was being nice, soft-spoken. Marjorie had a good ear; she could tell when someone was frightened.

Frank did not want to appear nervous. He wanted to appear calm and get right to the point.

"Can you guarantee I'll get my pension?" he asked.

Mike Peterson said, "Frank, if you do what we ask"—he glanced at Marjorie—"I've already told you, as far as I'm concerned, you've earned your pension."

Frank gave him a tired smile. "Listen," he said, "I'm not so dumb to believe that the two of you have final say on whether or not I get my pension. Let's say someone, anyone of the top brass, decides that I didn't do enough. Says to himself, hey, screw the cop. What then?"

"That would be obscene, Frank," Marjorie said to him.

"Obscene—whaddaya mean, obscene? That would be the usual way the Department does business. Ya think maybe they're gonna make me a hero? The hypocritical bastards are gonna wanna break my balls. And with all due respect, Captain, you're only a captain, not exactly a heavyweight."

"Frank," Marjorie said. "I know that for the most part the good things people do go unnoticed. But in this case you have my word that won't happen."

Frank grinned at her, gave her a quick glance.

She looked into Frank's eyes. They were soft and brown and full of worry. Those eyes had seen more than she had at first realized. And she wanted to tell him that she'd go to the wall for him, but she didn't.

Sergeant Peterson cleared his throat, a note of worry from the smoking presence on the seat beside her. Then

Peterson took an attaché case from under the seat and passed it to Frank.

"Take a gander at that," he said.

The case held a tiny recorder that fit neatly into a gray-brown pocket of adhesive. It was a body recorder, they told him. It worked best for close-in conversation.

Frank Bosco glanced over at Marjorie. She pointed to the pistol in the case—a two-inch-barrel Smith and Wesson, a fine new gun.

"Are you ready for this?" she asked. "Look. When you squeeze the handgrips and pull, it will transmit."

For a moment things got quiet in the cruiser. Frank placed the gun in his lap, opened the handle, then took out the batteries.

"Good, strong batteries last for a few hours, I guess."

"At least eight," Marjorie said. "And you'll be talking to me, Frank. I'll receive your transmissions."

"You sure you can get close enough to hear me?" Frank asked, placing the gun carefully back in the attaché case, seeing Marjorie's smile as she studied him.

"Put it in your belt now, and let's go to the precinct. You can make that report, tell 'em about the drug dealers at the Golden Door. We'll test the thing, see how it works."

Frank was aware of himself growing tense, the circus starting in his stomach, the pinching prick returning.

They drove away in separate cars. Marjorie tuned the receiver in the cruiser. She had told Frank to sing a song, and Mike Peterson would flash the headlights if they were receiving him.

Sergeant Peterson and Marjorie were treated to a soulful rendition of "Red Sails in the Sunset," another one of the four melodies that Frank knew.

Peterson giggled and reached for a cigarette. Marjorie opened her window. The headlights flashed.

Frank drove, and worried, and at Atlantic Avenue he caught a glimpse of the moon over Staten Island. It was full and the size of a silver dollar. Frank decided that maybe there were tougher women in this world than Captain Butterfly. They do exist, he thought, but only a few, and they live in West Beirut.

Frank knew before he entered the precinct that he wouldn't do what he had to do well.

And he didn't.

Nervous, his heart bouncing in his chest, his mouth so dry that he could barely speak, he walked up to the desk sergeant, twitching and moving his shoulders as if he had fleas.

"What the fuck you doing here, Bosco?" the sergeant said. "Today's your day off."

It was dumb to come into the precinct on his day off. Pretty thoughtless of these IAD people to send him in here on a day he wasn't working.

Three cops whose names he didn't know stood around and stared at him, stared at the loony who'd come in on a day off—to do what? Report a couple of major drug dealers?

Frank read all this on the faces of the cops he didn't know, and the desk sergeant, who tilted his head to the side and stared at him like he was a boil about to explode all over the station house.

"Some big-time dope dealers, the *biggest,* are hanging out at the Golden Door, staying there with women. They have two matching El Dorados. Two Cubanos, up from Miami, are laying down skag and coke all over our precinct. I got confidential information," he told the sergeant. "I got solid information. The best, the very best. What do I do? Who do I tell? Where are the forms I'm to fill out?"

"It's your fucking day off," the desk sergeant shouted, and the three cops whose names he didn't know cried out, "He's here on his day off." And it caught on; two clerical guys from the 124 room came out drinking coffee from Styrofoam cups and toasted the fact that some nut had come into Red Hook on his day off to drop a dime on a couple of Cubanos selling skag.

Frank insisted that he was just passing by, and thought he had better get this hot information into the precinct. Just passing by on his way to New Jersey to do a little shopping.

The desk sergeant began talking seriously about burnout, that police work was only for the young and stouthearted. He said, "Old cops begin to go a little fuzzy in the head after fifteen, sixteen years, and the only solution is early retirement in a place that's warm and sunny, like Florida."

"Florida," Frank shouted, "is where the Cubanos with the skag come from!"

"Drugs," replied the desk sergeant, "are a symptom of a sick society. We're a nation on the very brink of death. Say, Frank," he whispered, "why'nt ya go home, take a Valium, and get some rest. I'll do the report for you.

"And, Frank"—the sergeant nodded—"you should consider allowing Jesus Christ into your life. Valium is good, Frank, it works, but only the Holy Spirit can bring light and understanding and tranquillity to a soul in pain."

One Jew in my head is more than enough, thank you, Frank thought. He had enough trouble with Murray.

If it had been possible for Frank to feel anxiety about anything after leaving the precinct, he would have. He knew that he could not escape it, could not separate himself from this duty, this frightening duty that had somehow been given him to do. He thought about Ronnie, about Murray, about his wife and daughter in Florida, about Captain Butera, about a monk-faced sergeant who'd found Jesus, about Janesky. He thought and he thought, but now everything was simply too far gone for him to stop. The only thing he was certain of was that he was in one major trick bag.

When Frank, breathing hard, got into the cruiser, Sergeant Peterson was grinning. Captain Butera wagged her head and gave him a worried look.

He said, "Did ya hear all that? Did ya get it?"

Marjorie said, "Shhhh, that place is batty. That's a bad scene in there."

Peterson nodded to Marjorie and said to Frank, "You'd better be careful."

Frank Bosco loved to sing. He sang country songs, sixties folk, "Blowin' in the Wind," and "Puff the Magic Dragon." When he sang along with the radio, he remembered all the words and melodies. Murray had loved to sing, too, had a great voice, almost professional. Almost.

Murray's favorite was ol' Blue Eyes, Sinatra, the Chairman of the Board. "Can the man sing, oooh, and the pussy, Jesus," Murray used to say, "Jesus, can you imagine the amount of pussy the man had in his time? A thousand pounds, easy. Yup," Murray used to say, "Ol' Blue Eyes musta had a thousand pounds of pussy, easy."

Frank was singing now as he eased the Toyota into his driveway, singing soft, tears in his eyes, thinking how sad it was that Murray was dead, and Bobby Darin too.

Frank opened the side door and went through to the kitchen. The house was dark, too quiet. He knew Ronnie was gone. In his daughter's upstairs bedroom a radio played softly.

He took the steps three at a time. She was gone. There was no one there. He was alone.

The note was on his daughter's pillow, neatly folded.

He shut off the radio and returned to the kitchen.

He leaned his face on his hands and read.

When he finished reading, Frank stood for a long time looking out the kitchen window, out at his picnic table. Now and then he would glance at the note.

I'm outa here, Frank. You hadda know I'd go.
YOU KOOOK!!!!!
Look—I know you tried to do what's right. A lotta people have tried. I ain't so bad, ya know. My life ain't bad. Well, I like it—so there. What ya don't know, Frank, what ya don't understand, is how much I love

ta get high. That's it, and you ain't never gonna understand. Now let me be, don't you be comin' around, comin' after me, don't do that. Okie doke, I'll probably see ya on the street, you bein' out there all the time.

Luv,
Ronnie

P.S. I took the dollies, you don't need 'em. And, Frankie, I liked doin' it with ya, ya do it good, where'd you learn to do it sooo good?

He thought of her blue eyes, her soft white skin, the little smile that seemed to go on forever. Frank Bosco knew he'd failed again. He sat down on the kitchen chair. His heart began to race, and he held his hand out in front of his eyes. He was not too steady.

Can't cry over a dumb junkie skel.

He was thinking about the hard red-and-black nub on Ronnie's arm. How the point of blood shone in the light of the candles. He was thinking that Ronnie smelled like baby powder.

"I'll find her," he said. "I'll find her and make her well."

Chapter Nine

Frank Bosco went to work a half hour early the day after Ronnie disappeared. He took a quick turn through the Hook, down Water Street, and up Gene past the Bombay, hoping he'd run into her. He didn't.

When he walked into the precinct and crossed the muster-room floor to head for his locker, he wondered if his brain was working right. Up on the chalkboard, near the stairs to the second floor, was this message: "P.O. Bosco to C.O. forthwith." Five other officers' names were listed as well.

Frank read the message, then he read it again. The desk sergeant came alive and called out, "Hey, Bosco, the old man is waitin' on ya."

Frank was pretty surprised to see his name on the message board, especially in the same company as the other names. They were all to see Chief Janesky at the same time.

The station house was full of noise, with the seven A.M. to three P.M. platoon trickling in. The eight-to-fours would be right behind them, and most of the four-to-twelves were already there.

He stood for a long time staring at the board, ignoring the cops bullshitting each other about the day's tour.

Finally he went to stand outside Chief Janesky's office. He was dressed in his black corduroy slacks, his gray crewneck sweater, and his one and only lightweight zippered jacket.

Since he was ten minutes early, he made himself comfortable by leaning against the pea-green hallway wall, hands in his jacket pockets, head back, eyes closed, pretending he was lying in the sun somewhere, the warm sun easing the aches in his tired body, giving him life.

It was exactly this attitude, this ability he had to separate himself from his surroundings, that used to anger Murray. Frank could be quiet and wait, still as a rock, for hours.

"It makes me wonder," Murray would say, "what goes on in that gloomy head of yours."

Frank heard a sound beside him. "Hey, Bosco," then, "Hey."

He opened his eyes and saw Adams, Rivera, and Banks. He nodded, then closed his eyes again. He figured he could grab at least another five minutes.

"Shh, this old fucker is sleeping. Can you believe this shit?" said Adams.

"Resting my eyes," Frank said.

Rivera laughed. "An ol' hairbag like him needs to rest his eyes, Monty."

Then he heard, "What's happenin' here? Anybody know what's goin' on?"

A woman's voice—the Supremes were here too.

When Frank first met the tallest of the Supremes, whose name was Lorraine Needham, he thought to himself, A pretty dyke.

She had the look—tall, not a touch of makeup, short-cropped hair, hard-looking in a quiet way. Frank had watched her walk—a street roll, up on her toes. Lorraine had one of those high, turkey, runner's cans. All muscle.

Her partner, Doris LaMott, wore red earrings, small and round, dangling below a neat, natural Afro. She was small, maybe a touch overweight, with heavy breasts and full lips. Her breasts ballooned under her uniform shirt and caused an unusual number of cops to clear their throats when she sauntered by.

"Hey, we're outa the bag tonight, men," Adams said calmly. "Gotta stash these uniforms, 'cause I've got a feeling we're gonna roll on something special."

No one questioned him; no one spoke.

There was a long silence—it lasted maybe two, three minutes. Lorraine broke it by saying, "Hey, Adams, you ever notice I ride sidesaddle, smell like lilacs, and piss sitting down?" Then she walked toward Monty Adams, giving him a hard, cold grin. "When me and my partner are standing right here, and you say 'men,' I figure you gotta get a hold of yourself. That maybe you're slipping a bit. Or maybe you're just one nasty prick."

Doris, the small Supreme, was laughing, her hand over her mouth.

The door to Chief Raymond Janesky's office opened, and Frank backed up.

Standing in the doorway was a man Frank hadn't seen before. He said his name was Jim Casey, and put out his hand, asking, "Frank Bosco, right?"

When their eyes met, Frank watched the guy hesitate, as if Casey were trying to see right through him. Casey maintained a pleasant expression, but Frank knew right away there was something different about this guy. He couldn't figure it out. A seedy-looking hummer, he thought.

Adams led them into the room with his head up, a strut to his step.

They stood in a semicircle around Chief Janesky, who sat at his desk, his chin resting on his hand.

Janesky was a perfect picture of military neatness. No one Frank had seen in years wore the uniform with such presence. But why, he wondered, was the guy smiling at him? And this character Casey, who the hell was he? Frank did not like the way Casey watched him.

The five officers remained standing. Casey had taken a seat to the right of Janesky. Frank watched the way he sat, the way he crossed his legs, the way he held a cigarette, the way he smiled with lightless eyes, the way he sort of sniffed before he spoke. Frank hated sniffers.

Janesky said, "Officer Bosco, here, turned in a suspected-premises report. He came in on his day off and turned in the report. What do you people think of that?"

No one spoke.

"Well," Chief Janesky said, his voice as smooth as silk, "I'll tell you what I think. I think if I had more cops that gave a shit about this place, my job would be a whole lot easier."

Casey nodded grimly.

"You all know Jim Casey, here. Bosco, you don't. So let me tell you a little about the sergeant. Jim is my precinct-conditions man. He's the one that has his finger on the pulse of this beast of a precinct. He's the one who knows all the unusual conditions that exist here. Jim is my eyes and ears. I'm buried with paperwork, but Jim is out in those streets, those streets that no sane person should walk on."

Monty Adams was fidgeting.

Ramon Rivera stared straight ahead.

Officer Banks seemed to shrug.

The Supremes' eyes were closed.

"Bosco," Chief Janesky said, "let me ask you something." The muscles of Frank's belly knotted; he spread his legs and cleared his throat.

"Where in the hell does a uniformed cop get information like this?"

Frank had to play it with a knot in his stomach and a pinching prick. He had to play it out, but he wasn't going to give up Ronnie's name.

"Someone on my post came up to me and told me."

"Why, tell me why," Janesky said.

"Tell me who," said Casey.

Frank thought it was possible he might faint from the pain in his gut. He tried to answer by not answering.

Casey went after him, pushing him. "C'mon, Bosco, nobody comes up to a patrol cop and gives up big-time connections. Where'd you get it? Ya got a friend at Narcotics or something?"

"Some girl in the street, she called me over and told me that there were these guys, these Cuban guys up from Miami, doing big-time dope from the Golden Door Motel." Frank shrugged. "I don't know why, she just told me."

Lorraine, the tall Supreme, said, "It's that little bimbo. That blue-eyed hooker from down on Water Street, Ronnie something. I bet she told him. She's always hitting on him. I see her hitting on him all the time. You know her, Sarge, has a crib on Gene Street, runs with that little shit Pennyweight."

Frank Bosco closed his eyes.

Sergeant Jim Casey smiled gratefully.

Chief Raymond Janesky, sorting through a mound of unusual-occurrence reports, said, "We need to know if the information is legit, that's all we need to know."

The officers standing to either side of Frank looked at him sternly. And Frank, he felt that pain shoot from his lower gut into his groin.

"Okay, look," Janesky said slowly, "Sergeant Casey will set you up near the motel. We'll give it a couple of nights. Maybe we'll get lucky, trip over something."

Janesky rapped his knuckles against the desk. "Jim," he said, "it's worth a shot, don't you think? This could be big-time, a newsbreak, you know what I mean?"

"I suppose," Casey said doubtfully.

"Shouldn't we call Narcotics?" Frank said very quietly. "I mean, whadda we know about chasing drug dealers?"

"Fuck Narcotics, what do we need Narcotics for?" demanded Janesky. "You carry a gun and a badge, you're cops just like them. You go out there and do the job. Narcotics. Screw them! Man, would they love to come into my precinct and hold a press conference. That fat old fuck, the Narcotics C.O., Regan, would like nothing better than to embarrass me."

The last thing Frank Bosco wanted to do just then was ask another question, but something made him.

"We're gonna be sitting on the motel in what, Department cars, our cars, in what?"

"Geez, Frank," Monty Adams said, exploding, "we don't have unmarked cars here. Of course we sit in our own cars, unless you wanna use a blue-and-white."

"Oh, no, no, no, that would be foolish. Sorry. Stupid of me," Frank said. *Christ.* Myths, Frank thought, myths are made of loonies like Janesky.

The voice of Chief Janesky filled the room. He seemed to be growing angry again. His eyes grew wide. His cheek trembled.

"You people are fortunate," he said. "I'm happy for you. You're getting a chance to show what you can do. There's more to policing than riding around in sector cars. You can have impact, real impact. Goddammit, you can do something meaningful."

Janesky looked up at the ceiling with resigned disgust.

"Like insects on the surface of a once fine and clear lake, they pollute us. They bring us dread diseases, they carry plague."

Sergeant Jim Casey nodded.

Officer Rivera seemed to be in a state of standing sleep.

Adams watched Janesky, wide-eyed.

Officer Banks was giving Janesky his full attention. Like a dreamer on the trail of a nightmare.

The Supremes openly held hands.

"That's it," Janesky said. "I'm asking you to skim some of the surface of the lake. Will it help? Maybe so, maybe not. Remember, one thing leads to the next, roses from weeds, if you get my meaning. It's American genius that we can burn the slums and make roses from weeds."

Officer Frank Bosco scratched his nose and closed his eyes, thinking: Wacko.

"Okay," Jim Casey said, "saddle up and be in the muster room in ten minutes."

Five minutes later Frank was sitting in front of his locker. The room was quiet. The four-to-twelve platoon was already in the street.

He was wearing the pistol transmitter, but he wanted his service revolver, the one he carried on patrol. It was a heavy-barreled Smith, a damn good gun. He could carry them both, no strain. And it was a lingering thought of Murray that made him reach for the Kelvar vest hanging on the hook near his gun belt.

Murray had a thing for bulletproof vests. Memories.

Murray'd said that it'd be a bitch to be shot dead. And that in all his years on the job, the Department had done diddly-squat for the poor patrol cop, the heart of the force. "At last they gave us bulletproof vests, it's a dark sign," he'd said.

Frank pulled off his sweater and put his bulletproof vest next to his skin.

He wasn't sure at first just how to carry both guns. Finally he decided on a shoulder holster for the transmitter. The heavy-barreled Smith he'd wear on his waist.

Frank closed his eyes, feeling that Murray was truly gone. Gone from his head. He was on his own. He felt himself start to smile, thinking that it had ended right. Hoping that Murray had found peace and was happy.

The teams assembled in the muster room in front of the desk sergeant.

Adams was adjusting all the walkie-talkies, saying, "These radios suck. They always suck. Are we ever gonna get some decent radios?"

Sergeant Casey spoke. "I want everyone to have a radio, not just the teams. Rivera and Adams will ride together. Banks, you'll ride with Lorraine and Doris. Ain't nothin' worse than a black and white team on a stakeout. You three look good together. Bosco, you mind, you'll ride alone? So will I. This way we'll have four cars. We could set up a tail if we hadda. Besides, I like riding alone. How about you, Bosco?"

"Oh, so do I," said Frank, "so do I."

"Listen," Casey said, "there's a gas station directly across the street from the motel. It's the Shell station with half the shell busted off the sign. Ya all know the place. We'll meet there. Okay, let's roll."

On the sidewalk in front of the precinct, Officer Rivera called out, "Hey, Sarge, whadda we supposed to be looking for, anyways?"

Jim Casey answered him by saying, "Fuck, Rivera, if you don't know, ain't no way I can tell ya."

Lorraine Needham said, "Don't be so sure of that. I don't know what the hell I'm supposed to be looking for, either."

They all stood still, waiting.

Frank's stomach ached. He breathed out and rubbed it.

"We're gonna get on two El Dorados with Florida plates. We're gonna get on 'em and see what happens."

"What rooms are these assholes in?" Adams asked.

Casey said, "For Chrissake, they're in Room 7A, on the first floor. Didn't we go over this?"

"Sarge," Frank said in a low voice, "we've gone over shit."

"Well, now ya all got it, don't ya? Two El Ds, Florida plates, two Cubans in Room 7A. We get on the cars and watch the room. We sit out there and spend a night off the street. Ain't shit gonna happen, for chrissake. The boss wants us to do this, we'll do it. But we ain't gonna see shit, take my word for it."

"A pity," Adams said, "but I think you're right."

The Supremes shrugged, and Banks said, "Hey, a night off patrol."

Frank stared at Casey, who looked back at him hard, like he knew something.

Frank smiled at Casey, and thought, This guy's a hummer, a real fucking hummer. He'd better scope him real close.

The streets were crowded and heavy with traffic. The night was mild for March. But there was a rush to the night air that made Frank think a change was coming. A fresh breeze, like a river of cold air, was rolling through the streets of Red Hook.

For no reason Frank could put a name to, he felt frightened.

They moved along Water Street, one behind the other. They passed the Tee Pee Bar and the Bombay. Ronnie's apartment was around the next corner. Frank peered into the street as they went past. Nothing but darkness.

The line of cars toured through the streets of the Hook, heading for the Golden Door Motel at the far end of the precinct. The walkie-talkie rested on Frank's lap like a small black pet.

A voice came through the radio. It was one of the Supremes.

"A brown El D with Florida plates just hung right off Third Place. What'll I do? Maybe that's one of 'em."

"Get on it, get on it, get on it!" Casey cried. "You, too, Bosco, get on that car. That's one of 'em. The rest of you, go straight to the meet."

Frank didn't see the El Dorado, but the Supremes were right in front of him, tooling along pretty good in a silver Subaru.

Feeling no small degree of excitement, Frank picked up the radio and said, "Okay, ladies, let's stay with 'em."

Nearly a minute passed before Frank realized they were heading out of the precinct.

"Subject heading out of the command. Advise?"

"Hey, that shield you got says City of New York. Stay on that guy."

Frank could hear noise and building static. He answered Casey by saying, "Okay."

And one of the Supremes said, "Shee-it."

Frank got a good look at the Caddy as it entered the Brooklyn-Battery Tunnel. The driver was wearing a cowboy hat.

"He's wearing a cowboy hat," Frank said.

"Uh-huh," Lorraine said, her voice easy to recognize now.

"Where ya think he's going?" asked Frank, then feeling it was a dumb question, he said quickly to the radio, "I bet he's heading uptown."

The brown Caddy made a right at the tip of the West Side Highway and went around the Battery to the FDR

Drive, picked up speed, and soon exited the drive at Houston Street.

On Avenue D, the "cowboy" parked the Caddy and got out, his hat back on his head, his leather jacket with its collar up, tight pants tucked into boots. He danced across the avenue to enter a bodega.

"Ya see that sleazeball?" Frank said, sounding cool now, detectivelike.

Lorraine said, "I seen 'em. He looks pretty hot to me."

Frank could hear the small Supreme, Doris, giggle. What a high, silly giggle, Frank thought.

Frank rested his head back against the seat. His thoughts jumping to Ronnie, seeing her in the candlelight staring down at him, her breasts shiny and wet, and the smile when she leaned a shoulder to him, brought her breast to his lips, and the way she rode him, slow motion, her chin in her chest, her eyes wide, looking at the place where his black hair and her blondness joined.

"That hot boy's moving," Lorraine's voice announced.

Frank shook his shoulders, heard a buzzing in his ears that told him to get going. Don't want to lose this guy.

"Ya see what he put in the trunk?" Lorraine said.

"Naw, I couldn't see anything from where I was," Frank replied.

Lorraine said, "He put a brown paper bag in the trunk. He didn't bring anything into that store, but he came out with a brown paper bag and he flung it in the trunk. Whaddaya think, Bosco, our guy here picking up dope or what?"

At Eighth Street and Avenue D the El Dorado stopped again, and the driver went into a large supermarket. Out in less than a minute, he threw a shopping bag into the trunk. This time Frank saw it; this time he was paying attention, wasn't dreaming about nipples floating across his chest. And when he looked carefully, paid attention, like a cop should, he saw the gun butt sticking from Mr. Hot's jacket.

"He's heeled," said Frank.

"I seen it," said Lorraine.

Four more stops, two more supermarkets, two private clubs, four more brown paper bags.

Then they were heading back to Brooklyn, back to the Hook. The Caddy never slowed, made all the lights, and was back in the parking lot of the Golden Door Motel in fifteen minutes.

The phone was ringing as Marjorie walked into her apartment. It rang once, twice, then the machine took over.

"Margie, Andrew—listen, give me a call, will ya? I'm home."

Then his voice shifted for a moment, as if he'd suddenly become aware of a circling demon, a presence.

"Ah," he said, "maybe you should *go out* and give me a call."

For a moment she thought that Carow was a bit drunk. She replayed the message.

"*Go out* and give me a call." That's what he'd said.

She had a bad moment dialing his number, then decided that there was no point in speculating. Carow picked up on the second ring.

"Andrew?"

"You home?" he asked.

"Yes."

"Didn't ya get my message?"

"What is going on?"

"How are you feeling, Margie?"

"Cold as ice. Are you going to tell me what's wrong?"

"Wrong? What should be wrong?"

"You don't want to say what this call's about? Can't you talk? Is somebody there?"

They got this far into the conversation before the obvious struck her. Her phone was tapped. And Carow knew it.

She moved the phone away from her ear, took a deep

breath, and whispered, "Sometimes, Andrew, I feel like I could cry. Most times I feel like I want to scream."

"No need, no need," he said. "I mean, things are fine, in spite of what they seem."

"I'll talk to you soon," she said.

"I'll be waiting."

It was cool outside, not cold; still, Central Park West seemed deserted. A few taxis, one car, and three guys walking two poodles, laughing and clowning around, headed toward the Rambles.

About a block and a half from her building there was a pay phone. Marjorie walked toward it quickly, thinking as she went, *This is it, the payoff, this is all I can take. These sons of bitches put a wire on my phone,* my *phone.*

She began to feel herself falling into one of her back-alley black moods when she thought of how Carow had set it out so plainly to her.

Suddenly, alone on the street, she felt vulnerable. How serious are these people, she thought, how dangerous? When she picked up the phone to call Carow, she felt her anger dissolve into gloom. Carow wanted her to call on a safe phone. Obviously he's concerned. She considered that a moment. But he was still mixed up in this, wasn't he? Mixed up in what? she wondered.

"All right, Andrew," she said, "what in the hell is going on?"

"Margie," he said slowly to her, as he always did when he felt the need to consider an answer.

"Somebody has my phone up? Who in the hell would tap my telephone? Who would be that ballsy?" Then she shouted, "What is going on?"

"Look, I tried reaching you a couple of times today. You should be calm. Things could hardly be better."

"What are you talking about?"

"We've decided to get on board."

"On board?"

"I'm trying to explain, Margie. Ya see, Thomas fig-

ured it may be a little rocky, but it's either tie up with
Janesky and Reardon or start looking for work."

"On board, Andrew? Did you say we got on board?"

"Margie, this is not something we should discuss over
the telephone. Right now you should cool this Janesky
thing. I told them you'd be reasonable, that you'd listen
to me."

"You told them that?"

"Yes, I did."

"They're watching me like I'm a criminal. They tail
me, they've got my home phone up, these bastards. And
you told them I'd be reasonable." Marjorie paused. "Go
and tell your new friends to screw off. The people that
want to run the Department, the people that you've
joined up with, tell them I said they should fuck off!"

"Christ, Marjorie, I'm trying to help you."

"Tapping my home phone was the last straw, Andrew."

"I don't know that your phone is up. It's possible—"

"Andrew, stop this shit, will you? I'm going to scream."

Carow made a high scoffing sound. "Dear God, Margie," he said, "what in hell's the big deal?"

"Self-respect, Andrew, that's the big deal. Self-respect
and a concern that a bunch of asshole cowboys are out to
take this Department from under our noses."

Marjorie sharply hung up the telephone. She was angry and more than a bit frightened. All right, she thought,
how do you get through to people like that? More impor-
tantly, how do you stop them?

Marjorie's thoughts were growing more confused as
she went along. She got the storage-room key from the
doorman, Freddy. Standing in the basement, in front of
the telephone junction box, she began to feel danger-
ously depressed.

Something is fucked up, she thought. This is all wrong.
The arrogance, the total disregard for the law, the out-
right balls that it took to come into her building and
install an illegal wiretap on her home phone. She groaned,
thinking of some of the conversations she'd had with
Charlie, with Emi.

Shining the flashlight on the pair of set screws, she followed the phone wire out through the top of the box to where it joined the sleeved cable. It occurred to her that the tap might not be here but at a binding post one or two blocks away. That would be the right way to do it, the professional way. But to get binding posts you need the help of the telephone company, and you need a court order.

Marjorie was sure that whoever was on her phone didn't get help from the phone company, and certainly didn't have a court order. When she saw the slice in the cable, she knew what she was dealing with.

A little farther along the cable she saw a shape. It was a transmitter taped to her phone line. She was beginning to enjoy herself. She was good; she knew her business. A receiver and tape recorder had to be stashed somewhere nearby.

The image of the Department car with its tinted blue windows came to her. The receiver was in the trunk of that car, of that she was sure. She left the storeroom.

In a few minutes she was back with a stepladder, a pair of pliers, and a knife. When she removed the transmitter, she turned to smile at Freddy the doorman, who stood watching her, amused, and, Marjorie believed, more than a bit impressed.

"Isn't that against the law?" Freddy said.

Marjorie laughed with satisfaction. "You betcha," she said.

Marjorie carried the transmitter back into her apartment. She was keyed-up, experiencing that old investigator's need to get on with the game.

She took a small plastic bag from a drawer in her kitchen and placed the transmitter inside.

She looked at the telephone, then at her kitchen floor, and yawned.

Ordinarily, when her world seemed about ready to split in half, Marjorie reached for a tennis racket. Pound out a little therapy, was how she thought of it.

Sometimes she cleaned her kitchen floor.

Marjorie played tennis with a good deal of passion and a certain amount of joy.

There was no joy in doing floors. None. Forget passion.

Still, doing her kitchen floor had often served as a salve for her soul. Over the years Marjorie had come to greet her rare fling with the hands-on side of domestic life as sort of an achievement. She could do floors if she had to, and windows too. She could cook and clean and mend things, hang drapes, do the wash and iron. She could, if she had to.

She stood thinking about her world, and then she thought of all the women, with flocks of kids and husbands with dirt on their shoes, women that do floors, what, once a week, twice a month, every day? Screw that, is what she thought.

She didn't need to imagine problems; she had enough real ones. Marjorie couldn't get over it: Carow and Thomas joining up with Janesky and Reardon, as if they'd thought it was going to be that easy. Just tell her the game's over, they lost, now on to the next gig. Be sure to bring your fiddle, because from here on, you're part of the band.

There was a lot to think about.

Marjorie was thinking when the phone rang.

It was Frank Bosco. "I hope I'm not calling at a bad time, Captain." His voice was low and rushed at her. Frank was frightened.

"It's all right," Marjorie said quietly. "Take it easy. What's going on?"

"Well, for one thing, I'm in a telephone booth across from the Golden Door Motel, and I only got a minute to talk. I'm on a stakeout."

"A stakeout?"

"Yeah, right—me, after nineteen years, I get ta play snoop just like a real detective."

When Frank told her the guy running the operation was a sergeant named Casey, her heart dropped and she asked, "Wait a minute. A grim, bitter-looking guy, about five ten, talks through his nose like Stallone?"

"Ya know him, huh?"

She could barely hear Frank.

"Oh, I know him, all right. I worked with Casey in Public Morals. That guy's bad news, Frank. What the hell are you doing out there with Jim Casey? Shit! Tell me, Frank, have you had a chance to see Casey's car? What's he driving?"

"Huh?" Frank said. "His car? He's driving a Department car. I dunno, one of those unmarked cars. You know, the old-fashioned kind with the dark windows."

Marjorie asked him another question or two, then said, "You have that transmitter with you, I hope?"

"Sure thing, Cap. I'm wearing it."

"Good, that's good. Listen, I'll be there in a half hour. Just make certain you turn it on."

"By the way, Captain, this here Janesky, it seems to me that the guy's overrated. And this here Casey, he's creepy."

It's amazing Casey's still on the job, Marjorie thought, though maybe not so amazing. "Frank, Janesky's dangerous mainly because of where he is, and it turns into a real fucking nightmare when you know where he wants to go."

"Shit's beyond me, Captain. I'm just a simple cop, is all."

"Yeah—well, listen, Frank, don't you do anything weird till I get there, okay?"

"You're really comin', huh?"

"Hey, I'm not about to let my partner down. I'll be there in half an hour."

"How will I know you're around?"

"You won't, but I'll be there, trust me. By the way, Frank, has anyone notified Narcotics?"

"Hell, no. Janesky went bat-shit when I mentioned it. I said maybe we should notify Narcotics and he about took my head off."

"Careful, huh, Frank? You be careful out there."

Setting a new personal elapsed time record of five minutes, Marjorie was dressed and ready to go.

But there was a weight on her shoulders now, slowing her.

Get out there, she told herself. Get to Red Hook, get going.

Marjorie picked up the telephone, returned it, walked around the apartment. Charlie was still at the office. Call him, tell him, tell him everything. Somebody should know, in case. . . .

Her stomach was taut. She wasn't sure. She didn't think Charlie could sit on this, not a story like this. Illegal bugs, rivalry for power, covering up for a lunatic commander out to gain ultimate control over the Police Department. All the top commanders involved. A menace at this very moment rolling around Red Hook. Once again she was aware of the time; it was getting late.

She phoned Carow, told him where to meet her in Red Hook.

"I beg you," he told her, "don't rock this boat. I've been told that these people are not happy with you. You're leaving a very bad feeling. I can't protect you from yourself, Margie. That I can't do."

"Meet me," she said. "Just meet me there."

"Fine, if you want. But I hate to see you make a fool of yourself."

Marjorie picked up the telephone once more and quickly dialed Charlie.

"Charlie," she said, "two questions. You still want the story?"

"Are you kidding?"

"Wait. Wait till you hear the second."

"Go ahead."

"I call all the shots. And no bullshit. I'll give you the story, but it's on hold till I say so. And, Charlie, I may never say go."

There was silence on the line.

"Can I ask why this sudden change of heart?"

"Yes."

"Well?"

"There's this cop, a real sweet guy. He's caught up in this. He put himself way out for me. I told him I could protect him, protect his pension. I promised him things that maybe I shouldn't have. I really don't have the—"

"Yeah," said Charlie, "go on."

"Look, it's simple. I don't have the clout to guarantee that this officer, after all he's been through, will get his pension. I can take care of myself, Charlie, but to get at me I'm afraid that some Headquarters hotshot will try to hurt this cop, screw him outa his pension."

"Marjorie, did I hear right? Did I hear milady say she's afraid?"

"Oh, Charlie, we're all afraid," said Marjorie.

"Marjorie," Charlie said. "Whatever you want, whatever you need, I'm here."

"Charlie?"

"Yeah?"

"You're all right."

"That's good, huh? Almost an 'I love you.' "

"Yeah," said Marjorie, feeling it, meaning it, feeling good right then.

The Shell station was at the end of a lineup of wood-frame tenements, some with street-level stores; several of the stores were boarded up. Two, a candy store/head shop and a butcher, were dimly lit and doing no business. On the edge of the gas station's apron, the telephone stood near an old blue Dempsy dumpster infested with rats, spilling over a month's worth of garbage.

The station was open, and occasionally a car rolled in for gas. The attendant, a seventeen- or eighteen-year-old boy with green striped hair, glanced at the waiting cops without interest. In the station's office a huge pitbull banged its head against the glass door and barked ferociously when the boy walked out to service a car.

Frank leaned against the phone booth and watched as Jim Casey and Ramon Rivera came toward him from the direction of the Golden Door Motel.

The Supremes were parked on the near side of the street, facing the motel's parking lot. Monty Adams, in Rivera's blue Chevy, sat alone, across the street, nearer the motel.

They stopped in a dark spot near the dumpster, not far from the phone booth. Rivera stood with his head bowed and his arms folded. He kicked a beer can and watched as it rolled under the dumpster.

"Over there," Casey said, pointing to the motel's parking lot, "are the two cars. The people are there, the cars are there, and we got a problem. We got a decision ta make."

"What's that?" said Frank.

Rivera answered, saying "They're packing the cars, getting ready to leave. I mean, they're packing everything. These people are going home."

"He heard 'em talking," said Casey, "heard what they was saying. Go ahead, tell 'em what ya heard. Listen ta this, Bosco. Your information wasn't exactly top-flight, if ya know what I mean."

Frank watched him, fascinated at the way Casey's fingers were opening and closing, making fists. He glanced at Rivera and noticed that he, too, was watching Casey.

"Well, for one thing," Rivera said with a funny smile on his face, "these people ain't Cubans. They're Colombians."

"Go ahead, Ramon, tell him how ya can tell. This guy here is a lot smarter than he looks, Frank. Go ahead, Ray, tell 'em whatcha tol' me about the language and all."

"Naw," said Ramon Rivera. "It's no big deal. Latins are Latins to most people that aren't Latino, ya know what I mean? Now these guys here, they're Colombians, and well educated, no jerks. Colombians speak the finest Spanish this side of Madrid. Ya can't miss the accent, it's no big deal."

Casey nudged him. "Tell him about the other thing. Go ahead, tell him everything, for chrissake."

Frank was quiet. He looked at Casey, then at Rivera, and wondered if maybe he should feel guilty about something. He shrugged and said, "The girl told me they were Cubans."

"That's nothin', that's nothin'," said Casey. "One rice-and-beans guy is like another rice-and-beans guy ta me. This here's the part that tightens my ass. Go ahead, will ya, Ray, tell him."

Ramon Rivera smiled.

Ramon told Frank, "There's another guy around. He's not here now, they're waitin' on him. They call the guy Flecha Loca."

"Sooo?" said Frank, feeling a little desperate.

"Well, Frank, ya see, these here Colombians, from what I heard—now mind you, I don't know any of this shit for sure, I just heard it—well, they bring these crazy, wacko, lunatic, fucking Indians with 'em for protection. Ya know, from the Amazon, fucking savages, like we ain't got enough right here in Brooklyn."

"What makes you think that the guy they're waitin' on is one of these characters?"

"Flecha Loca, Frank. It means 'crazy arrow.' "

"Oh," said Frank, "you may have a point."

"Tell him the other thing. Tell him about the bike."

"I heard one of them say the bike's gone. That means Flecha is gone."

Frank heard the radio in Casey's pocket. It was Lorraine, and she was yelling, "Wait a minute. I think one of 'em is leaving. Yeah, he's going. It's the brown Caddy."

Frank heard Sergeant Jim Casey say, "Okay, the decision's made. Let him go, but get on him, then take him when he's out of sight of the motel. Let's jump these fuckers."

Marjorie scanned the area and could see that there was no way she could get much closer than one block from the motel. But Frank's transmitter wasn't working, or else he had forgotten to turn it on, because she was receiving exactly zip from him on her receiver. She heard the portables, however, heard the female officer's transmission and Casey's response.

Sergeant Jim Casey, still around, still doing his thing. Amazing.

No sense moving, she thought. Might as well sit and wait, and listen. Monitor the portables, she thought. Maybe Frank's transmitter will kick in.

From where she sat, Marjorie had an unencumbered view of the Shell station and the Golden Door's parking lot.

She watched the Subaru make a sharp U-turn and stop at the traffic signal. Behind the Subaru, a brown Caddy with Florida plates; behind the Caddy, Frank in his beat-up red Toyota.

Watching through her rearview mirror, Marjorie saw the Subaru hold fast as the light went from red to green, and then saw Frank pull the Toyota up tight against the Caddy's rear bumper. The driver of the Caddy turned, then turned again, as two black women pulled down on him, their guns held with both hands pointing at the Caddy's windshield. Next she saw Frank and a black cop come up on the Caddy.

"Don't move, motherfucker, or you're one dead Colombian cowboy," yelled Frank.

"Keep your hands on that wheel," Banks said to the Colombian.

For shit's sake, thought Marjorie, what in the hell is going on?

"Cops, like in *policia*," Frank shouted.

He wanted to reach into his back pants pocket for his goddamn shield. But he wasn't about to let go of the gun to do it. And he needed two hands. Frank always held his gun with two hands, even at the range, even when the range officers threatened to fail him if he didn't drop one hand. He held tight. Because when he shot, when he let go—man, was he good. Frank Bosco was great with two hands, couldn't hit himself in the ass with one.

"Let's not stand here," Frank said. "Get him outa the car."

" 'Scuse me," Doris said. "Ya mind gettin' outa the car? Put your hands on your head and come on out."

"Doris," Lorraine shouted, "how in the hell's he gonna get outa the car with his hands on his head?"

"Somebody's gonna go and open the car door," Doris said. "Frank."

All the nervousness, the excitement, all the frenzy of the moment changed, and suddenly Frank felt strangely strong and alert. His head was light, he could get it on—oh, yeah, if you had it, it showed! Frank felt immortal.

He opened the Caddy's door, took hold of the guy's leather jacket, and pulled. The cowboy hat rolled into the street alongside the sprawling Colombian.

Officer Banks made his move, putting a knee into the guy's back, twisting his arms around and cuffing him.

Frank got on the radio to tell Casey that they'd taken the guy. He sucked deeply at the night air to still his pounding heart. "Now what?" he yelled into the radio.

"Me and Adams just jumped the other one," Casey replied. "You find anything, come up with anything?"

"No, no, nothin', but we ain't had a chance to search yet," said Frank, rubbing his burning stomach.

"Okay, bring 'em back to the motel. Bring the prisoner and the car back to the motel parking lot."

Casey sounded irritated and uncomfortable.

Marjorie had been able to see the whole thing.

When she heard the exchange between Frank and Casey on Casey's transmitter, she wondered if Bosco was ever going to turn on his. She also wondered where in hell Andrew Carow was. It had been two hours since she'd called him.

Frank left his Toyota on the gas station's apron, and the Supremes parked their Subaru at the curb under the broken Shell sign. Then, one by one, they joined Officer Banks in the Caddy. Lorraine sat on one side of the

Colombian, Doris on the other. Banks drove and Frank rode shotgun.

The Colombian sat looking around, unconcerned, acting as if it were just another day at the office, just another roll in the gutter, as if he'd done this a thousand times before.

The Golden Door Motel was a two-story brick building without color or shame. A filthy place with slimy windows and twisted venetian blinds that rested on soiled and peeling window frames. The City dumped any number of welfare families in the place, paid a thousand dollars a month for filthy rooms and violent hallways. No sane person would spend a minute in its rat-infested rooms.

When Banks turned the Caddy into the parking lot, Casey was standing near the second Caddy. Behind him, they could see light coming from Room 7A. In the doorway, Monty Adams caught in their headlights and waved.

"He wants us to park next to the other car," Frank said.

"I see him," Banks said.

Everyone in the car was silent.

Adams had a gun in one hand and was pointing to a parking place with the other. Sergeant Jim Casey stood staring into the second Caddy's trunk.

The Supremes and Banks led the Colombian into the motel room.

Frank joined Casey, who didn't move or speak, just pointed into the car's trunk.

"Good Christ," Frank said after taking a look.

Maybe, Frank considered, somebody smarter, somebody more logical, someone less excitable than he could look at what he saw in the trunk and call it ordinary. But he watched in awe as Sergeant Casey took one brown paper bag after another and opened them, showing the contents to Frank. Then he opened an attaché case and a shopping bag.

"Okay," Casey said, slamming the trunk closed. "Let's see what's in the other one."

Frank took the brown Caddy's key from Banks, told him to come and watch when he opened the trunk, heard him gasp and cry out, "Oooooooweeeeeee," as Frank opened one brown paper bag. Then they both watched Jim Casey smile and say, "Fuckin' A."

Frank closed the trunk. He could hear shouts from the motel room, heard Monty Adams's voice saying, "You'd better just sit there and shut the fuck up, or both of you are gonna be doing the mambo."

In the motel room, the Colombians were sitting handcuffed on the bed, smiling.

Adams opened all the dresser drawers and began throwing stuff around. Shirts, underwear, a shaving kit, sweaters.

"Monty," Officer Rivera said, "we been partners a long time. I never see you as happy as when you're fucking people around. Geez, you're a pisser. What the hell are you looking for? Me and the girls went through those drawers. I tol' you, there ain't nothin' there."

The Supremes stood, arms crossed, leaning against a lime-green wall, watching Monty Adams play.

The Colombians were a matched pair, both in their thirties, both light-skinned, fair almost. The one with the cowboy hat had a band of freckles across his nose. The men looked as if they were related; brothers, maybe. Both trim and well-kept, clean-shaven, they seemed friendly enough, a couple of fun-loving guys from Bogota via Miami, here in the Big Apple to do a little street business.

"Do they speak English?" asked Casey, picking up clothes from the floor, stacking them neatly on the bed, opening and closing his hands, making Frank feel creepy.

When Marjorie first caught sight of Inspector Carow, she thought, He's walking as if he's trying to be cool and pass in the neighborhood. But Carow, who was nearly as wide as he was tall, looked for all the world like a cop. And he walked like a cop, uneasy in this strange, unfriendly place.

She flashed the headlights on the cruiser once, and he gave her a quick, short wave, then continued his cool walk, head down, hands buried deep in his coat pockets, a hurry to his step, just a neighborhood guy out for an evening stroll. She wanted to laugh.

As he crossed the avenue, coming toward her, she wondered where he'd parked his car; she also wondered if it was the old frightened Carow who'd come to join her.

Marjorie watched him open the door. He was smiling; his eyes were clear and he was smiling. A sober Carow. Perhaps a whole new Carow?

"Whaddaya got here, Margie?" he said. "Man, it's been a while since you and me been on something together. Feels like old times, eh?"

"Yeah, except in the old days we'd be watching pimps and bookmakers, number guys and hookers, not cops."

"Yeah—well, right. C'mon, whaddaya got?"

"I don't know."

"C'mon."

"I really don't know, Andrew. My field associate called me, told me that Janesky sent him and five or six other cops from the precinct out on a drug plant."

"Uniform people, patrol people?"

"Yes, but he sent 'em out in civilian clothes, in unmarked cars. And guess who's supervising them? Jim Casey, that's who. Old Jim Casey from Public Morals. You remember him, don't you?"

"He's in jail, isn't he?"

"Noooo, he's a sergeant, and he's supervising a drug bust in that motel across the street."

"Margie, holy shit!"

A motorcycle was coming. She could hear it when it was blocks away—no muffler. It roared past the cruiser and spun into the motel parking lot. It skidded to a stop, started up, and was gone again in a god-awful roar.

In the light of a street lamp Marjorie caught a glimpse of the driver's face. A strange face, a tough-looking character with shoulder-length black hair tied in a ponytail. More evil than strange, she thought.

A shiver passed through her. A feeling came to her breast, a dark and private memory of a recurring nightmare that had come to visit when she was a rookie. As a young policewoman, the thought of dying in the street chilled her sleep and filled her with fear.

She watched the blank look come over Carow's face as he took notice of her expression.

In the nightmare she died of holes. Holes in her body from a knife; there was a geyser of blood, torn stockings. It was the stockings she'd dreamed of, torn stockings and blood and moans and sobs, little-girl sobs, her arms crossing her breasts, squeezing in the pain. People standing around, bearing witness to her agony. Street people watching the uniformed policewoman, and when she held out her hands, they turned away. A cop's nightmare.

It had been a long time since she'd had that dream, a long time since she'd really been frightened.

Carow said, "Sometimes, Margie, you get a mean line around your mouth. You ever notice that? You get this real mean line when you're angry." Marjorie blinked and shuddered but did not speak.

She was uncomfortable on the seat of the car. She'd been sitting for a long while. Her knees trembled, her back ached, her head was beginning to throb.

"That Janesky," said Carow with a chuckle. "He's a character, isn't he? I'll bet he never notified Narcotics."

She stared long and hard at him, then she had to smile. "What do you mean, Andrew? Who are you kidding, notify Narcotics? You don't really think Janesky would miss an opportunity for a line or two in the newspaper?"

Carow coughed, turned away from her.

She gently tapped him with her finger on his shoulder. "I know his game," she said, "and so do you. Janesky figures that his cops will make a big collar here, and he'll be six-o'clock news. Forget that his patrol cops don't know what in the hell they're getting into. That it's dangerous. I know how Janesky figures things. He's easy, Andrew."

"And you, what is it that you figure?" he asked. "What are you figuring on?"

The anger that had been growing in her turned hard and grew large. "I know that under pressure people do some strange things. And my intuition tells me that there are vibes in the air, and that something's coming that's going to make me choke."

"Margie," Carow said flatly, "that's a woman's way of thinking."

After a long silence she spoke in a very soft voice. "We'll see," she said. "We'll just sit around and see."

She would have said more, maybe really let him have it, but then she heard that ugly sound again, rolling thunder through the Red Hook streets. The Indian was back.

"Ya see that guy?" Carow said, flicking his finger toward the motorcyclist. "That's the sort of garbage that Janesky and his people have to deal with in this precinct."

"What in the hell are you saying, Andrew? I told you that Jim Casey is in that motel room. Everyone knows his story. The file on him is as fat as *War and Peace*, for chrissake. We both know the guy's a thief. And what does Janesky do with him . . . ?"

She watched Carow shake his head, watched as he smiled, heard the faint sound of music makers downtown. She watched as Carow danced.

"You know how the job is, Margie," Carow said seriously. "Sometimes you gotta be a little creative. I mean, as a boss you have to use your imagination. Now, Jim Casey was always a producer. You know that as well as I do. The guy made hundreds of collars."

"You're serious," she said. Carow touched his nose with the tip of his finger, settled back on the cruiser's seat, saying, "There's been some changes, movement in the Department. In a few days things are going to really start popping at Police Plaza. You could come up roses, Margie. It's possible."

Carow pointed to the motel parking lot. The two female officers were moving from one Caddy to the other, opening the lids of the trunks, taking out paper bags, shopping bags, an attaché case.

In the Shell station across the avenue, the dark man sat back on his motorcycle, watching.

Policemen shoot off their mouths way too much, a character trait of the breed, Frank thought. That really troubled him, because he had that transmitter, and some mindless bull could end up costing someone their job. So he'd decided not to turn the transmitter on, at least not yet.

Silently he sat on one of the two beds in the motel room and watched Jim Casey.

"Are you feeling okay?" Casey asked him.

"Sure, why?"

"Just asking." Then Casey turned to the Colombians and asked them, both of them, "Where in the fuck did you guys get all that money?"

The Colombians glanced at each other and shrugged.

"What money?" said the one with freckles.

"We got no money, man," said the other. "You think we be living here if we got money, if we got cash? Man, you crazy."

Casey bent over, hands on his hips, and looked into the Colombians' faces, first one, then the other. He said, "There's two trunk loads of money out in that parking lot. Where'd you get it all?"

"We don't know about any fucking money. You found money in those cars, then somebody put it there. It's probably counterfeit—you know, funny money. Man, it's not ours."

Frank Bosco cringed and looked away. He watched the Supremes, who were whispering with Officer Banks.

"Bullshit," Adams yelled. "That's fucking bullshit! And whaddaya doin' with this fucking gun here, and these books with numbers and initials? Whaddaya think, we're dumb or somethin'? You fuckers are doing drugs. We know, oh, yeah, we know your story."

The Colombian without the freckles said, "This place is dangerous, man. So we got a gun. It's registered in Florida. In Miami," he said with a challenge in his voice. "You allowed to have a gun in your car or your house. The gun is registered. And why you talking dope? You see any dope here? We don't fuck with that shit."

"The fucking money," Casey screamed. "Whose is it?"

Both Colombians wagged their heads. "It ain't ours."

"If it ain't yours," Ramon Rivera said in Spanish, "then whose is it? C'mon, men, you can't be busted for having money. Whose is it?" he repeated softly, offering the Colombian with the freckles a cigarette.

"Man, if it ain't ours, then it must be yours. Because whoever stuck it in our trunks ain't here to say it's theirs."

Casey gave a wave without looking back, then walked with his hands in his pockets, his shoulders hunched, to a spot just outside the doorway, facing out into the night. One by one the other cops followed him.

They stood in a circle around Casey. Taking deep breaths, Casey stared into their eyes, one after the other. Casey was looking for something in their eyes.

Casey was calm when he spoke. He continued to stare at them, and Frank expected him to raise a finger and touch each one of the cops.

"I don't permit anything to be done unless the decision is unanimous," Casey announced.

It was a statement, not a question. Still, Frank asked, "What's the question?"

Doris, the small Supreme, said, "Lorraine, what's he saying?"

And Lorraine said, "Listen."

"These people say the money's not theirs," Casey said.

Monty Adams grabbed Casey's jacket sleeve so violently that Frank thought Casey'd fall. "Sarge," he said,

"I mean, we know they're bullshitting, right? I mean, we know it's their money. Am I right here?"

Casey said, "Ray, maybe you oughta talk to your partner."

"Hold it, hold it, hold it," Ray Rivera said. "Does anybody here know what we're supposed to do with the money?"

Officer Banks was a quiet man who tended to go along with things, but he said, "I think we're supposed ta call the feds. You know, the IRS. That's what I think we're supposed ta do."

Everyone nodded.

"Yup," Ramon Rivera said. "We call the feds, and ya know what they're gonna do with the money?"

Everyone wagged their heads.

"I'll tell ya what they're gonna do. They're gonna give all that money to Du Pont or somebody, and ya know what Du Pont is gonna do?"

No one spoke.

"Look here, Du Pont is gonna take that money and make bombs with it. They're gonna make napalm bombs with it and give those bombs to the government, and the government is gonna take those napalm bombs Du Pont made, and they're gonna drop 'em on some small town in Nicaragua. Killing all the women and children and burning all the fucking goats and pigs. That's what the feds'll do with the money, and I don't know about the rest of you, but I couldn't live with that."

Banks said, "Fuck, no," and turned to the Supremes. "Uh-uh," he said, "not me. Right, girls, you don't wanna be responsible for burning up some town in El Salvador or something?"

Doris said, "Nicaragua."

Banks said, "Same thing."

Trying to make some sense out of the situation, Lorraine offered, "We're not feds. So we don't call the feds."

"Yeah," said Casey, "then who do we call?"

"The City, goddammit, that's who we're supposed to call. Some City agency that deals with tons of money nobody wants," cried Monty Adams, looking a little pale now and fidgeting with his holster.

"Yeah, that's it," Ramon Rivera said. "We call some City agency, and whadda they gonna do with all that money?"

No one spoke. Everyone looked to Ramon Rivera for guidance.

Sergeant Jim Casey stood and nodded.

Frank Bosco stared straight ahead. His breathing was uneven, a little labored.

Ramon Rivera said, "You all have to consider this . . . because now I will tell you the truth as I know it. If we give this here money to some City agency, they will take that money and turn it over to welfare, and welfare's gonna take that money and give it ta some turdbird whose gonna go out and buy a gun with the money welfare gave 'em, and he's gonna go and shoot some cop. Now," Rivera said solemnly, "if you all wanna be responsible for some cop gettin' shot—killed, probably— we'll take the money and give it to the City."

"Fuck, no!" everyone called out.

Sergeant Casey smiled.

Frank Bosco took hold of his pistol grips, squeezed, and turned on his transmitter. And just in time, because the Colombian with the freckles had jumped from the bed and walked out to join the circle of confused cops. "All this talk is depressing me, man," he said. "Whyn't you all take half the fucking money and let us get the hell outa here and go home to Miami."

Frank Bosco's jaw tightened, and his stomach seemed to soar up into his chest. He'd never been so frightened. Never. This conversation would turn everything loose. It would destroy these cops. And he'd done it, with a little flick of a switch.

Nineteen and a half years a policeman, always with good intentions, and this is how it ends.

Make sense, he told himself. Wasn't this the purpose, the goal?

Jesus, he thought, *am I doing the right thing here?*

"Well?" the Colombian said. "How about it, you going to let us go, man? We'll just go, we won't come back."

"Swear to God," said Jim Casey.

"I swear to fucking God, I'll never come back to this city."

"The man swears to God," Casey said, "and you and I know that these Colombians are very religious people."

The Supremes exchanged quick glances. Officer Banks mumbled something like, "The man swore to God, a man swears ta the Almighty, that's good enough for me."

Adams said, "I say we kill 'em, kill 'em and take all the money. You all wanna be fucking criminals, let's do it right."

"Jesus Christ," Ramon Rivera said.

Where is it written, Frank Bosco thought, that policemen have perspective? Like everybody else, even when they see it firsthand, they hardly know good from evil.

A sickness in his poor, nervous stomach had finally replaced Frank Bosco's fear.

In the cruiser, Marjorie could feel the blood leave her face. She turned to Carow, who sat wide-eyed. He seemed very near the point of a breakdown.

"Get me that recorder in the backseat," she said.

Carow turned away, saying, "Don't record it. We'll listen, see what happens."

At first Marjorie was so angry she couldn't speak. When at last she could, words would not come together. She was left with only a shout: "Andrew!"

"Will ya calm down?" he said. "Take it easy, we don't need a recording. We're both here and listening, we corroborate each other. You know what I'm saying."

Marjorie shook her head. "No," she said.

"I'm telling you to wait and see what happens. Maybe

nothing will happen. Maybe these cops are just talking. Cops are known for their ability to bullshit, Margie."

The sound of the transmitter carried through loud and clear. Casey was talking, telling Adams to take off their cuffs, telling the others to count the money.

"This is stupid! So fucking foolish, for God's sake. What in the hell is going on here?" Carow asked. "Janesky has already been promoted. It'll be in tomorrow's orders, for chrissake."

"What the hell have you been up to, Andrew? You trying to play some kind of double game here?"

Andrew Tony Carow slammed the dash with the palm of his hand. "Janesky's going all the way, Margie," he said. "There's a load of promotions coming down. This time next week he'll have another star, and Thomas, he'll be chief of ops. They moved out two people, Margie, right up to the commissioner."

"Really, Andrew, that's very difficult to believe. Now," she said, "will you please give me the damn recorder?"

Carow groaned and slammed his head with the heel of his hand. "I'm gonna get another star. You got any idea what that means toward my pension?"

"The recorder," Marjorie said again.

"And you, I've been promised! It's in solid! You could move up to full inspector! Highest-ranking woman ever! Margie, think what that means."

"I'm thinking that Janesky's an eyelash away from being police commissioner! Give me that recorder, Andrew, and give it to me now!"

"A major scandal in this precinct, in Janesky's command, could blow the whole thing. Turn everything around."

Carow looked away, put his head in his hand.

"I have a message for you from Thomas," he said finally. "He told me to tell you to please dance this one with him. He said you'd understand. And he said later you and he could make your own music. 'We'll be music makers' is what he said, Margie, and he said, 'Please, please do the right thing.' "

"Thomas is crazy like Janesky," Marjorie shouted.

Carow was talking hard, laughing a little; she hardly heard him. His eyes locked on her, a solemn expression. "This is our one big shot, Margie, yours and mine. Don't screw it up for us. That's how Thomas put it, 'Don't screw us.' "

"Andrew."

"What?"

"Give me that recorder."

"You don't need it. Why keep a record of all this bullshit if nothing happens? There's enough conversation going on to get all these cops canned. They get canned and Janesky's had it. They'll be such a fucking scandal, we'll all go up in smoke."

Marjorie was looking out, staring out the windshield toward the parking lot of the Golden Door Motel, dimly lit in the pale glow of the streetlight. There was movement. People were gathering around the doorway of Room 7A.

"I'm telling you, Andrew, now you listen to me. I've been sitting here hearing you make excuses for Janesky, for Thomas, and for Casey too. I can't believe this. I'm right up to here with incomprehension and rage."

"Margie, Margie." Andrew Carow's voice came on small; it made a croaklike sound.

"I found a transmitter on my phone line. It's a line bug, Andrew. The cheap kind we used in PMD. Not Department-issue, you know what I'm talking about. The kind *you* used in the old days, you bastard."

"My God, you think I bugged your phone?"

Carow trembled, caught between confusion and fear.

"Andrew, we've worked together for years. I know you couldn't bug your own phone. It was Casey, Casey's a wireman. You used him in PMD, and you knew that Janesky was using him, too, using him against me. You betrayed me, didn't you? You betrayed me to score points with these deadheads."

Marjorie could sense Carow staring at her now.

"Never mind," she said. "Something goes wrong here and I'm going to get you all." As she spoke, Marjorie continued to watch through the windshield, thinking about Frank Bosco, and Charlie, and damn music makers.

Carow said, "Margie," and he said it in a voice that was high and funny.

"It'll be woman's work," she said, "like cleaning dirt from the cracks in a floor." Her voice was calm now.

"We all have weaknesses, Margie, all of us."

Marjorie nodded.

The sound came from across the avenue. Backlit by the gas station and in the streetlight of the parking lot, weird shadows danced off the motel's walls. And through those shadows, on a roaring motorcycle, like a cyclone, his eyes blazing, his mind blitzed by the finest Bolivian dancing powder, came a Yahito from Santa Marta, and he came to party with a MAC-10 machine gun, a little party music.

Frank Bosco heard the roar. *What's happening? What should I do?*

His thoughts were shattered by the ripping of the small automatic weapon.

Shoot! Shoot the prick, he told himself.

Lorraine dropped the brown paper bag she carried and was the first to go for her gun. It didn't matter; she was way too slow.

A short burst from the first volley of 9-mm fire caught her, spun her, sent her tripping through the parking lot. Officer Adams, to her right, dropped to one knee and got off two quick shots. But the Indian was gone, roaring off into the shadows of the night.

Doris lost it.

"No!" she scream-shouted. "Wait, no, no, no!"

Doris pulled at her hair, and she ran, tripping, dodging among the parked cars. She fell, got up, half running, half stumbling.

Frank stood for a moment looking at her in the light.

Her gun bounced behind her. It fell at the feet of the Colombian with freckles. He bent, picked it up, looked at it, and fired point-blank into the side of Jim Casey's head. The Colombian looked happy.

Frank began shooting without knowing it. Without looking at Casey, he fired again and again into the body of the freckled face.

Then once again the sound erupted in the night: a mighty roar came from Water Street. The Yahito and his motorcycle were back.

Short, horrible bursts from the MAC-10 mingled with the thunder of the motorcycle. But Frank was not afraid. A terrible excitement filled him; he was at the center of a hissing inferno, very close to madness, a magical place.

Jim Casey was lying at Frank's feet, bleeding from his ears.

Then Rivera was hit. His arms went straight up in the air, and someone shot him again. Monty Adams, running, firing as he ran, chased the motorcycle.

A sharp crack and whoosh passed Frank's ear and he whirled. The second Colombian had found a gun and was firing from behind the cover of the brown Caddy's fender.

Officer Banks walked toward the brown Caddy, just walked, forgetting everything anyone had ever taught him, shooting his pistol, his gaze holding on the Colombian and the Caddy.

Frank was hit with a great concussion that slammed his eyes shut and fractured his ribs.

To his left he heard Banks holler at the Colombian, "Die, you motherfucker." The Colombian stood with both his hands in the air. Frank saw him smile. Banks brought up his .38 and shot the Colombian in the face. Then Frank heard shots, and more shots, and he heard the motorcycle, its ungodly racket filling his head.

Life is real, he thought, life is special. Life, all of it, is planned. There was no breath in him; he couldn't get air. He was down on his back, hearing Murray's voice, calm and gentle. "See," it said, "I told you to wear that vest. You'd always be fine if you'd just learn to listen."

"Murray," Frank said out loud, air coming to him now, "am I dead?"

Quick and agile, Marjorie was out of the cruiser in a flash. Carow stayed in the car and called for help. He radioed a ten-thirteen: shots fired and officers down.

Marjorie walked to the center of the street, holding her gun at her side, waiting to raise it when the time came to shoot that madman right off his goddamn bike.

C'mon, you fuck, c'mon.

He was half a block away and closing.

C'mon, you creep, keep coming.

To her left she heard Doris crying.

Marjorie could see the Indian clearly, hunched over, no windshield on his motorcycle, his arm extended, his ponytail in the wind.

Nine-millimeter rounds ripped up the street. She brought up her gun, two hands, feet spread, balanced and calm.

Marjorie aimed and fired once, aimed again and fired again, then she dived toward the curb. The motorcycle roared past, but there was a wobble. She saw the front end go. Still the bastard kept going, kept rolling on, right up the street toward the avenue.

She looked left and right. *I missed him! How the hell did I miss him?* Then she heard the explosion.

Out of control, the motorcycle, the rider holding fast, head down, flew across the avenue, slashed through the gas station's apron, struck the door, and went right on through, scaring hell out of the kid with green-striped hair and pissing off the hundred-pound pitbull. At first the dog snapped at the spinning tires, then decided he'd do a lot better with the throat of the driver and went for it.

Suddenly noise filled the cold night air. Screaming sirens, and whoopers, and more sirens.

Marjorie sprinted across the street into the motel's parking lot. Her skirt was torn, and dirt streaked her face. She saw Frank Bosco sitting up against a street lamp, his hands clasped between his legs, his head down. He was alive.

Adams had a hand over the big hole in Rivera's chest; a terrible sucking sound seemed to be coming through his hand. Adams was screaming for an ambulance, for help.

Blood flowed; it ran from Lorraine, mixed with Casey's, and spread out toward the wide-open eyes of the freckle-faced Colombian.

There was pandemonium in the parking lot.

Carow shouted orders that no one heard. Officer Banks had his arms wrapped around Doris, who was pulling at her hair and vomiting.

Marjorie, breathing hard, knelt on one knee in front of Frank. She looked at the hole in his jacket, touched it with her fingertips. "Frank, you're hit."

Frank shook his head. He tried moving his hands up from between his legs. He sighed and dropped his head back against the lamppost. "It never went through the vest."

"God, you were lucky," she said.

Marjorie took Frank's hand and sat beside him, leaning her head against the lamppost, closing her eyes, squeezing his hand and resting.

When she first saw Carow and Thomas, Chief Janesky was standing in the center of the parking lot talking with them. The two stood, heads bent, their hands in their pockets, listening as Janesky spoke.

A familiar scene.

Marjorie got up and walked toward them.

Ambulance attendants, emergency medical service people, and precinct cops were scurrying through the lot. She paid them no mind. She was going straight for Janesky.

At the entrance to the parking lot a large group of people from the Hook had gathered. Some walked toward the lights, toward the action.

Marjorie saw Janesky nudge Thomas and point his chin toward her. She watched as Carow extended his hand, motioned for her to slow, to calm down.

Carow knew her, knew the look, saw the anger taking hold, saw the line form near her mouth.

She was within arm's length when Chief of Detectives Thomas said softly, friendly like, "Everyone's talking about the shot you made. Christ, you'll be headlines tomorrow. And now, with your promotion coming . . ."

Andrew Tony Carow said, "Margie?"

She leaned in close to Carow and spoke quickly, "To hell with you, Andrew." Then she stepped back, looked hard and straight into Janesky's eyes. Carow had been right; there was nothing there.

At that moment Marjorie wasn't sure who she despised more, Janesky or Thomas or Carow. All three. It was easy.

Janesky was smiling. She couldn't believe it, the son of a bitch was grinning as he looked over the scene, watching the wounded and dead being carried off.

"The shame of this!" she shouted. "The fucking shame of all this!"

"C'mon, easy," Thomas said. "Take it easy."

"We're responsible for what happened here. Don't you know it, don't any of you feel any guilt at all?"

Cops standing nearby didn't know what the hell to do; they just stared at her. Passersby stopped, moved back out of the light.

"Hey," Chief Janesky said, "you're a captain, Captain, behave like one. Because if you can't, I'm telling you to leave."

"Oh, I'm going," Marjorie said sharply, and began to turn.

"Don't look at me like that, Captain," Janesky said. "I don't like it."

Chief Thomas just stood there, head down, hands in his pockets.

"Ya see?" said Janesky. "Ya see? Ya put women in a combat situation, and what the hell do they do? I'll tell ya what they do, they come apart. Whyn't ya go home and make babies, Captain?"

Marjorie took a deep breath and said, "I only do what I can, Chief, only what I can. But I'll tell you all what I can do. I can see to it that you answer for this. I'm going to make you all fucking famous."

"Answer to who?" said Thomas, coming alive now, standing hard with his hands on his hips. "Answer for what?"

And Janesky saying, "Ohhh, but dear lady, I'm already famous." And Carow joining in, saying, "Okay, Captain, let's stop the nonsense. It's gone far enough."

But Marjorie knew she had them, had them good. There was fear in Thomas's eyes, and a tremor in Janesky's tone.

Carow started to say something, but even as he began to speak, he knew it was too late. That line had hardened on Marjorie's face, and the smile was set, unyielding.

"What the hell are you still doing here?" Janesky said. "Whyn't you just fucking go and we'll leave it at that?"

The surprise was to see him leaning into her, threatening. She wondered what the hell he was thinking.

Finally he said, "You'll see, you'll see, you hateful bitch, you've been trying to make problems for me for months." His eyes narrowed. "You spiteful bitch, you lost, and there it is, there ain't no more, you're done here, finished in this job. You're all alone, girlie. When you look around, there ain't gonna be anyone there."

"Oh, you got it, Chief! You just put your finger on it."

"What?"

"I did look around, and it was the looking that made me sick, made me angry. You shouldn't have made me angry, Chief, because when I get angry, I look harder, and do you know what I found, Chief?"

No one answered, no one spoke.

She had to take it all the way now, before she thought about what she was doing. She thought about a trio of music makers. *This is it, this is the night the music dies.*

Chief Thomas said, "Leave it alone, Marjorie, just leave it be."

What she finally said was, "This is all so sad and absurd and pointless." Then, having said it, she knew it was a mistake, because Janesky turned to the others and spoke to them as though they were to witness a great event.

"There are dead officers in this filthy street. Heroes. And this woman describes their deaths as absurd and pointless."

Chief Thomas mumbled something inaudible and tried to smile.

Carow said nothing; his features were clouded.

Marjorie could feel police officers watching them from the shadows.

"The dead are here because of you," she said to them.

"You are one royal pain in the ass," Janesky shouted.

"I'll grant you that," said Marjorie, "and I promise, I'm going to be yours."

Turning now, his back to her, Chief Raymond Janesky, all stern and proper, had the last word.

"You have no power, girlie, none. You think you're hot shit? You're a woman cop, is all, and not even a good one. Get lost."

It would have been comforting for her to see Janesky as an aberration. But Marjorie had been around, and she knew better. She resisted the urge to run at him, to look in Janesky's face and damn him. She took a deep breath, gathered herself up, and began to walk. *The truth is,* she told herself, *you talk too much. Maybe that's been the problem all along. You can't negotiate with evil. It's not possible.*

"Hey," Chief Thomas called, "don't go away mad, huh, Captain?"

On her way back to the cruiser, Marjorie saw that Frank Bosco was still sitting up against the lamppost.

A few cops stood around him, and an ambulance attendant and a small, frail, blond girl were pulling at his sleeve, telling him to get up, to get up and get going, the ambulance was waiting.

"You kook," the little blonde shouted, "will you get the hell up?"

Frank just sat, his hands folded neatly in his lap. He looked so unbelievably peaceful.

Marjorie waved to him and he smiled. She kept on walking.

Frank was not fully conscious. He'd been hit with a steel-jacketed .38. Sure he was wearing a vest; still, the round had hit him like a sledgehammer to the solar plexus. His eyes followed Captain Butera as she walked through the parking lot. That woman's a mystery, he thought, a mystery with the heart of a lion. And Ronnie was talking to him, pulling at him and saying, "You're a hero, you're my hero. Please get up."

He had some pain in his chest, and his ribs hurt. He was anxious to get going, to be the hell out of Red Hook, out of New York. He cocked his head, looked at Ronnie, and said, "Ya know, Florida's not so bad. You could be happy in Florida."

"Oh, sure," said Ronnie. "You and me and your wife and daughter. We could all go to Disney World and play with Mickey's mouse. Are you crazy, Frank?"

Good question, he thought. Now that's a good question.

At the corner Marjorie stopped to let traffic pass. A uniformed officer, a rookie policewoman with a sweet face, approached her, saying, " 'Scuse me, but aren't you Captain Butera?"

Marjorie nodded once, then she watched as the woman's eyes got wide.

"You were in that shoot-out, weren't you?" she said, pointing to the parking lot. "I've always heard you were really something. It's nice to meet you, Captain."

"You just make sure you're careful out here," Marjorie said. "The trick is not to be surprised but to be a shadow in the shadows. See them before they see you."

"I can take care of myself," the policewoman said. "People always tell me I'm a survivor, and I figure it's true."

"That's a good way to think," Marjorie said.

Marjorie glanced around the sad Red Hook streets. The traffic signal turned green, and the policewoman gave her a great smile. "You make us proud," the policewoman called as Marjorie set out across the avenue. "Take it from this policewoman, Captain, you make us all proud."

Marjorie was hearing something she'd waited a long time to hear.

In the gas station, she looked at the shattered door, at the blood on the office floor, and shuddered, thinking of the Indian, his motorcycle, a new addition to her collection of nightmares.

From out of the darkness she heard Charlie's voice.

"Hey, big-timer, you never cease to amaze me."

"And you," she said. "Where in the hell did you come from? How'd you get here so fast?"

"Are you kidding? The police radio was on fire. I'm a good reporter. I head for the action."

Junkies, hookers, winos, blown-away souls of every sort, cruised along the street past them and watched with dead eyes as Charlie and Marjorie stood on the apron of the gas station.

"I spoke to my editor," Charlie said, "and do you know what he said? He said, 'Go for it! Get the whole story and you can have the cover. You can blow Janesky and the rest of those half-assed brass gods sky-high, right on the cover of *Metropolitan* magazine.' "

"Oh, Charlie," Marjorie said, "think about it. It's a lost war. And we know it. That's the nightmare—the war's over and lost. I never learned how to lose. Answer that one. How do I learn to lose?"

There were cops watching them from the gas station lot as they spoke. Charlie sighed and wiped dirt from Marjorie's cheek. "Oh, Marjorie, I never said that if you let me do this story, we'd change history. What matters, what's important, is that you survive. Doesn't it matter to you that when I do this story, it'll turn out that you did a hell of a job?"

"What matters to me is that this will all pass. In a week, two, maybe as long as a month, it'll be business as usual. Those are your words, Charlie. Nothing changes in this circus of a city. Remember telling me that?"

"Why in hell would you listen to me?" Charlie declared. "When I say simpleminded stupid things like that, pity me. Think of me as dumb and behind the times."

He was grinning.

Marjorie took Charlie's arm. He kissed her and they moved off.

Two uniformed patrolmen and a sergeant stood, arms folded, at the intersection. Marjorie nodded in their direction and held tight to Charlie's arm.

From their portable radios came the sounds of a Brooklyn night. Bar fights, prowlers, a man with a gun, a missing child.

The sergeant nodded first, then smiled, then all three wagged their heads. If it had been a different night in another place, the act would have been comic.

"Hey, Captain," the sergeant said. "I'm sure glad you're on our side."

Marjorie grinned. "Some goddamn job, eh?"

"The job's fine, Captain. It's the people that suck."

"Meaning?" asked Charlie.

Pause. Then, as Marjorie and Charlie watched, the three cops slowly raised their arms, and each of them made a great circle in the air. All three spoke as one. "The world sucks."

"Tell me we haven't failed," said Marjorie.

"I don't think you failed," Charlie said.

Chapter Ten

The city buried the three officers with an impressive and massive funeral.

Lines of blue descended on New York from cities as far away as Chicago.

And the pipers played.

For Sergeant Jim Casey it was "Irish Soldier Boy," for Ramon Rivera "Mi Viejo San Juan," and for Lorraine Needhan, in a silver, flag-draped casket, they did "Amazing Grace."

Captain Marjorie Butera let it be, let it all be, did nothing to blemish the day.

All the newspapers in New York covered the shootout. They did the stories with photos of officers in uniform. Good, clear photos, for their family and friends to keep and remember them by.

Within a week *Metropolitan* magazine appeared on the newsstands, and Marjorie was on the cover. Inside, Marjorie, in full uniform, looked dazzling, a rare beauty, under a caption that read, SOON TO BE HIGHEST-RANKING WOMAN COP. THE MAYOR'S FAVORITE.

The mayor had the wit to slide up to a good thing when he saw it. A photo opportunity, of a good two-handed handshake, and an arm around a beautiful, courageous woman, good for fifty thousand votes, easy.

The long article recounted the shooting in the parking lot, detailed Marjorie's career. There was a sketch with her standing in the middle of the street, gun raised.

It was all quite dramatic.

That had been a month ago.

On the day of her promotion Marjorie was dressed in full uniform. And when she walked into the Headquarters auditorium, she heard soft whistles. The crowds of police and their families, milling about, all seemed cheerful enough.

Inside the auditorium, a stereo was playing "East Side, West Side."

Everywhere rookies, recent graduates of the Police Academy, searched for seats in class platoons. Some threw Marjorie quick, unsure salutes.

There were also a great many civilians. Friends, relatives, all very happy to be there to hear the mayor speak and to applaud the promotions.

Marjorie resisted an urge to search the sea of faces for Janesky, Carow, and Chief of Detectives Thomas.

Eventually the Super Chiefs came from behind a curtain and took seats on the stage.

Earlier, Marjorie had felt pleased as she climbed into the passenger seat of Charlie's car. This would, after all, be her day.

Emi, effervescent in the backseat, seemed to be thrilled for her.

"Well, what do you think?" asked Emi as they pulled away. "Will the mayor announce your appointment to first deputy police commissioner today?"

"I think so. He told me he would."

"And the police commissioner," Charlie said, "when will he announce the appointment of the new PC?"

"You once called the mayor a clown, Charlie," Marjorie reminded him. "Well, let me tell you, our mayor's a slick piece of work. He'll know when to drop that bomb."

"Well," Charlie said, "we'd all better watch ourselves, because lightning is going to bounce through the halls of One Police Plaza when the mayor announces the appointment of a black PC."

Charlie was joking, but Marjorie nodded soberly.

"They're not going to be happy," she said. "The Super Chiefs are going to be good and pissed when they find out the mayor went to another city to recruit him. And when they hear I'm to be first deputy—"

Emi reached over and touched her cheek. "I'm so happy for you. I'm proud and happy for you."

They drove on in silence for a while.

It had been a month since the night of the Golden Door shootings. After the magazine story appeared, Charlie's publisher had arranged a meeting for Marjorie with the mayor. She'd fully expected the police commissioner to be there as well. Cocking a grave eye at her, pointing a finger, calling her traitor.

She was wrong.

It came as something of a shock to find herself at one A.M. in the kitchen of Gracie Mansion, elbow to elbow with His Honor, fighting chopsticks and lobster lo mein.

So many emotions surged through her that night, she had felt dizzy, had made no effort to hide her discomfort.

Marjorie supposed that the mayor would view her as a whistle-blower, a hard case who was probably a bit twisted.

Wrong again.

The mayor was clearly happy with her, both for her performance at the Golden Door and for keeping some of the dirty facts from the press.

That, of course, was not entirely the case. Actually, Charlie knew everything. But he didn't print it all.

Her first instinct, after the night of violence and death at the Golden Door, was to spare the surviving cops.

The recording she had made would have been evidence enough to indict and prosecute Officers Adams, Banks, and Doris LaMott. But it would have required the sworn testimony of Frank Bosco, and the consequences of days on the witness stand, pointing a finger at fellow cops, to Frank's mental health, was something she'd prefer not to chance.

By the time she spoke to Frank, she'd already decided that if Banks and LaMott retired of their own accord, and Adams resigned, she would hold off any criminal prosecution. The three would also have to be willing to give sworn statements as to Chief Janesky's malfeasance, a felony in this city.

Marjorie struck the deal with her PBA attorney. Frank Bosco, grateful and impressed, was allowed to retire with full pension.

And though Charlie's story suffered, he, too, thought it ultimately correct to withhold the incriminating conversations from his article.

The mayor studied all the facts. It was simple justice and baroque politics; he loved it.

And then he told her about a big new broom coming to town to clean house. A big black broom from San Francisco, coming to New York to be police commissioner.

"A black broom is far better than a full-fledged investigation of the Department," he had said. "Don't you agree?"

And Marjorie told the mayor of the City of New York that anything is better than bloodletting. And historically speaking, investigations of the Department tended to be political footballs. The invisible Headquarters establishment never got into that game, not a mark on their uniforms.

The mayor smiled. And it was then that he insisted that it could happen this time. Quietly. He told her it had been arranged. She would be the new commissioner's first deputy. A stroke of brilliance, he felt. A stroke of mayoral brilliance. A black PC with a woman first deputy.

Marjorie could not think of one good reason to say no.

As first deputy she could settle all accounts, clear the books.

While Charlie found his way to the underground garage at Headquarters and parked the car, Emi said, "I've a great idea."

"What's that?" asked Charlie.

"Well, I think you two should get married."

"Thank you, Emi," said Marjorie. "You're a great help, sweetie."

"No—no, listen. All relationships have a beginning, a middle, and an end. Now, you two are long past the middle, so you have no options. It's either split or marry. Now, c'mon, I can see it in both your eyes. You two are in love. Go for it."

Charlie turned to Marjorie, tried a smile.

"Emi," Marjorie said, "mind your own business."

Charlie said, "Oh, me, isn't she something?"

Ten minutes later Marjorie went up from the audience to anchor the row of Super Chiefs on the stage. The mayor stood at the podium, solemn, a rock of wisdom.

And when he spoke, the words came easy, an experienced ringmaster, all aglow in TV lights.

As he leaned into the microphone to speak, Marjorie faded. She thought about Charlie, and she thought that he was different. That he was not your ordinary, average, run-of-the-mill, fucked-up male. And she did have a true passion for him, and passion, when you get right down to it, is important.

Still, she could not yet bring herself to say yes to marriage.

The mayor was going on about the Big Blue, the greatest police department in the world, he said, bar none.

Applause.

All in all, she thought, at age thirty-eight, she was fairly happy. And, to that small portion of the civilized world that did not condemn a woman for not really wanting to raise a family, successful.

Now the mayor was talking about promotions, and changes, real growth for the Department. New leaders who embodied the best of the Big Blue.

Small applause.

Marjorie was staring into the audience. Emi waved to her. At Marjorie's nod, Emi pointed to the empty chair beside her. Charlie was gone.

Suddenly Marjorie felt herself overwhelmed by an emptiness. Charlie was gone.

"This is a great day for the Police Department," the mayor said, "a great day for the women and men of the Department. Today, we the City of New York, for her unstinting valor, elevate Captain Marjorie Butera, first to the rank of full inspector. She will hold that rank, and then be granted a leave of absence so that she can fulfill the obligations of the civilian rank of first deputy police commissioner."

The crowd of cops erupted in applause, but not a sound from all that brass and gold seated beside her.

Marjorie leaned forward in her seat and continued to stare over the expanse of chairs filled with applauding cops. She was truly a wreck. She'd checked row by row, seat by seat, and no Charlie. Maybe that little exchange with Emi finally chased Charlie off.

It was a real possibility.

Marjorie shook her head in disbelief.

"Oh, Charlie," she said out loud, as though she were embarrassed.

Later there was a receiving line, the mayor at the head. He took her hand, asked, "May I?" and gave her a sweet kiss, a sweet political peck. Then he moved on.

Next came Chief of Detectives Thomas, wearing a suit that had set him back an easy five hundred, and a mean little grin.

Marjorie smiled, took his hand.

"Well," he said, "this is quite a turn, isn't it?"

"Indeed. We'll be working closer now, won't we? We'll be a team."

"Absolutely," Thomas said unhappily.

After a moment Marjorie turned and said, softly enough so that only Thomas could hear, "Well, that's not quite accurate, is it? The truth is, you'll be working for me."

Chief Thomas blinked.

Turning back to face him, Marjorie studied Thomas. She watched as his face came apart.

"Look," she said, "you can throw in your papers."

Thomas spoke at last. "Never."

"You could also finish your career as a patrol captain in the South Bronx."

Chief Thomas walked off a bit, then, looking at her, he said, "You're serious."

It would have been easy not to say anything.

"I'm not your friend, Chief. You sold me out. You can believe I'm not your friend."

"I'll fight you," he said.

"That's not your reputation," said Marjorie, and she smiled at her own remark.

Next came Andrew Tony Carow.

"Ahhh," he said, "my girl's done it. Honestly, Margie, I'm proud of you."

Marjorie gave him a good two-handed shake, a gentle tug, pulled him to her, whispered in his ear. "Ninety days, Andrew. In ninety days you're out of your office and collecting your pension. You'll have to go, Andrew. I'm sure you can see that you'll have to go."

Carow stood in numb stillness, said, for the very first time in the fifteen years she'd known him, "Marjorie."

"It's best, Andrew. Take it from me, it'll be best all around."

Marjorie watched him leave. He looked back at her, and she did not look away.

Then she turned to Chief Janesky.

She could hear Emi calling to her from somewhere down front, but she didn't look around.

She was watching Janesky as he came toward her, smiling the phony smile of an old enemy unable to ignore you at a family ceremony.

Evil smiles when evil's beaten.

She experienced a brief surge of panic.

He said, "Oh, this is good for you, eh? Makes you feel good all over. Well, let me tell you something—"

She cut him off with a smile of her own, and a gesture.

"No," she said evenly, "you can't tell me a goddamn thing. In a week, Chief—in one week you're gone. If not, I'm going to the U.S. Attorney. And when I tell that prosecutor all I know, when I show him all that I have neatly filed away, he's going to want to indict you, lock you up, take you away in chains. You pissed me off, Chief, and you really did yourself in."

Marjorie said it all so quietly and with such finality that Chief Raymond Janesky took a step back. He looked at her strangely for a moment. His eyes seemed ready to explode. A man in mortal terror, his career ending, his power gone.

Marjorie looked around into the audience of cops, smiles rippling all their faces.

Janesky moved past her, stopped, a stricken man. "I'm not done," he said. "Don't think I'll roll over and crawl off. The righteous are *bold*. Lady," he said, "you're not through with me."

Marjorie held up her index finger.

In a minute she was out in the audience. There was brisk traffic to the door. Charlie, she thought, must be out there somewhere. Then again, maybe he wasn't. *He has his story, and I have mine.*

Please, God, is what she thought, and she thought it with a quiet sadness. Then she spotted Emi.

"Hurry, Marjorie, will you hurry?" she said brightly.

"You've seen Charlie?"

"Yes. Yes, I've seen Charlie. He told me to tell you to hurry. He's waiting in the plaza."

Marjorie kissed Emi, then made her way through the crowd to the auditorium door. The crowd closed in around her, and she tried to move with strong, sure steps. But there were too many people, far too many surging to the single door. So she stepped aside.

Waiting, she leaned a shoulder against a wall. She caught a glimpse of a figure moving to her left, and it wasn't till she felt the hand grip her shoulder that she realized he had been moving toward her for a while.

"Chief Butera," the voice said, "by Christ, lady, you're tough to catch."

A tall, broad-shouldered man with green eyes, he wore the finest tailored suit Marjorie had ever seen.

"I'm Dan Kelly," he said.

"I know. I've seen your photo."

"Really?"

"It does you no justice. My God," she said, "you're gorgeous. You look like a movie actor."

"Well, well, now. Thank you." He was almost flustered. Marjorie could feel the blood rush to her face.

"Listen," he said, "I'm in town looking for an apartment. I came by to watch your promotion. Quite a show."

"A circus," said Marjorie. And when she said it, she thought of Charlie waiting in the plaza.

"Listen, Commissioner, I need to go. Someone is waiting for me."

A happy smile lit his handsome face.

"Not commissioner yet. Next week but not yet. Tonight the mayor's giving a party for me."

"I have to go," she said. "I'm sorry, but I really have to get moving."

A group of uniformed cops, the last of the crowd, and Emi stood by the door.

"Well, listen," he said, "you'll have to show me around. I'm staying at the Saint Regis. Give me a call."

"I'll call you. Commissioner Kelly, I'll be in touch. Jesus," she said, "I love your name. It's perfect. Kelly."

"It is, isn't it? Well, maybe they owned the plantation."

"And I bet your great-great-great-grandfather did more than just a bit of housework," she said wickedly.

"You'll call me?" he said.

"Certainly."

She was aching to get away from him. Charlie was waiting, and here she was flirting with the new police commissioner.

"Are you crazy?" Emi told her. "Charlie is double-parked out in front of the building, and you stand around schmoozing. Who was that gorgeous man?"

"That was Dan Kelly."

"The new commissioner?" Emi put her hand over her mouth. "Good God, Marjorie, you're in trouble."

Charlie sat waiting on one of the cement benches in the plaza, about fifty feet or so from the five disks of iron that depicted the five boroughs of the city. He studied the disks. Originally they had been black, but exposure to the rich, thick air of lower Manhattan had ripened them to an unhealthy red-orange. He looked up to find Marjorie waving at him. He began to rub a manila envelope against his knee.

In the early-afternoon sunlight, Marjorie thought about all the frantic activity that filled this plaza. This was her world now, and soon she would make her presence felt. Queen of Police Plaza, no more Captain Butterfly.

And Marjorie, in full uniform, felt a bit like Joan of Arc. Heady stuff.

She began to run toward Charlie. They could do it. Yes, they could. They would make it work. *Yes,* she told herself, *now I'm happy. Yes, indeed.*

Charlie ran to meet her, lifted her in the air. No small feat.

"I love you so much," he said. "Please marry me, please come away with me and let's get married."

They whirled wildly through Police Plaza.

"I have tickets here, a reservation, three weeks on a cruising yacht. We'll sail the Windward Islands off Venezuela. I have the tickets right here, Marjorie. Let's sprint."

She laughed. It was a strange laugh, almost not her own.

"Oh, Charlie, how could I leave now? You know, with the new job, a new commissioner. There are expectations. People expect things of me."

"I expect things of you. I need you. And you have needs too. You need a rest. Christ, Marjorie, it's only for three weeks. When we get back, it'll be spring, and all the assholes will be in bloom."

"How can I go right now?"

Marjorie watched as Charlie's face closed down.

"And what of your dream?" he said. "You see, I've always known about your dream. Tell me, Marjorie, what is your dream now? It can't be of this snake-filled plaza. That can't be your dream."

"Stop!"

"No, I won't stop. I'm packed and ready to go. Emi's already packed for you. Our things are in the car. What you don't have, we'll buy."

Suddenly the air was filled with pigeons, wave after wave of gray-green, brown-and-white ratters. Gutter eagles, dirty things. Some settled in the plaza searching for bits of pizza. Some swept into the plaza's leafless trees. The two at Marjorie's feet pecked at their lice-covered bodies, too sick to fly.

"I can't help the way I feel."

"And how's that? How do you feel, Marjorie?"

"Confused."

"You're kidding?"

"Why do you say it like that?"

Charlie shook his head.

"They've won, you know," said Charlie with a benevolent smile.

"What are you saying?"

"Can't you see they've killed your dream? You may have won the battle, dear heart, but the ultimate victory is theirs. You are now a full-fledged member of the band. How's that sound? Marjorie on the French horn."

Charlie folded his arms and looked at the afternoon sky. Slowly he began to back out of the plaza. "This is all yours now, this place of wonder and power. Does it satisfy your ego, your selfishness, your stupidity?"

"Charlie," she shouted in a shaky voice, "don't be such a dimwit."

"It's yours, all yours. And, baby, you can have it. I'm gone."

Charlie clapped his hands, and pigeons' wings beat the air.

"Let's hear a tune, First Deputy Commissioner."

Charlie turned and walked toward the street, out of the plaza, out of her life. Probably forever.

Oh, Charlie, she thought. *Don't do this to me.*

"Go!" she shouted with murderous rage. "Just go on and go. Go take your damn cruise. You can't even fucking swim."

Marjorie ran—slow and easy at first—then she picked up the pace and moved full out until Charlie was directly in front of her. She grabbed him by the shoulders, turned him.

"I'm here," she said. "Charlie, I'm here. I just remembered you don't know how to swim. You can't go on a sailboat."

"Who says I can't swim?"

"You—you told me you never learned to swim. When you told me you played baseball all summer, made all the all-star teams. Poor boy never had time for the beach."

"I lied."

"I want to come."

"Too late."

"For chrissake, Charlie, I'm here and I want to go. I want to go with you."

"Okay," he said, and took her hand. "Let's run."

Hand in hand, they moved out of the plaza, heading for Charlie's double-parked car.

"Don't look back," he said. "Don't you dare look back."

"Did you bring my camera?"

"Sure."

"Charlie," she said, "I'll grant you ego, and maybe I'm even a bit selfish. But, Charlie, if you ever again make the mistake of calling me stupid, I'll injure your testicles."

"I can accept that."

Marjorie watched as Charlie smiled a perfect smile of understanding, and as she watched, she wondered if she loved him more for his gentleness and honesty or because he was simply Charlie.

"Sometimes," Charlie said, "you do and say bad things, Marjorie, but most times you're quite a lady."

"What's that mean?"

"Hey, Commissioner, it means nobody's perfect. It means that you're my life and I love you."

"Not commissioner *yet*, Charlie, just Deputy Commissioner."

"Oh, no!" Charlie shouted.

"You bet your ass, Charlie," Marjorie put in quietly. "This Butterfly has learned to fly."

"Perfect," Charlie said. "That's absolutely you, it's perfect." And he said it with a small worried smile.

You are invited to preview the following
excerpt from

SWEET BABY
JAMES

the spine-tingling suspense thriller by

Bob Leuci

coming soon from Dutton

One

Running through a light sunrise drizzle, the jogger slipped, listed to his left, righted himself, then jumped a small treacherous, mud-filled pool, and entered Malcolm X Park just below Beekman Place. He wore the hood up on his Redskin sweatshirt, khaki shorts, and tennis shoes without socks. Suddenly the rainy mist gained force and started coming down hard, carried on a fresh June wind. The runner paused by a wet bench, then sat. Motionless and pale, he gazed up at the gray morning sky and roared, "Fuck this!"

The jogger was homicide detective Scott Ancelet, and normally Scott would have preferred to be burned alive than to exercise. But the day before, a face on Fourteenth Street had rung a bell and his partner had shouted at the guy, "Hey, hey you!" and ba-bing, they were off. Scott started out quick, stayed with the guy for an acre, maybe two, then he faded, which is a nice way of saying he stone quit. He didn't know if he should laugh or cry watching the guy go, knowing full well that the long-legged bastard hadn't touched second, forget third gear. Then the sonofabitch pulled up in front of a store window, turned sideways to look at himself like he was the star attraction, and gave a closing Big Mo, a Who, me? look. Then he was in the wind faster than you could say, two old cops that run like Raymond Burr ain't shit.

This morning Scott had woken a half hour before daybreak and told his skinny, aging body Welcome to a whole new life, sports fan. He grabbed his clothes, his gun and shield, then headed for the park.

Scott was young-looking and he'd always been a bit of a jock. He smoked, but he knew it was nothing to stop—hadn't he done it a hundred times? Of course, he had no way of knowing just when the old system would go, but he judged from recent pains in his legs and chest that it couldn't be much longer. There were times when it seemed a demon lived within his chest and leaned with a clenched claw against his heart. Not a killing pain, just an attention-getter.

Soon, he thought, feeling the pain creeping across his chest, I'm gonna be a goddamn old cop and this here police work is a young man's game.

Scott stood for a moment and ran energetically in place. Running is good, he told himself. He sat back down on the wet bench and grabbed hold of his ankles, did a little stretch. Began twisting his body, rolling his shoulders, feeling cool and loose. That's when the wind really started whipping the rain around. Scott scowled, throwing up his hands. Humping through a trail in the pouring rain might be okay for a young hot-dog super cop, but not for him.

"And why not?" he said aloud. "How bad can it be?"

He decided he'd come back later. Wait for the sky to clear, he told himself, hit the trail when there are other human beings running, maybe get a shot at watching some tits bounce.

Thinking over this offer to himself, Scott remained sitting where he was for a moment, thinking.

From nowhere a short, heavy, dark-skinned man chugged along the trail like Ishmael in search of adventure. In fact, he was moving with such panicky haste that Scott jumped when he saw him.

The man stopped, looked down at Scott, and nodded like they were in the tropics and he was a fine-feathered bird atop a golden palm.

"I need a phone," the man screamed, holding his chest and panting. "Where can I find a telephone? In the name of the Lord Jesus," he said, "I've never seen anything like it. I have to call the police."

258

"Whoa, pal, easy," Scott said. "Listen, I'm a cop. Why do you want the police?"

"You're no cop."

Now, early mornings before daybreak were not easy for Scott. He was never sufficiently awake before ten. He got to his feet, his voice soft. "I am," he said. "I'm a detective."

"You do have an honest face," said the man, "but I'd like to see a badge, an I.D. or something."

"For chrissakes, I'm running," said Scott, taking a step toward the little fat guy, who stepped back into the darkness.

Scott was now lapsing into an evil mood and beginning to feel real annoyed with this little fat fucker who looked at him as if he were a creep. Overhead the wind shifted and the rain eased. Scott could hear the horns of cars off in the distance.

"Look," he said, "there's a bank of phones about an eighth of a mile back up the trail off to the right."

"You really a cop?"

"Yes, I'm really a cop. What's your problem?"

"Too skinny. I didn't think they made cops so skinny."

"Lean's the word, and that's not what I'm asking. Why do you need the police?"

"About a hundred yards that way is a green rolled-up carpet. And sticking out of that carpet are two dead feet in sneakers."

Scott had known by the panicky gait of this little fat guy that there would be trouble coming.

"Man, at first I thought it was just somebody sleeping in the park."

"Wrapped in a carpet, you say?"

"A black kid in red sneakers. He's wrapped in a green carpet right down there."

"Get to that phone and call 911. Tell 'em to send a scout car, tell 'em an officer needs assistance."

The little fat guy stood still and rubbed his face with both hands. "Nightmares, I'm gonna have nightmares," he moaned.

"It's likely," said Scott.

Scott trotted disgustedly down the trail, thinking that he'd be forced to endure the odor of a bug in a rug when he had his heart set on smelling some fresh baked biscuits, bacon, and eggs. Then his right foot slipped to the side, and he went sprawling, skinning his knee and yelling at the darkness. If he had been twenty years younger, he would have made it without falling, but Scott Ancelet was forty and way out of shape. He could smell dirt and grass and the thunderous odor of dog shit. He got to his feet and began walking fast, purposefully, his attention fixed on the wet dirt trail.

The first rifts of blue began to show in the morning sky. The rain had ended. It was the beginning of a bright day full of light and promise. Scott was beginning to feel a bit queasy.

More quickly than he'd hoped, he found the rolled carpet. Stepping into a clearing he caught sight of a pair of red tennis shoes at the end of thin brown legs protruding from the roll. He took a deep breath, swallowed, and was instantly sick.

Scott turned away and looked up at the morning sky, now bisected by wet and dripping branches. He studied the sky for a moment, then his gaze returned to the ground in front of him. The feet of the body were crossed at the ankles as though whoever the carpet contained had grown tired of the effort to be free and had surrendered to sleep. How old was he? Scott wondered. It didn't matter. It was all bad business and Scott had already decided he'd unroll the carpet.

He took hold of the edge. It was wet and slimy, and the air was heavy and perfumed with the stench of death. He turned to glance back at the trail.

Detective Ancelet, a veteran police officer, understood that he had no business stomping around a crime scene. Yet despite this, things do happen when a homicide detective gets real close to a corpse.

The main problem, he decided, were the foot imprints. Discounting the guy who had stumbled over the body, he figured there were probably two, maybe three sets.

He put two hands on the carpet and pulled it open.

He felt a sudden careening inside his head and knew this was a mistake. It was bound to be bad, it's always bad. But you look, you feel the sickness rise, you shake it off and make yourself look some more at the happy work of some evil scum.

It was a youth, a black boy, and the second thing Scott noticed after looking at the horrible throat wound was that the pubic hair had been shaved—probably a day or two before he had been murdered, because there were new sprouts of hair rising. Other than the Fila basketball shoes and blue rolled socks, the boy was nude. Scott made his age at thirteen, fourteen at the most.

A bluejay with its wings spread sailed from a tree through the clearing and lit with a sharp bark onto the ground near the carpet.

"Hi there, asshole," a voice called from behind him. "Put your hands on your head."

Scott mumbled something about never being able to find a cop when you need one. But he stood real still, his back to the trail, not wanting to be shot dead by some rookie who thought he had come upon a killer. "I'm a cop," Scott shouted.

"Scotty?"

Turning, Scott recognized the hawk nose, the pockmarked face, and spooky grin of the Mad Hatter. His name was Tony DeStefano and he worked Fourth District patrol.

Steady as a rock, both his hands locked around his new Glock 9mm., the Mad Hatter grinned his famous nutty smile and said, "What in the fuck you doing here?"

"Running," said Scott.

The bird leapt into the air and sped past the Mad Hatter's head. Swooping between two pine trees, it wheeled and came at the uniformed officer on strong wings.

"Spooks," shouted the Mad Hatter, "this park is full of spooks."

"Put the gun down, hah, Tony, and come over here."

"Come over there? What I wanna come over there for?"

The Mad Hatter had moved behind a disease-ridden cedar tree and was now playing peekaboo.

"C'mere, will ya, and hold the edge of this carpet so I can get a good look at this kid."

When the Mad Hatter finally moved from his tree, he came out making whooshing sounds like he was a wind tunnel.

Scott said, "The guy that did this should be riding a Mongolian pony. I've never seen cut wounds like that."

The direction and velocity of the blood stains along the boy's body and on the carpet indicated to Scott two things: a strong arterial spray, plus the boy had been standing when he was slashed. A man who cuts like this, Scott thought, has some bad rage inside him.

Scott studied the bloody body for a moment, then noticed that the boy's arms were crossed, his palms turned outward. Suddenly, for some reason or other there was absolute silence in the clearing. The sun had risen with exquisite brilliance, and now light and shadow dappled the dead boy's face. Scott felt his mind would explode, so crowded was it with unwanted memories of dead faces.

"Hey, Tony," he said finally, "look at this."

"Why do I gotta look? I don't need this trash before breakfast. And besides, that dip shit Sperling is supervising, and that rib sucker'll have my balls for dancing through a crime scene like this."

"Look, will ya? This kid's eyebrows have been plucked clean off."

The Mad Hatter took a deep breath and opened his eyes. "Yeah," he said, "and he shaves his balls. He's a fag hustler. I usta run into em all the time in vice."

"I never seen one," said Scott, feeling the full weight of the sickness rising now. Suddenly he wanted to call Maryann. Maryann should be free this afternoon, he thought.

"They're all over this town," said the Mad Hatter. "Fags and fag hustlers, they're everywhere."

"I want this case," Scott muttered. "I wanna nail the sonofabitch that did this."

The Mad Hatter remarked with a huge grin, "The kid's neck looks like a chunk a bad steak, don't it, Scotty? Whew," he said with a happy smile, "somebody was real pissed at this boy."

Scott could feel the rage rising, filling his chest, making him crazy. He certainly didn't need another whodunit, not with the open fourteen he and Big Mo carried.

He shook his head slowly, and he twitched when the Mad Hatter took hold of his shoulder, saying, "Hey, Scotto, you don't look too good, old buddy."

"I'm gonna find the guy that did this," said Scott, "and when I do, I'm gonna tear open his chest and rip out his black heart."

The Mad Hatter chuckled agreeably. "You're funny," he said, "No shit, Scotty, you say the weirdest things. But I think you're terrific."

To be thought of as someone special by the Mad Hatter, Scott concluded, was nothing but a bad omen.